The Gift
Of Love

"Le Cadeau De L'amour"

ABOUT THE AUTHOR

I am the only son in a family of four; born to a working-class family. We were poor in financial terms but we inherited a rich and interesting history from our ancestors.

Family gathered and the stories of the past thrilled me as a child. There were real life stories of raw emotion and events born out of actual experiences and learning.

I have been on a lifetime journey; personal experience led me to a spiritual pathway and I actively pursue this as an integral part of my very being.

Acknowledgements

I would like to say thank you for their true friendship: In their support and understanding for their care, consideration and kindness, for hearing me. For their strength and courage, In their truth, honesty and transparency, without an agenda. In their patients, their trust and loyalty: consistently and persistently. And being my true friends....

I would like to thank those of wisdom and knowledge who shared.

"This book is to fulfil a life's dream...."

"A Labyrinth of an intertwining journey of...
Kindness & Understanding,
Emotional Growth & Loyalty,
Laughter & Humour,
Romance Love & Affection,
Tears of Joy
Psychosomatic,
Paralleled Existences
Tears of Sorrow
Jealousy & Deceit...
Intrigue & Mystery...
Encompassing a Thrilling Twist...!
Spiritual
Spirituality"

"The Gift of Love"

"Some people look
But they do not see...

Some people listen
But they do not hear...

Persevere"

"A Dream is but a Dream
A Desire generates an Intention
Intention Manifests in to an Action,
Beware of your Desired
Intention….!"

The Gift of Love

Written by

Mr Steve Sullivan

Chapter 1

The Réaction

"Come along, Chloe darling. We've arrived home now. Come on, let's get inside quickly, no doubt the press will be converging and will set up camp outside on our bloody door step soon enough, and I'm sure we will get a visit from the Police asking more bloody questions, As if they haven't seen and know enough already. There will be no peace now not for any of us. And the future looks very bleak here now. There's no future for us, not here my love, no more," said Fred Miller, seemingly composed and unruffled. This probably came from his years of experience in the service of his country.

"How can you be so calm after what has happened?" said Chloe, with tears rolling down her cheeks. "How, Fred...?" Her eyes were puffy and her mascara was all over her previously beautifully applied make-up. In the classy manner that would be fitting for the occasion. Now her face was a total mess.

"Calm...? I'm certainly not calm. How could I be calm after what I've witnessed today? I'm devastated, I'm burning up inside. My life... our life... all of our fucking lives are in ruins. It will never be the same. I'm horrified … in fact I'm in a fucking state of shock," said Fred Miller. "And we know who will get the blame."

Mr and Mrs Miller had arrived back at their lovely home in a black taxi cab. Mr Miller paid the fare of the cab journey to the driver through the glass partition, as Mrs Miller slowly raised her head and glanced out of the black tinted window.

They both got out of the taxi from the same side, kerb side, by their front garden gate. They had requested to the driver to pull up that way. Mr Miller opened the gate and they both scurried up the pathway. Before entering the front door of the porch, instinctively they both turned round and stared at the other five houses on their small estate.

To think they had been there seven years, such happy times, and such fond memories.

They stepped inside the porch, opening the inner door.

But before entering the sanctuary of their home, they took just one more momentary look, their eyes surveying the grass common and pond. Then beyond to the houses they had visited, frequently, openly, lovingly, so many happy times.

They stepped inside and closed the doors firmly behind them.

Mrs Miller went into their front room lounge and collapsed onto the settee, while Mr Miller went into the kitchen and made himself a carafe of very strong coffee and his wife a pot of Darjeeling tea, her favourite brew at times of stress. Mr Miller then returned to the lounge, and going straight to the drinks cabinet he proceeded to pour out two large brandies, placing them on to the tray with the coffee and tea and the decanter of Courvoisier. Mr Miller crossed the room and sat next to his wife, placing the tray on the coffee table.

Inadvertently he sat on the remote control, which had been partially hidden by a cushion. The television flicked on, as did the video....

Mr Miller was sitting on the sofa, and he gently placed one arm around his wife's elegant divested shoulder. His other hand was clasping the large crystal brandy glass. Offering it to his lips, he took a large gulp, swallowed hard in one go and started to pour himself another large brandy. His wife had followed his example, downing it in one, and she was gesturing for her empty glass to be equally refilled. Without raising his head or taking his eyes off of the crystal glasses, in one motion he moved on and half-filled her glass, and they sat there in silence, both sipping there cognac.

The video recorder started to play. They both sat there captivated by what they were watching. At the sight before their eyes, they shuddered...

"If there is a God in heaven... Why? Why, Fred? How? How! How the fuck could this happen, Fred? Hooooow? Why? Nooooooo!" screamed Chloe as she hurled her glass full of cognac across the room.
Then rising to her feet, purposefully and with uncontrolled tears streaming from her eyes down her face, she screeched: "NO!!! WHY!!!" and simultaneously

swiped her arm out in a rage at the objects of the coffee table. Cups, saucers, coffee pot, tea pot, sugar bowl, milk jug, brandy decanter, glasses and tray swirled across their so elegantly designed room, ending up strewn everywhere.

"Stop Chloe " remonstrated Fred Miller... "Stop this now. Stop this destruction, Chloe, please ... Darling, please ... I cannot cope with this as well ... Have we not had enough devastation and carnage today...?" he continued, trying to control his hysterical wife, trying to manage her rage and cocooning her in his powerful arms, holding her arms at her side as gently as he could, as though to protect her.

"I don't know why, Chloe. I have no idea how such a dreadful thing could happen. It's insane. No sense in this happening whatsoever. I cannot explain why or how. One thing I do know: in all the brutality and cruelty, senseless loss of life I witnessed in service, this is by far the most macabre, premeditated act of violence."

Gradually Fred gathered his wife that he loved and cherished so dearly into his arms. Her submission was futile.

After her outburst of rage, Chloe was listless, exhausted.

"I'm so so tired, Fred," she said.

Fred cradled her in his arms, manoeuvring her tenderly into sitting back down on the settee.

"Chloe, my darling, my love, I have no idea, no answers," he said.

The silence that followed was deafening and although it only lasted momentarily, it seemed an age.

"Was it us, Chloe?" continued Fred. "Is it our fault? Should we have done more? Could we have done more? How much more love can you give? Are we guilty? Are we to blame? Did we love too much? Should we have stayed where we were? Did we give too much?"

Tears started to stream from Fred's bloodshot eyes, down his face. Once more there was silence. They sat on the settee, cradled in each other's arms, holding on tight to each other as if their survival, their very existence depended on it. They had lost everything they believed in and lived for.

"Questions, questions, questions," whispered Chloe. "So many questions, there are no answers Fred, At least none that we have. No-one could have predicted these events! Do you really believe you can love that much, give too much?"

Fred pondered for a second or two, maybe a minute. Time was irrelevant now.

"No, Chloe, I don't."

Chapter 2

They were both in their new wedding suits.

Mr Miller had his morning suit on, looking very dapper. He had placed his top hat and gloves on the table in the entrance hall, before heading to the kitchen. Then returning to the lounge, he nestled onto the settee.

Mrs Miller was already sitting on the settee. Wiping her eyes, she snuggled her head against her husband's shoulder. She was wearing her new electric blue dress, and her matching jacket which had been discarded across the armchair. Chloe had placed her matching cream hat and gloves, and a box of confetti on to the side board cabinet, when entering the room.

Chloe Miller had bought it on a pre-wedding shopping expedition with Martha Jackson and Joan Childs. They had all treated themselves to new outfits and they had had a very lovely day in the West End on their shopping spree.

They had left home early.

"Come along, girls! Early bird catches the worm," quipped Joan Childs.

"Excuse me! We are not birds, we are ladies," retorted Martha Jackson "Even if it's only for today!"

There was a quick look at each other followed by an explosion of laughter.

"Oh! Ladies, are we? If that be the case, *first class my dears ... tallyho and this bird isn't for eating no worms!* ... Actually, girls – sorry: ladies – my taste buds are doing overtime for a very large fillet steak in pepper sauce, with sauté potatoes and asparagus. Mmm! With a very palatable red wine, Barolo, I believe" stated Chloe Miller with a combination of a rather posh accent to start, with an American twang slipped in, "*this bird isn't for eating no worms,*" finishing off with a very down to earth I-know-exactly-what-I-want statement.

"Fillet steak, no less," emphasised Martha.

"Palatable red, if you don't mind. Barolo!! And what's wrong with a Rioja V?" Joan said mockingly.

The three ladies went into a simultaneous chorus of "*Ooh! Don't you know!*" taking the rise out of themselves as they generally did.

"Breakfast is the first port of call. Set us up for the day," said Martha.

"So be it. Three BLT baguettes and coffees all round?" asked Chloe, as they queued in the station deli.

Getting onto the main line train they ate their *à la carte* breakfast in the buffet car, ordering extra coffees on the way while reading the magazines they had bought for the journey.

"Hmmmm! Scrumptious...!" Joan said with total satisfaction.

Then on they journeyed, on to the Underground making for High Street Kensington, Knightsbridge, the entirety of the major stores, the exclusive individual boutiques, hat shops, shoe shops. They made a full day of it, stopping off for lunch in a little Italian restaurant.

"How was your fillet steak, Chloe?"

"Wonderful Martha, How was yours?"

"Great!"

"Yours Joan...?"

"Mmm... lovely... divine...."

"Three large espressos please waiter..."

"And the cheque... please..."

And then they were back out again as only women can, shop after shop after shop.

"Let's go back to that shop, you know, the first one we went to," said Martha.

"Ah yes...! That was a lovely shop..." mused Chloe....

"You should have bought that dress and jacket," added Martha.

"It Looked like it was made to measure for you."

"For that price it should have been made to measure," slipped in Chloe.

"Sod the expense. Put it on your gold card," Joan said firmly with a wry smile and a wink.

"At this rate I'll need a gold *mine*!" said Chloe.

"Platinum one will do," Martha said excitedly.

"Gold *tooth* would do me," laughed Joan.

"Come on now, it's their wedding day!"

"Yes you're right!"

"No expense spared … *ladies*!!"

And the infectious banter and shopping went on all day, until all the ladies had expensed their cards on obtaining their special chosen attire.

Chapter 3

Fred and Chloe Miller had bought a brand new house, one of six on a prime development surrounding a duck pond, with grassland, trees and a picnic area. It was a private estate just on the edge of a village.

They had both signed up for the forces straight from school, had done their basic training at different camps, and had been posted for service all over the world, at times involved in action.

Fred was an electronics engineer. He had learnt his trade from the Army and was highly qualified, gaining promotion steadily, but his big passion was guns: automatics, rifles, handguns, bazookas. You name it, Fred could fire it with great accuracy, always on the firing range with his comrades shooting at targets. But deep down Fred was a peaceful man who deplored violence, which was strange for a man in the Army doing service.

Chloe had always wanted to be a nurse but she also wanted to see the world, so what better solution than to join the Army? She was a very conscientious, caring, sensitive lady who held the care of her patients above all else, and after her training and regular nursing she went on to become a sister in rank. She was also known for having a wicked sense of humour. Some said it was necessary in her profession; some said it was necessary to be with Fred! For her relaxation Chloe took up archery and became good enough to represent the Army.

Both Fred and Chloe had been deprived as children, being the victims of broken, violent marriages and suffering emotional, mental and physical abuse. So they had joined the Army to get away from it, to feel wanted, to belong.

They had met while both doing a term of duty in Ireland.

Fred had been caught in crossfire, being where he shouldn't have been, so to speak. He had been shot quite badly in the legs and it was left to the lovely Chloe to nurse him better.

The coincidence of it all was that Fred was shipped home to an Army hospital, and Chloe having done her stint in Ireland was transferred home to Fred's camp hospital. In next to no time romance blossomed and needless to say with so much in common once Fred was up on his feet they were soon wed.

Fred was unable to go overseas due to his injuries but continued to work from the base, and Chloe carried on nursing at the base hospital, where they were given married quarters, soon to hear the patter of little tiny feet. Sophie was a beautiful baby and in turn a lovely child and everyone on the camp liked her.

From their time overseas Fred and Chloe had picked up their share of languages and taught their daughter to count, to talk, to spell and she picked it up quickly. At nursery school, in the infants' class, she would chatter away in German, French, Greek, with a little Arabic and Portuguese.

She was good, and even the Colonel would joke that they would sign her up for counter-intelligence. But she was never showing off … it was natural, pure talent, fluent. She also liked to be out with the other children on the camp playing.

Fred and Chloe still had their passion for guns and archery and would take Sophie with them to show her it can be fun and weapons don't have to be used for violence. They had both enjoyed the army but were ready to move on and wanted a different life for Sophie.

Fred had done his time and so had Chloe and they were given a golden handshake and a well-earned pension. They moved into their new home. Fred was doing some part-time consultancy work and Chloe was doing part-time at the private hospital. That's where she had met Martha Jackson, and Sophie was going to the same school as Tommy.

It was a Brave New World for them, but they were so happy together and they were sure Sophie would settle.

Mr and Mrs Jackson had moved out of East London to Essex and had also bought one of the new houses.

"It was an ideal place to bring young Tommy up," Mrs Martha Jackson had said. "We'll move in during the six-week summer holiday so Tommy can start his new school at the beginning of term with other new kids."

Tommy and Martha Jackson had been uneasy about taking Tommy away from his friends and surroundings, but Tommy senior had earned a big promotion to senior management at his company's head office in Essex.

Martha Jackson was a qualified physiotherapist and was going to turn the utility room into a treatment area and work from home once she had built up a client base. In the meantime she had acquired a post in the local private hospital.

They had great hopes for Tommy, who was a bright kid, easy-going and very likeable, and even at this young age he had a rare talent for football. He could juggle the ball with his feet umpteen times, dribble, control, tackle, shoot. It was like the ball was stuck to him, and when you saw Tommy you saw a ball. A football, a tennis ball, a golf ball, a beach ball, it didn't matter … he'd be practising.

They had managed to get Tommy into a nearby school that had high grades in the league tables, and had checked out some local football sides for Tommy to join, and even at this age Tommy had been spotted while playing for his school and local sides in London.

"A very rare talent indeed" Eager eyes were watching his progress.

It was tradition to support your local side in East London, win or lose, fighting against relegation. Your hopes and dreams of having a good season, maybe winning a cup, that's been known...! – It was in your veins.

Tommy senior was a good semi-pro in his younger days but never made the grade.

As soon as young Tommy was old enough, his dad took him to home games with his team's shirt, shorts and socks on, and he loved it. He would mimic his heroes in the garden or in the park and he knew who he would like to play for.

Mr and Mrs Jackson were certain it was the right move and they would all make friends and Tommy would settle down, that he would be OK and he would make new friends.

Geoffrey and Joan Childs had bought the third and last of the six houses to be snapped up.

Geoffrey Childs was a lawyer, but he had done it the hard way. His parents were hard-working, middle-to-working class, salt of the earth people. They wanted to give Geoffrey every chance, and he grabbed it with both hands, studying every hour possible to get the qualifications to go to university. How proud his parents were to see him receive his scholarship.

However, he loved nothing more than to be with his dad helping him to build a wall or put a roof on. His dad owned a small building firm with ten or so workers, himself included, and after the work was done, they were down the pub.

"Will we win the World Cup" was their favourite conversation, but he also loved the law and was good at it and had got a job with a very reputable company. He would also look after his dad's legal dealings, and that made him very proud. He was well on his way to becoming a partner in the law firm. "Well thought of" was whispered in the corridors.

It was at university Geoffrey had met Joan. Apparently she could down a yard of ale as good as the next man, which was quite surprising as she was a tiny petite young lady, although in a debate she had a tongue like a viper and a brain twice as quick.

Joan's dad never encouraged Geoffrey. He was a judge from the old school.

"Riff-raff! He'll never make anything of himself. He'll live off our Joan and me," he was heard to say. Well, he had to eat humble pie and Joan and Geoffrey never let him forget it, in the nicest possible way.

The night Louise was born the old judge lost his wig to a bottle of 12-year-old malt. Did they wet the baby's head that night!! "DRUNK IN CHARGE OF A WIG" Geoffrey's dad accused the old judge of.

All except Joan, that was … but she made up for it at the christening; one after the other, drink after drink. She stood with Geoff's dad and the lads. She loved Geoff's dad and mum – "salt of the earth" – and she could hold her own in court or at the bar.

Louise was angelic; so affectionate and loved her cuddles, but clever so clever. She picked things up straight away, remembered everything, never missed a trick and she loved to learn. She would study, read, write, and ask questions and then stop.

"Go out and play."

"Come back to that later."

As far as advanced as she was, she was never the snotty-nosed Miss Know-it-all. She loved to show how it was done but, in a nice way – the teacher or maybe the lawyer.

Even the judge had to admit he had been wrong about Geoff and was so proud of his granddaughter and was impressed with the new house.

Each of the families on the estate had in turn had a house warming party, including the other three families on their plot. Everybody got to know each other very well and all appeared to get on famously, inviting each other to their new homes, all expressing their gratitude and friendship.

"A good neighbourhood to bring the kids up in" was the favourite expression.

It was only the Jacksons, Millers and Childs who had children. So of course they all had something in common and spent more time entertaining, especially as the children were of the same age.

In between 'The Three Musketeers' as the children had become to be known as, a true bond was born, and it was 'one for all and all for one'.

Louise, Sophie and Tommy all started school together and were all in the same class. Right from the off the teachers could see there was a special bond that existed between them and they had warranted being placed in the top class. The teachers had decided to split them up and kept the kids separate around the classroom, sitting each one next to someone else, probably hoping their hunger for learning would rub off on the other children; but this never broke them up.

As soon as break time and lunch break came around there they were, 'the Three Musketeers'. This was their nickname, which had been started by the teachers in good humour, and to be fair was appropriate and the kids liked it. It gave them the feeling of belonging to each other, and when they got home from school full of themselves and informed their parents of their new title, they in turn could see the irony of it, and it stuck.

All three enjoyed school and didn't have any problems, for as much as they were 'The Three Musketeers; they were also very popular with the other kids and made many friends ... although no one could infiltrate the trio.

They were doing well in English, maths, languages, history, all the academics, plus the practical subjects like cooking, woodwork and metalwork.

Louise excelled in the academics far and beyond her nearest rival, who happened to be Sophie. This in turn was not a problem for the girls; it just inspired them to greater achievements.

Sophie without a doubt was the linguist; she was leaps and bounds ahead in the languages.

Tommy, it has to be said, was bringing up the rear but was holding his own in the top class. He was also captain of his school football team.

The first term passed very quickly and they were soon breaking up for the festive season. Christmas was here and everyone was excited in and out of each other's houses … and surprise, surprise, there was good old Fred Miller driving everybody crazy with his video camera.

Mr Childs decided to throw a big New Year's Eve bash, inviting his new-found friends the Millers (including video camera) and Jacksons and their immediate families.

Chapter 4

The television screen was alive as the video played on …

The Millers eyes were glued to the screen

They were watching the three children jumping about in the small swimming pool in Geoffrey and Joan Childs' garden which his dad had built for them as a moving in present. Geoffrey Childs was standing by the barbecue cooking *à la carte* burger and sausages. Joan Childs was standing by the picnic table preparing the salad. Tommy Jackson senior and his wife Martha were sitting at the garden table talking to Chloe Miller pointing and laughing at the three kids jumping and splashing around.

They were taking it in turns in dive-bombing each other, having races, and generally larking about. Young Tommy was chipping a football into the pool, splashing the girls and the girls in turn where trying to sting Tommy with the ball when throwing it back at him. All in all they were having a great time, and as usual whenever there was a celebration, a party, a gathering, a special event or even someone making a cup of tea, up would pop Fred Miller with his trusted side kick, his video camera.

He took an awful lot of stick over that video camera, but he loved every minute of it, and he would start it up knowing he would get a response and be ridiculed.

"Watch out, Spielberg's about!"

"No, it's Clockwork Orange, Russell."

"Looks like Warhol to me!"

"Bore...Hole..."

"No, it's Hitchcock!"

"Hitch *who*?"

"I certainly hope not!"

"You better get down that clinic, Fred Miller!"

"And then you've got me to answer to about that ... Hitch, my darling," Chloe Miller finished off with a very stern face a little wink and a smile, and they all burst out laughing.

"I'm saving these films until we're old and our kids are famous and prosperous," said Fred. "Then we will be able to look back on them, and reminisce... ah such good times... so young and gay..."

"Gay....! Something you haven't told us Fred...."

"So you're coming out of the closet Fred"

"Need to get it off your chest Fred..."

"He loved all that dressing up in those uniforms..."

"About time..."

"You won't laugh and chastise... when I bring these films out of the archives' and share them with the world...."

"Here he goes again with the films... business...."

"Films no less...! Get hold of him," said Tommy senior.

"The world... if you like..."

"He wants to take over the world...!"

"When our children have grown up and they are world famous... people... the world will want to see these, to see what they were like as kids"

"Chloe, you've created a monster since you bought him that camera," stated Geoffrey.

"Here we have Fred Miller reporting for Pathé news," Martha said mockingly with a smile on her face.

"It's Sky News Live with our very own Fredrick Miller," announced Joan.

"This is the Oscars, and tonight, ladies and gentlemen, a very special award is being presented to … And for outstanding achievement! Beyond the call of duty! In extreme danger for his own safety! For film and camera work…. to the one and only… FRED MILLER!!!" Announced Tommy senior, imitating a presenter...

And so the laughing and mocking went on, and on went Fred videoing his audience; and while they made their acting performances Fred was bowing and taking their applause.

"I've got you lot on film," he said.

"There he goes again... with that film business...."

Everyone was clapping him and smiling.

At this point he had sauntered down the pathway and across the lawn; Fred positioned himself by the pool's edge. Now he was videoing the kids, and as they had been instructed they began to splash him, to everyone's delights including Fred's, who had a great sense of humour.

"Oh, I see! Conspiracy in the ranks! Mutiny on board!! Kiss me Hardy!!!" roared Fred in a pirate's voice. And all at once, everyone, including the kids, bellowed back at him in unison a chorus of *NOT SO BLOODY LIKELY!!"*

Which of course he was expecting; it was a well versed party piece.

Fred being Fred, and as he conveniently only had his trunks on, he placed his beloved camera down out of harm's way and dived straight in, dive-bombing the kids, but fully aware of where they were, no harm done and they all began to laugh and splash.

"Grub's up!" shouted out Geoffrey Childs, and Joan called the kids and Fred out of the pool.

"Come on you lot! And Fred, you're a bigger kid than them! Come on, dry off and eat."

Fred Miller loved his video camera and continued to film everyone, everything..... Even though he was still dripping wet, when he got out of the pool...

Videoing everyone as they got served and began to eat, he gave a running commentary for his own amusement, giggling to himself.

"Here we have the family Jackson, a species from the East End of London town. Well versed in survival and protection of their loved ones and friends. *Here's me hand! Here's me heart, son...!"* Fred said, trying hard to impersonate an East End accent. "Which, when translated roughly means: I rather like you, you're a jolly good chap, and I'll look after you," he said in a well pronounced voice, smiling at Tommy and Martha.

Martha and Tommy... took it all in good heart... indeed a backhanded compliment... and flashed big broad smiles back at Fred...

"Deeper into the wilds we find the more shy and retiring Childs brood.

Elegance personified... That is, until you upset them. Then... By hook or by crook,

"Childs law will win...."

"And don't take meekness for weakness. Straight from the hip... shoot you down with a look or a word.... And thank God they are on our side," commentated Fred in a very Attenborough tone of voice.

Joan and Geoffrey smiled sincerely... Joan curtsied and Geoffrey bowed...

"Now we have left the feminine member of the Miller family," he continued, "My high priestess, my queen of the jungle. She who will be obeyed... the rock... nay the jewel in the stone...."

"And of course we have the families' cubs ... gathered together, living together, nurturing and caring for each other, animals of the jungle, able and willing.... living in peace and harmony. Like birds of a feather ... we flock together!"

"My God, it's Tarzan with a video camera in the jungle and a poet," protested Geoffrey.

"Naaah!! He thinks he's Jacques Cousteau now!" quipped Tommy senior....

"No. Stingray, I'd say," said Martha.

"Attenborough's got competition now..."

"Man from Atlantis, more like!" mused Joan

"Spielberg beware...!"

"Tarantino must be shacking in his boots..."

"He's my Adonis," said Chloe.

"Oooooooh... Adonis Adonis... Adonis...!!!" was the joint chorus echoing from the rafters... from all of the others in accord, but all thinking: "*how lovely...*"

"Looks more like Jack the Flipper to me," roared Geoffrey Childs' dad, who had just turned up with his wife.

So it went on, the barracking and the laughing, and Fred gave as good as he got. Once they had all eaten, the kids were straight back to the pool to continue their fun and games, and on went the video...

Chapter 5

"It Is So incredible." "It is just amazing." "Oh, how lovely it is."
I'm sure they are telepathic...." "They are... Without a shadow of doubt... in my mind.... soul mates..."

This seemed to be the general census of opinion, and everybody agreed upon it.

"These three kids are so close, and in coming together, how they gelled"... "How they work for each other"... "How they look after each other and protected each other." This was recognised by their teachers, new neighbours and local people, and even by the local vicar.

After the upheaval of moving away from all their old stomping grounds... their familiar surroundings, their schools, their clubs..... Everything they had been use to, to know and trust, and most of all their pals, their friends.
That would have been the most difficult thing to do, to understand and accept, to leave there friends behind, the best friends they think they are ever going to have.
"Why have we got to move?"
"Why have we got to go?"
"Why can't we live here?"
"But that means I'll never see …!"
"Look, we know how you feel. It's the same for us and we'll all have to make new friends," said their parents caringly.

"Mum! Dad! You don't understand …You haven't got any friends!" said the children collectively yet individually, miles away from each other.

"Of course we have friends and we will keep in touch with them and make new friends!"

"Once we have settled in your friends can come and visit and stay the weekends"

"But it's so far away!"

"It's not that far away. They can treat it as an adventure."

"Oh yeah!"

"Look at me, please. Look at me and listen. You will make new friends, I promise, and all the friends you have now can come and visit."

"I won't know anyone there, I don't want new friends, and I want the friends I have now."

"THEY ARE MY BEST FRIENDS IN THE WHOLE WORLD!!!!!"

"We are moving and you will thank us in the end."

"Oh yeah...! Right! Of course I will!"

"*Excuse us*, but don't talk to us like that. Show some respect. We are your parents, and you can cut out the strop right now."

So it went on, the whingeing, the sulking, tantrums, no understanding.

"At their age it is the biggest thing in the world to them."

"I know they think they are going to the end of the earth."

"That is as far as they are concerned."

"But we are right."

"Try explaining that to an eleven-year-old."

In the end, all the three families had moved onto the private estate within a week of each other just six months ago, and now these kids were inseparable. See one see three.

It could not have worked out much better for the parents, as it took a lot of pressure off of them in making their kids happy, but it could not have worked out much better for the kids either. They were thrown together, not out of choice, but as a result of synchronicity, and now they were together.

So they were not isolated, and as they knew nobody else they soon teamed up, which made them stronger.

It wasn't just that they did not know anybody else. It was as if it was meant to be.

Three families from different walks of life, with three children all of the same age, purchasing new homes at the same time on the same project, from different parts of the country.... Coincidence Fate, Synchronicity.

On a balmy evening with the parents sitting in the local pub garden enjoying a few drinks, the conversation moved on to their children and the actions that they themselves had taken.

"There is something special in their relationships," mused Chloe, mystified.

"Even at their age they have a bond, a connection," added Martha.

"Such friendship has grown so strongly," Joan said, inquisitively.

"Hmm. Very strongly," Tommy joined in, in a positive tone.

"And … soooo quickly," puzzled Fred.

"But that's good, isn't it?" confirmed Geoffrey.

"It's become so apparent that they have forgotten their old mates and don't even miss them," reassured Fred.

Geoffrey started to talk as if addressing the judge and jury. "Well, what's quite apparent to me is that ..."

"Objection, my Lord! Council is leading," jumped in Tommy with a big smile on his face.

"Overruled Council may finish his statement," ruled Fred.

"Thank you, my Lord. As I was about to say before I was rudely interrupted, maybe they would help each other grow," finished off Geoffrey mockingly, but sincerely.

They all sat in stillness, nodding their heads in approval.

"Yes, you're right. I'm sorry Geoffrey," said Tommy, winking and nodding his head toward Geoffrey, realising he was speaking earnestly and that he had interrupted him.

"So here's to growing," said Joan, raising her glass and glancing with a nod at Tommy in appreciation for his magnanimous gesture towards her husband.

"Here's to growing," saluted the gang as their glasses clanged.

"It was meant to be," was their second toast with another clang of glasses as the parents reassured themselves it was obvious how well the children got on.

Their parents were quite chuffed with themselves.

"I knew it was the right move all along," said Martha with a twinkle in her eye.

"It was the right time," endorsed Joan.

"Hear hear!! The kids were at the right age to make the move," exclaimed Chloe. "If we hadn't moved then we never would have."

"The way house prices have gone we were lucky we moved when we did," proclaimed Geoffrey.

"Wasn't luck it was judgment, a strategically mounted manoeuvre, sound action," reminisced Fred.

"Just think. If we hadn't all moved at the same time our kids would never have met and neither would we," said Geoffrey, being quite profound.

"No, you're quite right, Geoffrey, and how lucky we – that is: you, your Joan, my Martha and me – are. We wouldn't be living next to a movie mogul, would we, Fred?" quipped Tommy senior, his humour in the right place on this occasion.

Tommy raised his glass and the others followed suit.

"To friendship, everlasting," he choked genuinely. Then in typical Tommy style, counteracting with a quip: "*here's my hand ... here's my heart, son*" in his roughest cockney twang.

They were all quite amused and it brought all of them back down to earth, closing their self-praise and self-appreciation circle.

Chapter 6

The plus side to this whole new adventure was that they got on so incredibly well together right from the off. It was as if they had known each other for years. They would listen intently and seriously and when appropriately candidly convey their feelings, express their humour with each other's yarns and experiences. Respectfully, with mutual understanding of each other's morals, ethics and principles, with honesty and truth, as was instilled into their children.

Sunday lunch time would become a ritual for the three dads. They would meet up at midday with their Sunday papers under their arms – the Times, the Financial Times, the Mail on Sunday, the Sun on Sunday, and the People – and take a leisurely walk down the country lane to the local.

"Three pints of real ale please, my darling," requested Tommy to the barmaid who by now had got used to them and their humour.

"In for the session, are we boys?"

"We most certainly are, madam," responded Fred.

"Are we expecting the ladies to be joining you later?"

"Most eloquently put, my dear. Most favourable to be allied to the ladies," expressed Geoffrey.

"In others words, my luv, we are in for the session and yes, our good ladies will be joining us for a tipple or ten," said Tommy in his unfussy manner.

Over the next two hours they would sip their ale and they would have a few, reading their papers intensely, front to back, back to front, swapping about, interrupted only with the occasional banter.

"I see your team won again, Tom," enthused Fred.

"Yes, my mate, a great result," replied Tommy, smiling.

"Was they playing the local girls school?" whispered Geoffrey.

"Here Fred, did you ever see photos of Geoff in his school outfit?"

"No, Tom, I didn't."

"He wore a wig then, only with a hockey stick in his hand and a skirt on."

"St Trinian's by any chance, was it?"

"You finished reading that or you still looking at the pictures?" Geoffrey quizzed Tommy.

"Now now, my Lord, you're too old to look at page three."

"It's like being in the Sahara Desert in here! You could die of thirst!" moaned Tommy senior, shaking his empty glass and winking at Geoffrey Childs.

"I suppose it's my turn again?" slipped in Geoffrey quickly.

"Again...? Again...? The last time you bought a drink it was VE Day," said Fred Miller from behind his newspaper, without raising his head.

"That's only because it was a tanner a pint," chuckled Tommy.

"You know he still thinks white fivers are legal tender!"

"He used to have a slate in his old pub you know," gestured Geoffrey to Fred pointing at Tommy.

"Interesting...! Did he ever pay it?" asked Fred.

"No. It got wiped out," stated Geoffrey.

"How come such good luck?" asked Fred.....

"Doodle Bug dear chap, Second World War," cracked up Geoffrey.

"I hope you're not insinuating that I'm mean?" asked Tommy through his belly laugh.

"Mean... as in tight... you mean... as tight as a ducks ......" Said Fred trying to keep a straight face..

"Quack.... Quack..." Geoffrey cut off Fred..... In his elegant voice... this was even more amusing to them....

"Well, Tom, now you come to mention it.... we did hear through the grapevine that you only breathe inwards," released Fred.

"And he wakes up half way through the night to make sure he hasn't lost no sleep," Geoffrey followed on.

At this point they were in raptures.

"Come on! My shout!" said Fred.

"Bloody hell...! He thinks he's back in the naffy...!"

"Or the supermarket...! This week's special offer: buy one, get two free," quipped Tommy.

In between the witticisms and satirical humour, they would converse and debate every subject, opinionated, dogmatic, and candid and then leave it, agree to disagree. Martha, Chloe and Joan and the three kids would join them for a Sunday lunch time bevvy and the good-natured banter would continue.

They would have lunch at the pub or back at their houses, and Sunday lunch would be prepared by the ladies helping and preparing a sumptuous gourmet meal. Then midweek they would meet up for a pint or six after work while the ladies went to the gym and yoga or a wine and cheese evening at one of their homes. They would go to concerts, the theatre, the cinema, they had busy workloads and social lives, but they would always include and make quality time for the kids.

Even though they had all come from such varied backgrounds and upbringings, they enjoyed each other's company immensely and the most important thing to them all was the happiness and the welfare of their children.

They all got on really well with their other neighbours in the remaining three homes on their small estate and in the village.

"Good morning."

"How's the wife?"

"How's the husband?"

"How are the kids?"

"The Times, please"

"Good evening."

"Three pints please"

"How are you?"

"Fine, thank you."

All the familiar pleasantries of village life.....

In addition, of course they were invited at times to some of their social events and some of their parties, which they attended.

The families were popular on the small estate and in the village.

They could mix easily with one and all; yet the close relationship the three families shared remained the core of all that they did.

Chapter 7

Saturday morning had arrived and Tommy was playing football for the school, a top of the table clash with the winners winning the league.

It had been a very close contest all season with some wonderful football being played, bringing to light some awesome and outstanding performances from such young talent. This in turn created media cover for the schools and district sides, and on many occasions there would be a posse of talent scouts who would recommend the young boys to professional clubs.

Tommy's mum and dad and the two girls stood on the touch line. It was a grey morning, cold and rainy, the wind biting, not the best conditions for a football match.

Tommy never managed to score in this game but they won 3-0. However he created all three goals and controlled the game from the middle of the park. He was everywhere. His mum and dad and Louise and Sophie were going crazy, ecstatic. It was obvious who he belonged to.

Directly after the game, while they were waiting for Tommy, who was in the changing room, Mr Jackson was approached by four separate individuals, all claiming to be scouts for big clubs.

This never impressed Tommy senior, who said very politely, "Tommy is thirteen years of age; let him enjoy his football without the added pressure, please."

"We would like him to come and train at our club with all the other boys. He's quite special," said the scouts, all using the same patter.

"Yes, he is," smiled Tommy senior. "He's our son for starters. Secondly, it's not going to be trained out of him, and if you still think he's special when he's fifteen, and that is when and if he's still wanted, we will allow him to join a professional club."

Some of the other mums and dads whose boys were also playing couldn't help overhearing the conversations, and they were astounded. The following Wednesday evening Tommy was playing for the district side representing his Sunday morning league. The same four scouts were there, plus another two.

They won 2-0 and Tommy scored both goals and won man of the match. It was a full house. The Jacksons, the Childs and the Millers were all there in support of young Tommy. After the game Mr Jackson was approached by all six scouts, who this time had documentation to prove who they represented. They meant business. To be fair to young Tommy, Mr Jackson invited each of them to his home over the next week, to listen separately to what they had to say.

They all agreed to this arrangement, some saying they would like to bring their manager with them; this was now accepted even for a thirteen-year-old. Arrangements were made over the next three days by telephone between Mr Jackson and the club managers, who had been advised of the situation by their scouts.

Most of the managers already knew of Tommy's reputation and had taken it upon themselves to watch him play a couple, several, or numerous times, depending where they were travelling from. Even so, the managers had instructed their scouts to keep an updated dossier of Tommy's progress.

So the auction began for young Tommy Jackson's signature.

Each of the managers set aside one full day in his diary to sell himself and his club, on the basis that they would offer to look after Tommy's future; that they would keep his welfare at heart and nurture him, protect him, guide him and make sure he would enjoy his football; and that they had long-term ambition for him.

Tommy senior and Martha, be it at short notice, both took the next week off, allowing Tommy to do the same so they could all be together to listen intently to what the individual managers had to say, to see if they took to him, and to see if they liked the club's policy. They had discussed it, and decided Tommy should be there with them as this was his future.

Over the next six days managers from the five top clubs in England arrived.

The manager from the club the family supported – which it has to be said isn't considered a top club, an under-achiever in its history – was placed last on the appointments list. This was not an indictment of them. It was the way the family wanted it, and they had their reasons.

In fairness, it had attracted some big names in the past, mainly players in their swan song looking for Easy Street and a pension. It did, however, have a great reputation for its youth policy and had produced a wealth of talent over the years. These players went on to play for the top teams in England, playing in Europe and representing their countries.

Sadly, though, it had also become known as a selling club. The new owners and manager were trying to change all of this; and with their new policy of no more golden oldies and hanging on to the young talent, what a scoop Tommy would be! Tommy, Martha and Tommy junior were all very excited at the prospect of meeting all these famous people, and they intended to sit and listen to what was being proposed for young Tommy.

The incentives being offered for young Tommy's signature were unbelievable, not only for Tommy but for the family as well.

"A nice holiday would probably be appreciated, Mrs Jackson."

"Have you been to America?"

"All expenses paid and a lump sum."

And so it went on.

"OK," said Mr Jackson to each and every one of them, when they had finished their bartering and had offering their golden chests for the signature of his son. "This is the deal. Tommy is staying on at school until he has finished his A levels. Obviously we would like to see him become a professional footballer as much as he wants to become one."

He paused.

"But he must complete his education. His career could be cut short before it's even got going by one mistimed tackle; and he must have something to fall back on."

He paused again.

"We want you to leave him alone for the next two years. You can come and watch his progress and you can invite him to games to show him around your grounds and the training facilities. But he will not be signing for any of you now. If you are still interested in him when he is fifteen, he will pick who he goes with, where he goes to train. But he will not sign any forms until he is sixteen and completes his education. So we thank you for your wonderful offers of gifts, but Tommy is not for sale that cheaply. We don't mind you phoning to see how he is doing and keeping in touch, but if you persist in pestering him or us, I will personally make certain he will never be joining any of your clubs!"

"Mr Jackson, if you do allow Tommy to join us we will make sure he completes his education."

"Let him come to us and we'll look after him and of course we will be very grateful to yourself and Mrs Jackson."

"The patter's the same," said Tommy snr to Martha. "Like a recording... No respect."

"What do you think, Mrs Jackson? Wouldn't you like young Tommy to come to us?"

Martha Jackson looked the agent square in the face.

"I believe for the position you hold you're not a stupid man. But please don't try to divide us. You heard exactly what my husband has said, and said quite eloquently if I say so myself," she stated quite proudly.

"Mrs Jackson, no … please, hum, no … please, you've misunderstood me."

Tommy Jackson senior stood up from the table.

"We have not misunderstood you," he said, "and I'm sure you're not misunderstanding us. It's time for you to leave".

Young Tommy always knew where he wanted to go and so did his mum and dad, but they would go through the procedure of seeing every one that was interested and then Tommy could decide.

Before the manager of the team that Tommy and his dad supported turned up, they had a quick tidy-up, taking the team's photographs and rosettes down, moving his flag and scarf out of sight and making sure his football kit wasn't on the line, so as not to give him an advantage.

They listened to what he had to say with great interest and liked what he said. Mr Jackson reiterated what he had said to all the others and waited for his response.

"Obviously, it goes without saying, we are disappointed in not having Tommy join us now," said the manager. "That is, of course, should he have wanted to come to us. It is your decision and we will adhere to it. But we would like you all to come as our guests to a few games this season. Whenever you want, just ring and we will arrange it … we would like you to come to our training ground and see our facilities, watch training and our methods ... we will keep a watchful eye on Tommy and if it's OK with you we will phone now and again to inquire as to how you are all keeping."

Tommy and Martha looked at each other. They had their own sign if they agreed on something or liked something, and they also had a sign if they didn't like something without speaking a word.

Martha twitched her nose twice, Tommy twitched his nose twice, and they both smiled. Tommy looked at his son, who had been watching both his mum and dad, and winked. Young Tommy then looked at his mum, and she winked at him too.

"We like what you have had to say and the fact that you respect our feelings," affirmed Martha.

"We would like to see the training facilities and your methods and we would love to come over and watch some games," avowed Tommy.

"We didn't inform you before, as we wanted to hear what you had to say without being influenced," acknowledged Martha.

"I have supported the club since I was a kid, and so does Tommy; and we – that is the wife as well – go as often as we can. So long as you wanted him you were always going to be Tommy's first choice," said Tommy snr genuinely.

"GREAT!! That's great!! Wonderful!!" said the manager, trying to curb his exuberance. "What the hell!! I'm over the bloody moon!!" he said. "Sorry for the language. I'm … I'm so pleased. I think your Tommy has such a great future and I'm so bloody pleased he wants to come to us."

Martha, Tommy and young Tommy were all looking at him, smiling.

"Oh!! Sorry for the inappropriate language again"

"That's all right," said Martha. "A deaf man would like to hear it."

"And I'm sure we'll hear a lot worse," added Tommy.

"Not when they're kids, madam. Maybe when their older," he smiled.

"OK. If you still want him when he's fifteen and he still wants to come, he's coming to you," said Tommy Jackson, holding out his hand.

"Fine...! We will keep in touch and make arrangements," said the manager, and they all shook hands.

Chapter 8

The years rolled by with the families going on summer holidays together or the children going way on holidays and breaks, with each other's parents.

Learning inner growth, individually and as a group, independence and trust...

One of their favourite destinations that they visited annually, mostly as a group, over a number of years, was Portugal.

The Algarve, a place called Carvoeiro once a sleepy little village with load's of character. With some seven bar's, a few restaurant's and a disco, all very laid back, but over the years it had expanded into quite a big town and some could say not for the better.

They would rent a villa with a pool and spend lazy days lying around soaking up the sun.

They visited the local Water Parks and took part on all the rides, which was a bit silly for a boy in Tommy's position, with such a great future.

Although in the main he was quite sensible.

Or they would travel out to some of the more popular beaches with water sports on. Over the years they had also found some beautiful sandy coves with small beach bars or restaurants for sun drenched lazy days….

They sampled the fresh fish, sardines, prawns, and squid with a garrafer of local wine.   Or perhaps the chicken piri piri, that would make their lips tingle from the chilli, washed down with ice cold beer or in the kids' case coke.

Then come the evening they would go down town where they would enjoy another meal at one of the local restaurants.

Then on to their favourite music bars, the kids were allowed to go into most of the bars as it was tradition there.

Their favourite bar was in the town centre, not far from the beach, it was very unique in as much as the back of the bar had been dug out of the rock, deep like a cave............ fossils and shells imbedded...

It was all very family, orientated: music, dancing, competitions, quizzes and the traditional football team, made up of local lads, residents and holiday makers... uniting as one, the penalty for talking shop... whether you where a resident or a holiday maker, would be a shot of Madronier "fire water."

This was kindly supplied by the owner and it had to be said he was a very charismatic character; handsome, suave, sophisticated, debonair, very respectful, but with a risqué sense of humour, and of course extremely modest...! or at least that is what he told everyone, plus he always had the last say, or you had the Madronier.

Over the years they enjoyed their holidays very much and became increasingly friendly with the restaurant and bar owners.

Eventually when the kid's were grown up they would return on their own.

Chapter 9

They would have regular sleepovers at each other's homes.

They went to the parks and the swimming pool together. Shopping and the cinema always together, youth clubs and dances together; they lived in each other's pockets.

They always seemed to be together, obviously this was not a bad thing as it never interfered with their education or their individual talent and they never once fell out.

They were just like most children they would have different opinions and views, but somehow they would always sort it out.

They never fought; they shared their intimate thoughts, ideas, dreams, ambitions, C.D's, even their clothes fortunately this didn't include Tommy, right down to their ice cream.

It was incredible there were never any fallout's, sniping, or bickering, which you would expect from kid's at their age, in this cut throat world of competition and pressure, certainly amongst talented children, at such young ages.

"As if they aren't under enough pressure already"
"From parents and outside influences"
"Come on you must be first, you must win"...
"It isn't any good coming second"...
"Who remembers losers"...
"Achieve, achieve, win, win, study, study"
... Pressure, pressure.

A blessing for Louise, Sophie and Tommy was that this never went on in their households.

Their parents also showed a great deal of interest in their outside activities; encouraging the children, encouraging their teachers and their trainers, in their pursuit of excellence, but always there with a protecting supporting arm and an encouraging word and more so a word of comfort and discipline when they thought it was deemed necessary.

They taught them fair play; to be competitive and to be magnanimous in success. There was no competition between them, any jealousy, selfishness or siding.

True friends brought together by chance who cared for each other deeply and they always would put their friends' feelings first, before their own.

Chapter 10

As the years went by Tommy Jnr. was turning into a very good football player, playing for the school and being picked for district and county matches.

Tommy was turning into a super prospect and was being noticed by more professional clubs.

Tommy loved his football; he trained twice a week and played Saturdays and Sundays.

The girls would come down and watch him play but after the game or training and in the rest of his spare time he would be with the girls, nothing would break their allegiance.

Sophie was doing very well at school; excelling in English and languages but like her parents her passion was also shooting and archery.

Her dad belonged to a Gun Club and her mum to an Archery Club.

This was obviously where her skills came from.

There was friendly rivalry from her parents as to which she was best at but Sophie excelled at both to the point where she made the local teams and also won some junior tournaments.

Tommy and Louise would go and watch Sophie in competition clapping and cheering their great mate on.

She was becoming a dead shot.

Louise was the academic; maths was her forte but English language, business studies and history were of the top notch.

This young lady was destined for university and the City but all through the years it never changed her. She would help her two friends with their homework – never doing it for them but coaxing them, teaching them.

Even as the years went by and the exams became more important and right up to their final exams before leaving school, Louise had the ability to simplify difficult subjects and this enabled her friends to pass with flying colours.

She knew one day that this gift may send her away from her friends but dismissed it to the back of her mind.

The Three Musketeers, the name had stayed – one for all ... all for one, progressed through their school and at no time had they found a prospective girlfriend or boyfriend, they never seemed bothered.

They would go to cinemas, dances, clubs and parties together making associates along the way but no one could infiltrate the bond they had for each other.

Even their parents would joke that they would end up buying a three bed roomed penthouse.

They had great aspirations for their children and why not?

Chapter 11

Tommy Jnr. was picked to play for England schoolboys at Wembley.

What a day... "WEMBLEY" the mums and dads and the two girls were there.

A number of clubs had wanted Tommy to sign but Tommy had picked his local team the one he had supported as a child. Plus they had kept all their promises which pleased both his parents and in turn pleased him as it allowed him to join them as they still wanted him.
They were in the premier division and he fully intended to help them stay there.
 That was the place to be for him to fulfil his ambition to play for his beloved Club and to represent his country at the highest level.
That in turn was great as it also meant he didn't have to move away, for now!

Boy, he had a cracker of a game, scoring two in a 4-0 whipping. What a result for Tommy and the team.
Tommy would make a top class professional footballer, already being touted as a future England captain with the world at his feet.
"Tommy Jackson England Captain" Tommy snr would whisper in Martha's ear.

Chapter 12

Sophie was winning trophy after trophy at Club and County level in the many competitions she had been entered for by her archery and gun clubs.
There where rumblings of Sophie representing England.

This was becoming more and more difficult and as both the archery and gun clubs wanted her solely for themselves. She was an outstanding competitor and prospect; this was making life difficult for Sophie.
There was little to choose between the two as she excelled in both and she didn't want to have to make that decision.
One way or the other it would disappoint either her mum or dad and she didn't want to do that as they had both been very supportive.
Sophie decided to let it take its own course.

She was also doing very well at school and at one of the many gatherings whilst discussing their children; Mr. Childs had stated, "She will do well in the City as a P.A. in some major conglomerate,"
"Either that or a latter day Robin Hood", quipped Tommy snr.,
"No Dick Turpin" Mused Joan, and they all had a little chuckle at this....

 Mum and Dad had secret ambitions of her representing England, the Commonwealth Games and maybe even the Olympics and the media had been pushing for her inclusion.

"So she could,"…

"She's good enough...." they'd said in private, and they joined in the laughter as they knew their friends were only teasing.

Chapter 13

Louise was beyond belief; she was frighteningly years beyond her age at mathematics English and business studies.

University was looming just around the corner.

"Wonder what she will achieve?"...
"The world is her oyster" mused Joan and Geoffrey.
"Perhaps she'll become a JUDGE!!?" said Joan with a wry smile.
"Do you think she's got the brains" answered Geoffrey they both glanced at the old judge, Joan's dad.
"I'll tell you this..." he stated.

They both started to giggle, there'd hooked him.

"That beautiful young lady takes after me for brains... and looks," ... he paused...
"I fancy her for politics, logical cute brain, Maths English, Business... Chancellor or Leader indeed"...

"In which case she should stay away from politics" said Geoffrey satirically.
"Her colleagues would have no idea what she was talking about" said Joan dryly.

He winked at them, he realised what they'd done and turned the tables and they all burst out laughing.
"Either way she will be going away....' said Joan sadly.

"Yes, indeed a sad day..."

Chapter 14

The Growing

There had never been any romance amongst the friends but they were beginning to develop and the hormones began to jingle after all they were into their sixteenth year.

Tommy had left school with O Levels in English and Maths thanks to the tuition of his two best friends.
But he had made his dream signing pro for "his team" already playing reserve football and occasionally substitute for the first team to blood him at sixteen and a half this was unusually rare, but he was beyond his years physically mentally and with an abundance of talent; what a future for Club and Country.

Both the Manchester's, Liverpool, Arsenal, Barcelona and Madrid; all the big clubs home and away wanted Tommy and were very disappointed when he signed for the team he supported as a kid, which had really pleased his mum and dad.

Tommy was beginning to look at Louise in a new light. She was no longer one of his two best friends, his feelings were starting to run much deeper but he tried to hide it as he didn't want to hurt Sophie.
This was becoming a harder task than he had imagined.

He desperately wanted to tell Louise how he felt.

He wasn't silly; he knew she would soon be going away to university and that day was beckoning.

There would be all types of blokes there and even a blind man could tell how beautiful she was and what a lovely person she was.

"What am I going to do...?"...

"I can't talk to Sophie about it"...

"What a dilemma"...

"Do I come straight out with it"...?

"Do I take the chance of upsetting Sophie"...?

"Or do I keep quiet and take the chance of losing Louise"....?

That thought didn't bear thinking about.

Chapter 15

Sophie had also left school and gone straight into the City working for a merchant bank.

She was a very popular girl and was doing extremely well in her field moving between various departments to gain experience.

Being a brighter than average student this was not a problem for her to adjust. Her bosses having the knowledge of Sophie's talent's, her fluency of languages they were keeping a very watchful eye on her.

She was being nurtured for the future; International monetary accounts, V.I.P. customers, world travel ….

Sophie would go to lunch with her colleagues to the local wine bar or brasseire.

She would be taken to special events and meetings by management and introduced to influential clients, already mixing in her future circles of work.

On a number of times she would be chatted up and asked out on dates, which she politely declined.

She was no shrinking violet or indeed no ugly duckling, but a rose bush in full bloom and a beautiful swan and Sophie only had eyes for…Tommy.

"How am I going to divulge this to Louise, God only knows"…

"I don't want to hurt my sister"…

"She'll understand"…

"After all Tommy and I have so much in common".

"In any case Lou will be going to university soon and she is bound to meet a nice bloke there, everything will be fine."

Sophie had continued with her archery and shooting at a very high level.

To the delight of her dad she had been chosen to represent her country in firearms, mainly pistols. Guns had finally come out on top but her mum was still so proud of her. And as ever the gang were all there cheering her on; she loved her two friends dearly.

Chapter 16

Louise had stayed on at school under special tuition so as to avoid leaving for University for as long as she could.

But she knew she would have to go sooner rather than later and what an emotional wrench that would be.

They were so close since they first met; just kids, they had never ever really been apart, they had grown together, matured together, and they knew everything about each other.

"What will it be like not seeing each other every day? Walking to school together, meeting up, going home together, spending our social time together, seeing Sophie in competitions, watching Tommy play football ....? ...Ha...Tommy...

Waking up knowing I won't see...Tommy...!" she felt sad at that thought.

She could not bear the thought of leaving her two friends especially Tommy. She had seen the way he looked at her and then quickly looked away.

The hair on the back of her neck stood up and goose bumps ran up her back; she had butterflies in her tummy...

"But how could she tell Sophie?"...

"Would she understand?"...

"We are the greatest of friends"...

"I'm sure Sophie would understand"...

"She loved her just like a sister."...

"Ho Tommy"....

They had promised as kids that they would never leave each other...

"All for one and one for all".... "The Three Musketeers..."

"But we were just kids"...

"We're grown up now"...

"We can still be together"...

"The grown up Musketeers."

Chapter 17

As a combined and belated, they had to wait for the end of the football season, 17th birthday present; "Well done on your achievements" their parents organised and paid for a two week holiday to Portugal.

The parents had got together in a clandestine meeting, behind closed doors.... with a few bottles of wine to get on with.............

"I do think they've done extremely well." said Geoffrey very proudly.

"They certainly have, my dear" agreed Joan.

"So what are we going to do for them...? Asked Fred...

"Maybe a party, a celebration" interceded Chloe.

"Not if that means Spill-the-video gets 'is camera out...." added Tommy snr.

"Portugal. We pay and send them to Portugal.... They are adults now" commanded Martha.

"Quite right" agreed Joan.

"Great choice" echoed Chloe.

"They would feel comfortable there" pronounced Geoffrey.

  "They know it well and they will feel at ease, first time away" affirmed Fred.

"So be it".... "Agreed" decreed Tommy.

"Agreed" "Agreed "Agreed" "Agreed" "Agreed."

The plot was planned down to the last factor...............

They had booked their flights and they would book the villa that they always stayed in. There was room in the event if Tommy decided to take a friend along. The villa came with a cleaner and its own pool, along with transfers.

When they informed Sophie, Louise and Tommy of the prize and celebration present they were ecstatic...
"Ho my God thanks to you so much..."
"Wow brilliant thanks... I can't believe it..."
"How wonderful, what a magical surprise..."

This would be their very first holiday away together, on their own, with no parents.
They decided against asking anyone else for as much as they got on well with their other friends they agreed their first holiday should be just for "The Musketeer's; their first adventure overseas."
They were well excited; they'd been out and bought their sun tan oils and toiletries.

Their bags were packed, the taxi arrived and off they went to Gatwick.
'Ok we have booked in."
"No delays."
"Coffee anyone?" asked Tommy.
"I think we'll hit the duty free first" said Louise.
"Yes we'll grab some perfume." added Sophie.
"The only thing you'll get hit with is the full price...!" Quipped Tommy....
"... And you better be careful of whom you grab or you'll get an unwanted admirer or 18 months."

Sophie and Louise made silly faces at Tommy "Comedian," they said together.

"When he's finished football, he could go on the stage."

"What as a sweeper." Both the girl's started to giggle.

They all trudged off to the duty free; Tommy bought a couple of different types of after shave and a few C.D.'s.

The girls bought perfume; they also looked at watches, chains, rings, personal C.D. players.... even though they both owned one.

"I'm off for a coffee"... Tommy said ... "coming...?"

"No we're going to have a look in the bikini shop."

"HA! Sounds good to me, in that case I'll come with you, buy myself a nice THONG" he winked.

"Oh, no you won't...!" said Louise.....

.... You go and have your coffee."

"We'll catch up with you in a bit" said Sophie.

"And if we see a nice THONG"... "We'll buy it for you," quipped in Louise.

"Large cappuccino please" ordered Tommy and settled down to read his newspaper back page first.

The girl's strolled along lazily chatting until they reached the bikini shop, "LETS SLIP IN." Sophie and Louise looked at each other pulling silly faces "nice name"... "Nicer bikinis I hope" and they started to laugh.

"Look at this one there's nothing of it" grinned Louise.

"I don't mind showing a bit of cleavage but we may as well stick two corn plasters over our nipples" grinned Sophie.

"We may as well do loop the loop with a piece of string round our boob's"

"Or go the Full Monty...?"

"Topless with a thong...!"

"And we'll buy Tommy one we will be known as THE THONGERTEERS"

"Or THE MUSKERTHONGS..."

The girl's bounced off of each other. They loved their party pieces, their one liner's.

"Seriously Sophie would you go topless...?"

"Well I had considered it Louise, would you...?"

"I'd like to..."

"Seems a shame not too"

"All that sunshine"

"Get a better tan"

"Get a much better tan..!"

"An all over tan...!"

"I am not going that far...!"

"What about Tommy are we going to go topless in front of Tommy...?"

"I don't know, do you think he would get embarrassed...?"

"Embarrassed...! Tommy, when does Tommy do embarrassed, I mean does the Pope Kiss tarmac, do bears pooo in the woods..."

"Hmmm I see what you mean"

"Do you think we would be embarrassed...?"

"Well we have done it before"

"Sophie we where twelve years old and the only chest we had was a Spanish galleon's ... SUNKEN CHEST"

"That's true, more breast on an anorexic chickens, than we had on us."

"Our shoulder blades where bigger than our boobs"
"I thought I had measles once with only two spots.... both on my chest, turned out to be my nipples."

The girl's looked at each other with wry smiles then burst into laughter as did a number of customers and the shop assistants who had been listening to their banter.

"You two should be on the stage" said the shop assistant smiling in admiration.
Sophie and Louise walked over to the full length mirror...
"Well we aren't twelve anymore"
"Size twelve...!"
"And they are not any pimples on our chest...!"
"Topless or not Topless...?"
"That is the bottom line"
"Top line dear"
"Will he mind...?"
"Will he be bothered...?"

They each looked at their opposite reflection in the mirror and said,
"NO"
"TOPLESS"

Nodding their heads in agreed approval.
They bought a couple of bikini sets each, reversible ones and headed for the coffee shop.

"We won't tell him what we are going to do"...
"SURPRISE, SURPRISE."
 "It's a double whammy...!"
"You speak for yourself, I quite like mine..." quipped
Louise smiling.
 "But we should sound him out."
"If he's against it...?"
"We won't do it."
 "We don't want to embarrass the poor boy."

They walked into the coffee shop and planted their bags
at the table.

"TOP UP Tommy...?" Smiled Louise...
 "Cappuccino please, what you two been up to...? With
those silly smiles on ya faces. You've bought the airport
up I suppose."
"No we haven't... would you like a couple of French buns
TOPPED with fresh cream with your TOP UP coffee...?"
asked Sophie.
 "Sounds nice" said Tommy looking at both the girls,
puzzled. They walked off together giggling and grinning
like two Cheshire cats.

The girls returned with their drinks and buns and they sat
around the table.

 "We'll let's see what have you bought, let's have a...
butchers hook... and did you get me a thong...?"
 "Tommy what do you think about topless...?" quizzed
Sophie being far from discreet, Louise sat there mouth
gaping. "Sophie!"

Tommy sat there with his chin in his hand and mused...

"Well, I'm not wearing a bikini top it would spoil my all over tan." The girls looked at each other; they couldn't believe their ears. Had he been eve's dropping out of sight....?

"TOPLESS sounds wonderful to me, everyone should do it… It will be topless; I'll just wear the thong."

The girls sat in silence. Had he...? Hadn't he...?

"WHY...?" pronounced Tommy looking alternately at the girls and smiling.
"Because" said Sophie delving into her bag of goodies....
"That's all I've bought you.' Pulling out a white pair of men's thongs and throwing them at him.
Louise was so surprised; she had not seen Sophie buy them.

Tommy stood up holding the thong against him "THANKS they're brilliant" ... "And you didn't think they'd suit me...?" He said looking at Louise.
"Well" said Louise looking at Tommy "YES... I actually did" and threw another white pair of men's thongs at him, which she had pulled out of her bag of goodies.

"THANKS two pair they're brilliant, both white, matching, good taste."

He put one pair over his head and held the other pair against him, dancing, "BRILLIANT."

Sophie was also very surprised; she had not seen Louise buy them either.

Sophie and Louise where both watching Tommy performing with his thongs they looked over at each other, big smiles appearing on their faces, they took each other's hand and clutched tightly at this point Tommy lent under the table taking two small bags from his duty free bag and throwing one each to Louise and Sophie.

The girls were startled at this action again they looked at each other puzzled, they opened the bags and both took out a white bikini...!
"I thought there'd come in handy especially when you've got a nice tan and I will be going topless....!"

Both the girls looked at Tommy "did he know...?"... "Didn't he know...?"

The girls jumped up and ran around the table and all three went into a great hug.

"The Three Musketeers" spent the next two hours walking around buying bits and pieces, looking in various shops, there was great delight and micky taking whenever they came across a store that sold bikinis.

Eventually their flight was called and they went through to departure gate 22.

They had another short wait and then they boarded flight 416A to Faro.
They had flown to Faro a few times but this time it felt different they were on their own, all grown up.
2 hours and 45 minutes to glorious beaches, beautiful sunshine, wonderful food and a great time to be had by all.
They all sat together; Louise claimed the window seat, Tommy in the middle and Sophie on the aisle seat.
They had breakfast on the plane as they had been booked on an early morning flight; they were sitting looking at their papers, browsing through the magazines. Passing time...

"I'm just off to the LOoo" said Sophie turning her head sideways looking at Louise, with a silly grin on her face.
Tommy bowed his head and grinned, this was a standing old pun, and he knew what was coming next, "Ho are you, and I thought you were going for a lay down on the SOPH...err" responded Louise as she screwed her face up.

In this respect the kids took after their dad's always jibing each other, but woes betide anyone else who tried it.

"Remember when we were kids Sophie...! ... Don't pull the chain...!" Tommy said without taking his eyes from his newspaper, with that he pointed his finger at her then moving his hand; he pointed his finger downwards "WHOoosh...!"

Sophie gave him a blank stare "MORon" and walked off to the toilet grinning to herself...............

Chapter 18

On their first trip to Portugal when the kids where twelve the three families all went away in a big group.... of friends.

Sophie had said "I'm going to the toilet mum"
"Ok dear do you want me to come with you...?" was the reply.
"Mum I'm old enough to go to the Looo by myself...! Sophie retorted with one of those looks at her mum and a quick glance at Louise...

As she stood up and edged into the aisle...Tommy had said "remember don't pull the chain unless you have both feet on the floor and your feet wedged against the wall and hang on tight to the rail with your other hand "
Sophie looked quite alarmed at Tommy..."WHY....?"
"You'll be flushed away pulled down with it, *the air pressure*..... Whoosh...!"
And Tommy was pointing his finger downwards

Sophie for a kid who lived overseas and had flown before, actually wasn't sure and had not pulled the chain.
When she got back to her seat her mum had asked "Did you wash your hands dear...? And did you pull the chain...?"
"Yes mum" ... "and no mum Tommy told me I would go down with it when it opens up and flushes."
"Sophie how many times have you flown" her mum had said and the three mums who were sitting next to each other all turned and looked over their seats at Tommy

shaking their heads with smiling eyes, Tommy's mum said....

"I wonder who you take after...?"

Simultaneously the three mums have looked at Tommy snr. Who was sitting in the middle seat behind the children "We wonder" They chorused.

So innocently, butter wouldn't melt in their mouths, Fred and Geoffrey sat pointing an accusing finger snarling... "YEerrr" at their mate....

Tommy who was an avid John Wayne fan sat there with a silly big smirk on his face soaking up the plaudits and with his John "DUKE" Wayne brogue he replied.........

"THAT'S MY BOY"

Geoffrey and Fred immediately started to bow their heads and hands chanting, "DUKE, DUKE, DUKE, DUKE" in mock approval.

"And you two are no better" said the ladies smiling.

Tommy sat there gently rocking, pointing his two index fingers into the air with the same silly smirk on his face.

The three kids started to laugh; the three mums' shook their heads,

"Sad"

"So sad"

"Don't sit there laughing encouraging him."

"I don't know who the bigger kids are...?"

Telepathically all six, the three kids, the three dad's, sat rocking gently, side to side pointing there index fingers

into the air with big cheesy grins on their face's they started to sing;
"Always look on the bright side of life, dada, dada"
"always look on the bright side of life, dada, dada"

As hard as they tried the mum's couldn't help themselves they turned fully in their seats perched on their knees facing the other six they started to rock gently, side to side, pointing there index fingers into the air, their heads rolling side to side, all nine started to sing....

"Always look on the bright side of life, dada, dada"
"always look on the bright side of life, dada, dada"

This show was abruptly brought to an end when an air hostess appeared, smiling she asked "is everything O.K...?."... "Can I be of assistance?"

"Now you come to mention it" said Tommy snr.
In his John "The DUKE" Wayne accent and a bigger smile on his face "You can little lady"... he paused.
"I'll take three gin and tonics please for the saloon gal's" pointing at the wives as they began to turn in their seats.
"Three beers and three whiskey chasers for us"
"And I'll take whatever the saucepan lids *"kid's"* want please"
"Coke" "Coke" "Coke please" echoed the kids.
"Three cokes please"... "And no chewing tobacco...they're too young !"

The stewardess smiled, nodding her head she said "It'll be my pleasure Duke" in a Dolly Parton accent…………..

Chapter 19

Sophie returned from the toilet *safely* "everything O.K. Sophie? ... Come here and rest your butt take a seat and rest your brains..." said Tommy frivolously

".... And did you wash your hands...?"

"Did you pull the chain dear?" quipped in Louise smiling at her.

Sophie sat down and glanced at her two friend's nonchalantly then looked forward, a grieved look on her face without replying she sat in silence.... staring into space, Solemn...............

"Sophie, are you ok...?" demanded Louise...

"Soph what's wrong...?" Tommy said concerned.

"Sophie, speak to us, please are you ok...?" echoed Louise.

"Is there something wrong....?" they both interjected.................

Sophie bowed her head and a wry smile appeared on her face then a grin.....

"Got ya"... "Let's go fishing ... Hooked and reeled in ..... Landed...!"

They looked at each other; they knew they had been had!

"You cow...!" sneered Tommy...

"You said it" confirmed Louise........

And almost immediately the three of them where gently rocking side to side and humming;

"da, da, dada, dada, da, da, da" "always look on the bright side of life dada, dada"

The hands automatically went to the side of their heads index fingers pointing up wards moving up and down in unison.

There'd never forgotten.

The rest of the journey was quite uneventful.

They sat silently musing over their own intimate thoughts.

The silence was broken "Bing Bong"... "This is your Captain speaking we will be presently preparing for our decent into Faro Airport as you can see it is a clear beautiful sunny day not a cloud in the sky, it is approximately 85 degrees Fahrenheit. The long term weather forecast is it's going to get hotter, so I would suggest you take care to make sure you don't burn and cover up in the midday sun".

"Cover up what about my thong...?" groaned Sophie,

"Cover up not likely" said Louise.

"Yep" said Tommy "It sounds better and better to me bring on the sun".

"Ladies and Gentlemen on behalf of the crew and myself, I would like to take this opportunity to thank you all for flying with us and wish you a pleasant stay".

Tommy, Sophie and Louise buckled themselves in as did the rest of the passengers and the Captain brought the aircraft in on a very smooth landing.

As they stood in the doorway of the plane ready to disembark, they skipped down the stairs and the heat hit them.

"Wow"

... "You said it"...
"And its early, it will get hotter"

They walked the short distance across the tarmac and went into arrivals through to passport control, where they queued patiently....

"Ola, bon Dias" said Sophie to the passport controller.
"Ola Seniorita, totabine...?" replied the controller with a smile on his face.
"Si commasta" replied Sophie
"Ferrias...?" enquired the official,
"Si duas semmanas, com duas amigos" answered Sophie
"Fella Portuguese...?"
"Um porco" Sophie said with a smile and nodding her head gracefully, the passport controller handed Sophie her passport back and nodded his head respectfully "Obrigado Siniorita, bon ferrias".

Next up was Louise; she passed her passport to the controller and stood there with a smile on her face..... He looked at her passport photo then at her, "Bon Dias Seniorita ... Ferrias...?"
"Ho yes" said Louise "Two weeks with my friends" pointing toward Sophie and back over her shoulder at Tommy....
"Totabine" passing her passport back to her he gestured her through.

Tommy waited until the controller beckoned him forward Tommy handed his passport through the counter..... The controller look at his picture then at Tommy, then at the picture then at Tommy again, Tommy looked a little apprehensive, then a wry smile spread across the Passport controllers face, "bon ferrias amigo, duas com amigos, Senioritas... munto bonnitto........" Tommy looked at him blankly.

The controller glanced toward the girls who were waiting for him, "Ho yes" nodding his head and once more the controller gestured him through...........

The three friends walked through to baggage claim, on the screen they saw their flight number indicating conveyor belt 3.

"Soph what was that all about...?" inquired Louise

"yer spill the beans, bi-lingual girl" chuckled Tommy.

"We were just being polite you know, hello, how are you, fine thank you, holidays,

Yes two weeks with my two friends"

"He said that I spoke Portuguese."

"I said a little."

"He said thank you have a nice holiday."

"He also said that... we two girls were very beautiful."

"A little" said Louise..."

".....Hooo did you say he said we are very beautiful, well there we are, a man with taste"

"....And by the way....You have A-level literature and fluent in the language.....".

"That's for sure... you have A-level in every language... that is except, "Cockney" said Tommy clapping his hands together

"Don't you Adam and Eve it our saucepan lid" replied Sophie in rhyming slang, "Me old fella done a bit of porridge with a geezer from the Bow Bells"

Tommy started to laugh "don't believe it our kid; your dad did a stretch in prison with a man from the East End of London."

"That is what one indicated wasn't it...?"... "Well ...no...? ... Wasn't it...? Yes...?" Retorted Sophie in an exaggeratedly, posh voice.

"Come along Del-boy and Rodney" said Louise "although I'm not totally sure whose who... here is our bags"...

"You know who that makes Louise" whispered Tommy to Sophie.

"Who...?"

"Uncle Albert" sang out Tommy and the three of them went into a chorus of...

You can keep the Algarve..... I'd rather be in Yarmouth with all the family"...

"I don't think so ... chicken piri-piri ... a garraffa of vino - verdi and fourteen days of sun"

They grabbed their cases threw them on their trolleys and headed out of the airport continuing with the ditto.....

"I don't think so... you can keep the Algarve... I would rather be in Yarmouth with all the family.... I don't think so"....

"GIVE US... CHICKEN PIRI PIRI, A GARRAFFA OF VINO VERDI AND FOURTEEN DAYS OF SUN"

"Taxi, Casa da Luz Carvioero, faz forvor"

An hour later they pulled up outside their villa, they had given the driver directions once they reached the town centre.

After all they'd spent many a good holiday based in this villa with its panoramic views overlooking the sea. It was a detached villa in its own gardens Bougainvillea climbing, flower beds and shrubs with an array of beautiful colours, six foot walls separating them from the villas either side giving them supreme privacy, idyllic.

A welcome pack as always was waiting for them.

They picked their rooms all though this had all ready been decided, Louise and Sophie went through the door on the left hand side of the living room and they came into a passage way, there were two bathrooms adjacent to each other and two double bedrooms at each end of the corridor.

The girls picked a room each.

Tommy entered the door on the right hand side of the living room the layout was identical to the other side again there where two adjacent bathrooms and two bedrooms, one double and one twin each end of the corridor, and Tommy picked the double bedroom overlooking the swimming pool.

They unpacked their bags quickly put on their shorts and tee shirts and took a leisurely stroll down to the town.

They picked up some food and bits and pieces had a quick lunch and headed back to the villa.

After depositing their goodies into the fridge and cupboard, the girls took off their shorts and tee-shirts, they all ready had their *bikinis* on underneath.

Tommy slipped off his tee-shirt and the three of them lay around the pool on their sun lounges soaking up the sun for the rest of the day.

The girls had decided not to go topless....on the first day.

That evening they proceeded to go out for a pleasant meal and a few drinks at a restaurant on the beach at Prior da Roacha.

Chapter 20

The following morning Tommy was up earlier than the girls, he made a pot of coffee and some toast and sat by the pool.

"Tommy would you like some breakfast...?"Asked Sophie, "well it's about time" answered Tommy with a laugh in is voice "a man could starve to death here."

"YOU You... You could have always brought us breakfast in bed" chirped in Louise

"I left you to enjoy your beauty sleep."

"Is that right, what are you trying to insinuate then" demanded Louise with a massive big smile on her face and hands on hips.

"yer pretty thing what are you trying to say" piped in Sophie,

"Well now you come to mention it" Tommy said quietly covering is mouth and lowering his head

"Ho yer!!" Both the girls replied instantly

"Only joking... only joking... only joking" said Tommy jumping to his feet and turning round to face them for the first time

"MELONS... melons"... "Ho my God melons" he stood there nodding his head...

Louise and Sophie where standing at the open patio doors... topless.

Both the girls burst out laughing "problem...?"... "Any problem...?"

"No" said Tommy regaining his control "none at all now you both sit down and I'll make you some fresh coffee, pot of tea toast and cornflakes" he stuttered.

"I think you need to sit down" said Louise "well make you some fresh strong coffee"
"And close your mouth before your jaw hits the floor"...
"You look like you're catching flies" said Sophie.
"You'd think this boy had never seen topless before"
"Well not since we were twelve"..... And both walked off giggling

They laid around the pool soaking up the sun every now and again taking a dip in the pool to cool down.

"Anyone for lunch...?"
"Sounds good"
"Shall we wonder down town to the beach...?"
"SARDINES...!!!"
"Bifana's..."
"On the beach... yes" they all joined in at once, quickly slipping shorts tee shirts and sundress on and off they set.

The first four days followed much the same vein lying around the pool soaking up the sun, lunch on the beach and going out for a meal and a few drinks at night none of them being particularly big drinkers.
They went to the local bars joined in the fun, but for the most they were quite happy to have a relaxing first few days and a few early nights or to sit around the villa in their own company, playing cards, monopoly, listening to music, very contented.

They were all acquiring nice deep tans and were looking pretty good and looking forward to the remainder of their holiday.

There was however a new energy between them there was a tension that had never existed before.

This was their first time away without their parents and a freedom to do and to express them self in the way they wanted.

This of course was empowered, stimulated and exaggerated by this: awakening, burning desire of emotional, mental and physical hormones that were stirring wildly, individually, inside each of them.

A sensing, a noticing, an appreciation, a desire, a passion, an arousing that was ready to erupt, so far on the surface controlled, but simmering just below the surface, inside, boiling, like a volcano ready to explode.....................................

Only in which direction...?

"Bar-B-Q tonight up in the Monchique Mountains" exclaimed Sophie

"Yes looking forward to it" enthused Louise....

"Get your glad rags on girlies; tonight we'll hit the town when we get back from the Ba-B-Q" claimed Tommy

"Yes, we could go to the disco" said Sophie excited.

"Sounds good but today, I'm not moving from this pool, rest is the order of the day" said Tommy.

"REST has been the order of every day since we've been here" quipped Sophie. "WONDERFUL isn't it" smiled Louise.

"And I don't think I'll be moving far from the pool today either" she added

"Well I suppose that means I'll be going down town on my own I've got to get some bits and pieces, do you need anything"

"No thanks Soph" replied Louise

"Could get me a paper so I can catch up on the sport..." said Tommy

"I'll head down in a bit then I can get back for lunch".

"About 2 o'clock... it will be on the table" Tommy said "my treat I'll do the honours" "that means we'll have salad rolls". mused Louise

"You don't want to bloat yourselves out girls Bar-B-Q tonight"

"True"

"OK ... I'll be off see you in a bit, bye-bye"

Sophie took a leisurely stroll down to town stopping off at the beach bar for a cool long drink, she then wandered around the shops picking up the things she needed.

Louise and Tommy laid effortlessly on their sun lounges soaking up the sun rubbing in their sun oils so as not to burn and enhancing their tans............

Tommy could not help himself he was constantly aware that he kept looking in Louise's direction under the cover of his dark sunglasses every time Louise looked up in his direction he would smile at her, then drop his eyes or close them pretending to be asleep.......

Louise without being too obvious and aware that she had caught Tommy looking at her....wondered "Why does he always look away"..."does he find me so unattractive".... she would sit sporadically gazing at him beneath her sunglasses, then close her eyes......

"God she is so beautiful"... *"Tommy Jackson"*..."I cannot take my eyes off of her"... *"You are such a handsome man"*..."What am I going to do...?"... *"What are you going to do...?"*..."how am I going to handle this, these feelings...?"... *"Do I handle this and show my feelings"*... "What can I say to her...?"... *"Say something Tommy...!"*... "Louise I must tell you" ... *"Tommy I've got to tell you something"*... "I can't stop thinking about you, night and day"... *"Tommy you are on my mind all the time"*... "I just want to be near you"...
"I want you close to me"..
These where the thoughts being shared between them..... Driving them insane.... But no words were spoken...... the silence was deafening....

Chapter 21

"What time do you think it is" asked Louise loudly

Tommy glanced down at his watch beside the bed and yawned a false yawn, and then he stood up putting on a big act exaggerating every movement looking at the sun guarding his eyes with his hand he said "Almost 1 o'clock".
"How can you tell by looking at the sun...?" quizzed Louise.
"It's easy I saw Crocodile Dundee do it" mused Tommy.
"You checked your watch first and then told me the time didn't you, you cheat" accused Louise.

Tommy shrugged his shoulders "exactly MY DEAR" and smiled
Louise shook her head and smiled "you're incorrigible".
Tommy winked at her and said "Don't you smile and swear at me in one go"
"Go and make the rolls gourmet" Louise said shaking her head and smiling.
"See you're doing it again bossy" said Tommy winding her up as he walked inside laughing.

Louise applied more oils to her front and closed her eyes. Picturing Tommy in her thoughts..........

Tommy went to the kitchen "*Ho Louise*" he washed his hands and started to prepare lunch...

"Salad rolls coming up, Plate Du Jour no no, Prate do Dia as in Portugal do as the Portuguese do.... Dish of the Day" he said to himself.

"Ham salad rolls one each, cheese salad rolls one each, little bowl of side salad each, crisps, olives and pickles"

"Looks good... bottle of white wine maybe two large bottle of iced water pot of percolated coffee and some almond cake"

"Hmmm salad rolls indeed there'll be impressed" Tommy looked at his watch "1.45 good timing"

"Louise lunch is ready are we having it out there or in here"

"Louise do you want to freshen up...?"

"Louise...?"

"Louise come on, move, its lunch"

"That's all I do here washing, ironing, tidying up, making the beds, slaving over a hot stove...cooking. Do I get appreciated...? No..... and as for sex, ha, forgotten about that haven't ya.... What about my needs...? I'm just a slave, in your castle", Tommy was having a right old laugh to himself....

And Louise could hear every word shaking her head, giggling away.......

"Nag Nag Nag" ... "I'm coming stop moaning...." Louise shouted out so Tommy could hear....

Which only inspired him even more "Nag Nag Nag I see that's how it is now, now I know what you think of me an old Nag".... Tommy retorted... sarcastically laughing to himself out loud.

Louise smiled and raised herself from the lounger......
she ambled slowly across the patio grabbing a narrow
strapped T-shirt from the chair...... she paused at the
doorway into the lounge area... pulling her T-shirt over
her head and down to her waist....... pushing the straps
down over the tops of her arms

Tommy skipped towards the kitchen door; still
giggling at himself as he learnt out to call Louise again...
"Louise...."

She stepped into the doorway right into his aura, into a
tight space for both of them.
They both glided and mirrored each other in a slow
motion action their own momentum took them back into
the kitchen, standing there Louise's back was touching
the wall next to the doorway leading to the lounge and
they froze settled
Against the wall that felt cool against Louise's back, the
only thing that was cool....

They stood there looking deep into each other's eyes
transfixed, tranquil, silent, the energy between them
flowing back and forth... electric.
One of Louise's legs then raised a little placing the sole
of her foot against the wall, she was biting her bottom
lip.... she was wearing just her thong and T-shirt ... over
her moist oiled body.

One of Tommy's arms was aloft and his hand placed on the wall just above Louise's head ...The other hand hovered beside her waist.

Tommy had the tip of his tongue between his teeth, Not a motion, statuesque....

A small bead of perspiration broke out on Louise's forehead; Tommy gently brushed it away with his finger tips and then flicked her hair back off of her face over her shoulders....

Then a single pearl of sweat rolled from her left shoulder flowing over the edge of her moistened thin T-shirt which was now translucent against her torso, it cascaded down her tanned oiled body, over her rounded succulent breast down to her waist, vanishing into the cloth of her thong.

Tommy watched it as it ebbed away down her beautiful fit body.

Louise watched his eyes follow the curvatures of her body and she noticed his, she went weak and sighed...

Tommy's eyes then returned to meet Louise's who had stopped admiring Tommy's firm physic.....

Once more both looking and both seeing each other in a whole new dimension.

Tommy was wearing just his shorts, his muscular tanned body, strong muscled legs, his hair pushed back over his ears.... they were close, so close.

They stood that *CLOSE, the energy and sensual tension between them was electrifying.......* rising

Louise straightened her leg; she licked her lips and said softly "I've got cramp in my foot".

Louise and Tommy were locked into each other's eyes as she spoke.

In a moment without hesitation he crouched down onto one knee never taking his eyes from her body, her firm succulent rounded breasts her slender stomach and slim waist, her curved hips, her well shaped legs.
His firm hands gently took hold of her foot; he cradled it into the palms of his hands and he massaged it.
Louise stood there motionless looking down at Tommy smiling, enjoying the moment, the intimacy, enjoying the way he was caressing her foot, the closeness between them, taking care of her.

Tommy continued to massage Louise's foot then leaving one hand holding the base of her sole, his fingers were gently pulsating, in out in rhythm... in out in out manipulating. The other hand he placed on her calf, gently stroking up and down the calf muscle, Louise gasped and swallowed deeply.
Tommy's eyes wondered upwards scanning the entirety of her beautiful tanned oiled body and their eyes met.
 Tommy slowly began to rise they were fixated with each other he brushed the hair from her brow with his left hand and tenderly fondled the cheek of her face with is right.

You couldn't slip a cigarette paper between them
Intimate, intrusively wonderful, for what seemed to be an eternity without any boundaries crossed..... Or any reservations

"Thank you" whispered Louise

Putting her right hand on his shoulder and placing her left hand on top of Tommy's right hand...

"My pleasure Louise any time" whispered Tommy as he continued to brush her hair and stroked her face……………..

"HELLO, HELLO I'm back" shouted Sophie "where are you...?"... "There you are"...

"Ho my God is anything wrong...?"... "What is going on Louise, are you O.K....?" she quizzed.

"Yes yes I'm fine I've got cramp in my foot"... said Louise "I should say I had cramp in my foot" she added...

Tommy looked over at Sophie startled, "lunch is ready it's on the table Soph"

He mumbled lowering his head and combing his fingers through his hair.....

Tommy stood there for a few seconds really not knowing what to do or say. Then at once it all became quite apparent as to what he should do and quickly, because he was suddenly aware and embarrassed by his body's reaction, showing in full proudest.

He turned away very quickly so his back was toward both of the girls hoping, praying no one had noticed, he moved rapidly towards the table trying to cover his pride and sat down.

"Excuse me" ... Louise went to her bedroom she sat on the edge of her bed for a minute or so to regain her equanimity.

Wiping the oil and sweat from her body. "Wow"

Sighing deeply her emotions were all over the place, breathing erratically then deeply, taking stock of what had just happened and calming herself...

Once more in self-control and poised, she then put a Bikini top on and shorts, a dry tee-shirt, before returning to the kitchen.

She smiled at both of them and sat down opposite Tommy.

Unknown to Louise and Tommy's knowledge, Sophie had been there quite a while longer than before she had spoken and interrupted them.

She had returned to find no one by the pool.

Curious at their disappearance and slightly concerned, "where are you...?" she mumbled.

Alarm bells went off in her head and butterflies started to jingle in her tummy.

A sickly feeling rose from inside her, nausea..... "Where are you...?" she panicked.

"No noise, silence, perhaps they have gone for a kip or a shower" she thought more hoping..

Sophie had entered the room via the patio doors and was heading for her bedroom when she saw their reflection in the mirror on the lounge wall.

She stopped instantly; the nauseous feeling increasing in maintaining the angle and positioning herself into a view point that they could not see her.......

Although there was little chance of that, their attention was fixed on each other, it was ... magnetic

...... Observing this very close encounter and had indeed witnessed their moment.

"Cramp wow my god that's painful" said Sophie "I only thought sports people got it" she mocked ... "good job his lordship was here to give you a helping hand" she added as she unpacked her bags, full of goodies for them.

She then went to her bedroom to remove her personal stuff and to get changed returning to the kitchen.

"Still at least Tommy was on *HAND* to help out" she quipped again "is it ok now...?"

"Yes fine thanks it only lasted a moment" answered Louise coyly

"Yes the muscle wasn't that solid ... TIGHT" piped in Tommy wishing he hadn't said anything as he slightly started to blush putting his head down.

They sat around the table eating making small talk the best they could but there was a tense atmosphere, awkwardness and embarrassment between Louise and Tommy and brusque from Sophie.....

"Was there many people down town Soph...?" asked Louise

"A few..."

"Were the shops busy...?" inquired Tommy

"Did you buy anything nice for yourself...?" quizzed Louise

"Did you go into Sully's for a drink...?", added Tommy

"Blimey this is like the third degree...

     ... Good cop ... bad cop...

      ... What's next the thumb nails ....?" retorted Sophie cynically

"Slow down tiger" ... snapped Tommy

"...... We are only interested Sophie...." said Louise with a tone, an edge to her voice

"I went down to the beach bar first for a coke and the beach was very busy.......

    ..... No the shops were quite empty......

   .... I saw a few things I liked but I didn't buy anything...

    ..... I thought maybe we would have another look tomorrow......

    ..... I popped into Sully's and had a bottle of water before starting back..."

Answered Sophie sarcastically and tersely.....

".... Well that certainly told us" ... quipped Louise with a strained smile on her face....

"In no uncertain terms..." said Tommy lightening the mood trying hard to bring some levity and humour into the situation...

"Is anything wrong Sophie" asked Louise genuinely concerned and completely unaware that she had witnessed their liaison...

"Has something upset you Sophie...? Or has someone upset you...? Because you are a little bit jumpy...." again genuinely concerned.... inquired Tommy

Sophie was slightly taken aback and overwhelmed by their genuine concerns even though given she had been snappy and terse, sarcastic and rude to them in her answers.

She looked down at the floor..... And she thought to herself.....

"... Have I over reacted"....

"...Ho no I could have got it wrong"

"... Have I misconstrued the situation....?"

"... Perhaps it was all innocent..."

"... What I saw was nothing more than Tommy helping Louise..."

"...Why am I so angry ...?"

"... At what I saw"

"...Why did I feel a tightening in my tummy and feel sick...?"

"... Are you winding us up again..." mimicked Tommy

"... Are you going to pull that silly face and start laughing in a minute...? Smiled Louise

" ... She is fishing...." Tommy added

"... and landed us...." confirmed Louise

Sub-consciously.... and consciously this is what they were both hoping for and it was happening... it would alleviate their own pangs of... guilt and embarrassment releasing them from their responsibility.......... in having to face up to what had really happened between them.

This infuriated Sophie, "They are diminishing my feeling?"... This was her first thought...

And the feelings came flooding back into her emotional response of what she felt when she saw Louise and Tommy so close, so intimate.............. Too close ... too intimate......

"... NO I'm not winding you up...

    .... Or fishing...

      ... Or landing you...

    ... No nothing is wrong...

... And No, no one has upset me..."

Trying hard to regain her composure... as she spoke......

   Tommy and Louise looked at each other curiously and then at Sophie.....

You could cut the atmosphere with a knife... Fraught to say the least

Tensions were running high...

 Something these three had never experienced before between them...

 ... A whole new experience.....

There was a prolonged silence.....

Eventually Tommy stood up now feeling more comfortable now that his hormonal reaction had died down and his attire wasn't so tight... He said... "I'm going to have a lay down in my room have a kip before tonight see you in a bit" and walked off.

The two girls sat at the table finishing their drinks they watched Tommy as he rose from the table placing his cup, glass and plates into the sink then heading for the kitchen door and leaving.

 "Yes that sounds like a good idea I think I'll go and have a lie down as well before we go out" Said Louise and she too went to her room.

"That makes good sense have a sleep and wake refreshed" said Sophie and she also retired to her room.

Chapter 22

Tommy entered his room looking around shaking his head; he placed his head into his hands "God she is so beautiful..."

"I've never really realised how beautiful Louise is, we were so close"...

"I've been close to her before but, but that feeling, that closeness was different, very different".

Tommy looked into the mirror, "how am I going to handle this...?"

"And what's all this with Sophie's actions and why is she was so angry....?"

For one fleeting moment he thought.......

"Did she come in and witness us that close...?"

"No because she shouted out where are you........!"

Tommy lay on his bed thinking about Louise......

"It's all I think about lately"

"Her eyes, looking into her eyes, so deep so beautiful"

How he kept looking at her, how beautiful she is, how slender and shapely her body is, the curves, her gorgeous breasts, her hips and her long shapely legs.

Touching her... foot... her leg.....

How she touched my hand..... My shoulder

What had gone on in the kitchen....?

God how close we were and it felt so right....

And how his body had reacted towards Louise......

He had been embarrassed but very excited as his body had told him; "I hope they never noticed my shorts getting so tight...!"

"Lunch is on the table.... LUNCH IS ON THE TABLE"
Tommy shook his head.
"I could have thought of something better than that to say"
"Hi Sophie how you doing...? How was town...? By the way Louise has got cramp I'm just sorting her out" ... "I mean massaging her"... "I mean releasing the tension in her..... Ho shit..."

He could not get the picture of Louise's face and body out of his mind nor did he want to and again his body reacted, aroused and suddenly he was excited and he was tingling, pulsing and tense all over. "Ho shit...!"
 Tommy jumped out of bed and went for a very long cold shower;   this   remedy   didn't   rectify   his arousing.................. So he did... then showered again

He patted himself down and He covered himself in moisturiser!
He returned to his bed and eventually slept dreaming of..... Louise.

Chapter 23

Louise slumped onto her bed "I've got cramp I'VE GOT BLOODY CRAMP...!"

"I could have said something other than **THAT...!**"

"My intellectual brain, the brain of Britain and that was the best I could come out with"

Louise pulled her tee shirt over her head tossing it into a corner she slipped her shorts off gently laying on the bed her mind started to wonder and oh how she was so close to Tommy.

"I've been close to him before but I've never been that close before his muscular body so firm but gentle, the way he took my foot into his hands, safe *"I felt so safe"*...

Louise could not get Tommy out of her mind her every thought was of Tommy how close they where, his eyes the way he looked at her, his touch the way he touched her, she began to perspire and her body reacted like it had never done before.... tingling , pulsing, throbbing...

She jumped from her bed darting into the shower, a cold, a very long cold shower, but still her thoughts were only for Tommy.

She patted herself dry and started to rub in her after sun moisturiser. Into her face and neck, into her shoulders, her breasts, her stomach, her back and eventually into her long shapely legs, looking at herself in the mirror. She closed her eyes and imagined Tommy holding her in his arms and she laid back down on her bed, eventually going off into a moist fantasy dream.

Chapter 24

Sophie followed Louise from the kitchen across the lounge and into their separate rooms.

She looked around the room and noticed the mirror, looking at herself; she resonated with the feelings and re-ran the events in her mind like a video show....

The way they looked at each other...

The way Tommy wiped Louise's forehead...

The way Louise rested against the wall... lifting her leg and Tommy was too... and so close

The way he knelt down and caressed her foot and leg...

She unbuttoned her short sun dress and hung it on the back of a chair, she had nothing on underneath.

She sat on the chair looking into the garden through the window very pensive …

Cramp…cramp….that was more than cramp, now what was that all about...?.

Where did that come from...?

Is there something going on with Louise and Tommy...?

Is there something they need to tell me...?

Wouldn't I know...?.

Wouldn't I have sensed it...?

I don't know...!

They never wanted to come into town with me!

They wanted to be on their own!

Why where they in the kitchen together at the same time...?

Why In that position...?

Was that planned....?

No I'm seeing too much into it mind you they were close, **to bloody close**, *no stop it, we're friends and we are all friends...!*

"THE THREE MUSKETEERS" and in any case if something like that was to happen... it would be me and Tommy....

*   ...After all said and done we have so much more in common".*

"...In any case Louise will be going away soon; of course he was just helping her with cramp....

*   ......If I needed help I know Tommy, he would be there for me, I know he would, he said we would always be together....!"*

Chapter 25

Tommy rose from his bed not completely refreshed... He had tossed and turned all afternoon, dozing off and then waking, dozing off and then waking. Louise always in his thoughts....

"...Something happened between us..."

"...there was openness... between us..."

"There was a connection..."

"...there was a feeling..."

"...something deep..."

"... Something new..."

"... I've never felt like that..."

"...and I want more..."

"...it was enchanting spell binding..."

"...magical..."

"..."mysterious..."

Silence..............

"Bar-B-Q night, tonight... better get ready...." Tommy said to himself....

"What about Sophie....?"

"How will she handle this... if there is a... this...?"

"There is a... THIS...."

"...Louise felt... it...! ... I know she did...

...or is that wishful thinking....?"

"And Sophie, yes Sophie she will have to deal with *this* situation that's arising..."

Tommy went into the kitchen stopping long enough by the wall to reminisce; smiling.

He made himself a strong coffee and a cold glass of water and went and sat on the patio...

Chapter 26

Sophie woke up feeling confused still unable to correlate the events she had witnessed.... unable to place everything into context she was feeling mixed emotions...

Betrayal...? "Why"....?

Cheated...? "Why"....?

Rejection...? "Why"....?

Resentment...? "Why"...?

Hurt...? "Why"....?

Angry...! "Why angry"...?

Isolated...? "Why"..................?

 "Why ...Why ...Why...?"

"You know why Sophie. You thought you would be ... wanted to be with Tommy"...she whispered and admitted to herself......

"They were close"...

"My two best friends"...

"I should be happy for them!"....

"...can I be..."

"...happy for them...?"

"How would Louise feel if it was *Tommy* and *Me*...?"

"Slow down you don't know if anything is going on......"

"...bloody cramp...!"

"I'm going to have to deal with this"

"Right let's get a drink and get ready Bar-B-Q night and hit the town"

Sophie slipped on her shorts and top entering the kitchen she couldn't help but glance... at that site...

She made herself a coffee and headed for the patio...

Chapter 27

Louise was lying on the bed; she had been awake for some time... thinking ... pondering...

"Something happened between us... that I know..."

"... and it felt good..."

"...it felt right..."

"...it felt magic..."

"... and I know Tommy felt it..."

"...how will he deal with it...?"

"...How will I deal with it...?"

"...How will Sophie deal with it...?"

"...How would I feel if .... mmmmm..."

"...if it was Sophie with Tommy..."

"... A sickly feeling rose inside Louise's tummy to the point she thought she was going to vomit..."

"...Ho I hope my God, helps me..."

"...I'm going to have to deal with this...!"

Louise slipped her shorts and t-shirt on...

She went to the kitchen and a shiver and goose pimples erupted through her body when she walked through the kitchen door and just hesitated as she passed *that wall......... she smiled!!!*

She made herself a cup of tea and a fresh orange...
And headed for the patio...

Chapter 28

Tommy was sitting quietly sipping his coffee; the silence was wonderful, peaceful and calming, little moments of solitude.... he so enjoyed

"Hi you ok...?" Sophie enquired... "...all right to intrude....?"
"Yep ... why not...? Tommy replied frowning inquisitively
"All right.....?" She asked
"..Yes good thanks.... you?
"Good"

They sat in silence both sipping at their drinks..... Admiring the view out to sea.....

"You two ok...?" Louise asked as she joined them.
"Enjoying the peace and the view..." said Sophie
"Come and join us..." encouraged Tommy
"Thanks..."

They all sat in silence, a comfortable silence soaking up the ambiance of the aromas coming from the bougainvilleas, the warmth of the evening sun.
The rippling of the pool and the view of the vast peaceful ocean, a cool breeze ruffling the trees......

"Good kip.....?" Sophie broke the silence looking and smiling at Louise
"So so....."
"So so... big night... tonight...." inserted Tommy

"Bar-B-Q...." enthused Sophie

"Mmmm chicken piri piri" Louise said licking her lips

"Spare ribs...!" Sophie put in

"I'm starving ...I could eat a scabby horse....." giggled Tommy

"You may well do....!" said Louise

"Shergar ..." added Sophie

"With any luck... help me run faster....!"

It was a balmy early evening

"The Musketeers"... sat by the pool finishing their drinks

"What time does the coach pick us up...?" asked Sophie...

"7.30... outside the hotel in the square..." answered Louise...

"Take 15 minutes to walk down... don't want to be late".... added Sophie

"Time for the three...S's then...." smirked Tommy...

"Tommy...! Objected Louise...

"Ok...two S's....

Louise gave him a look...

"Keep your third S in the privy that's private...!"

"Shave and a shower...! He smiled at Louise

"I'm showering... but not shaving"... joked Sophie

"Mmmm 5 o'clock shadow..." said Tommy smiling

"Well I might shave ... but not shower..." Added Louise

"WHOooooo... Lonely girl....." Chorused Sophie and Tommy

"Won't be standing downwind of you".... said Tommy grimacing his face

"Plenty of perfume"... added Sophie pulling the same face as Tommy...

"Come on let's get a mossy on ..."

"... 45 minutes... enough time...." added Tommy
"Don't wait for us..." instructed the girls together
"Up... up... and away..."

With that they scattered like mice.... in to their rooms.....

Pruning, preparing, showering...... shaving..........
Dressing and admiring themselves individually in the mirrors in their rooms
And changing at least three times...

"What shall I wear?"
"Summer dress or ..."
"Skirt and top or ...?"
"Does that look right?"
"Do those sandals match... do they go together?"
"This dress is see through ... where's that slip I packed"
"Shall I put my hair up or down?"
"Earrings ...mmm, studs or loops?"
"Necklace...? ... yes or no...?"

"Ok nice pair of white dress shorts, loose purple shirt...
... and mules comfy on the feet, no maybe trainers, could be uneven ground"

Tommy looked in the mirror one last time...
"What do you think Lou..." he said to himself.

He left his room and walked into the lounge.

"I'm ready you two come on ... move it... you going to be much longer...?
... If we miss the coach....."

"That will do...!"

"Eat your heart out world"

"Tommy will notice me tonight ...?

"I hope Tommy likes this dress ...!"

Sophie had chosen a white loose fitting pleated cotton skirt, and matching embroidered buttoned blouse ... and white sandals.....

Louise had chosen a white loose fitting cotton summer dress and flip flops....

Chapter 29

"The Three Musketeers" sauntered down to the square in town.

"No time for a quick drink the coach is waiting...."

They climbed aboard and found a seat...

The coach was almost full and started its pursuit up to the Monchique Mountains; it took almost an hour... to arrive at the venue...

An old Manor House in its own land; approximately 10 acres of woods, a fresh water lake and stream with some out buildings that had been renovated to a high standard, now self contained apartments keeping as much of the old character and artefacts.

It was now used for tourist events, corporate events, weddings and other functions.

It was inspirational yet a tranquil setting.... it could be ... whatever it wanted to be......!!!

The coach pulled off of the turning, twisting, ascending road of the mountain. The high rise trees lined the earth and rock banks to the sides. On the coach went through a set of 8 foot high wooden gates along the gravelled drive way....

The Manor House was an imposing site.

There was a stage set up for the bands to play.....

... And of course there was room to dance....

There were a number of erected bar areas for beer, wine and sangria....

And the food area, where there was a number of Bar-B-Q's with the aroma of.....

.... Chicken piri piri ... spare ribs.... burgers... sausages... Bowls of freshly made salad... pasta... jacket potatoes.... freshly baked crusty bread..... Stimulated their taste buds.... and filled the air

... And of course no sign of a scabby horse.....

The coach pulled into an allocated parking area where there were a number of other coaches all from different resorts along the Algarve.....

... And there were a lot of people... who had all come to party...

The trio departed from the coach, firstly to gather their bearings and identify meeting points should they get separated....

"Ok who fancies a drink and then....?"

"....Grab some grub" interrupted Tommy I am Hank Marvin...."

"Ho the dear boy's starving"

"Yes look at him he'll fade away, tin ribs"

"You go and get lining up for some food and Louise and I can go and order some drinks"

"Good idea what do you want Tommy a beer...."

"Sounds good.... thanks"

"We'll meet you around here pointing in a general direction"..."there are plenty of tables" organised Sophie

"Sure thing what you going to do about your food....?"

"We will no doubt be served before you, so we will come and join you in the queue, Queue jumpers"

And off they went.....

As much as they were getting on there was still an undercurrent from events to earlier in the day. Embarrassment, no one is looking each other in the eyes...

So on meeting back up and beers and wine in hand, a table full of goodies they tucked in....

"That was beautiful"

"I'm stuffed..."

"Wow... my mouth is on fire"

"There are chillies living in my mouth..."

"That was so spicy but so Moorish!"

"A few Sagres later and that burning sensation will start to diminish"

"And so will our inhibitions..."

"Then we will party"

A more relaxed atmosphere was in attendance as were the little glances and the catching of the eye...

Tommy was looking at Louise when she got up. "Where you going...?"

"Just to look at the band playing, I'm not going far"

His eyes would followed her, not that she strayed too far because she had noticed a couple of girls eyeing up Tommy.

She had also noticed they had come into Tommy's radar but he showed little interest, in fact he extinguished their flirting flames and attentions with a smile and a wink putting both his hands on top of the girl's hands with a little squeeze.

Louise watched Tommy when he went to the bar or to grab a bit more chicken... it was Moorish....

... She would watch his every move smiling at him and follow his return;

"Where you going...?"

"Getting a bit more chicken want anything...?

He in turn didn't want to stray too far... as he a noticed that there were a couple of blokes in their early twenties who were pointing and suggestively gesturing their ideas... in the direction of the girls.

Sophie had not missed a trick; she had watched Louise's and Tommy's interest and awareness of each other's movements.

Although it has to be said Tommy was attentive toward Sophie, which was so it wouldn't be too obvious, it wasn't too blatant for his feelings in Louise's direction.

"Do you want some more food Sophie or a drink...?"

"No thanks I'm good, ho ok I'll have another beer"

Louise also was conscious that she had to make more effort in communicating with Sophie the same as she had always done in the past; before her feelings became alive for Tommy.

"Sophie do you want a beer I'm getting one or some wine...?

"I'll have a beer please"

It was also apparent that both the girls in turn could not help but observe the unwanted interest of the two guys who were not shy in demonstrating their desires.

"Clowns..." insinuated Louise

"Pissed Clowns..." Sophie said turning her face away from them and her back towards them.

"Morons..."

"They are beginning to wind me up girls, to be truthful...!"

"Ignore them Tommy"... pleaded Louise

"Come on let's go dance..." added Louise

"That's a good idea... slurred Sophie"

"You go on I need the toilet and I'll get some cold drinks..." instructed Tommy

"Ok... don't be long..."The girls headed for the dance floor...

Tommy headed for the toilet.... then the bar...

... As soon as Tommy got to the bar alone

The two scrutinizing enthusiasts made a bee line for him...

"Hey handsome ... it's nice to see you at last all on your own...!"

"Good looking man like you shouldn't be left... to fend for yourself....!"

"Thank you girls but I'm not on my own my two beautiful ladies are dancing..." Tommy informed them gesturing with a movement of his head to the dance floor

"Ha that's nice; there are not enough gentlemen about..." snarled one

Louise had watched for Tommy and saw the two birds of prey hovering sizing up their intended feast...

"Munchies for the night... is their appetites..." said Louise to Sophie

Sophie had also been keeping a watchful eye of proceedings... well at least one eye as she was a bit tipsy... and not impressed...

"Slappers what do they want...?"
"...Well it isn't his spare ribs... Sophie." Confirmed Louise
"...NO obviously...they want the meat on his bones" counted Sophie

 She was drunkenly interoperating the episode....
"Why doesn't he take any notice of me ...? She thought to her self

As too did the two drunken dregs...
For has soon as the two prey mantis's moved in on Tommy....

They, the two vultures swooped in on the girls...

"Fancy a good night out girlies..." slurred one
"Yer leave the little boy to them two tarts..." added the other
"He might as well lose his virginity to them ... two"... hic
"Everyone else in our hotel as..." hic... hic...
"You can come back with us... for a drink and some fun"
"Yer try a real man ..." hic...

Instinctively Tommy stopped the small talk and swivelled round.....

 His eyes glued on Louise and Sophie.....

"Come on big boy leave your little entourage ...behind and show us the rest of those muscles....!"
"It's time for you to enjoy an experience show us what you're made of; your girlies will be looked after..."
"...Or maybe not, not with them two pricks, there'll be safer with them than having their chastity belts on"
"Considering they haven't been able to look after anyone else there always to pissed"... one of them said speaking from experience
"That's for sure" the other one laughed out....

"They are not my entourage they are my two best friends and I care and love them both very much....
.... So why don't you run along and get some more notches on your bed post or another tick on the tree you frequent ... or where ever you ply your trade...." Tommy gave them a very quick gaze and then turned his attention back to the situation in hand.

That was enough... and they walked off.... muttering....
"Faggot..."
"Lady Boy..."

Louise was conscious Tommy was in touch with them... in his radar...

 "Why don't you crawl back under the rock you slivered out from!" commanded Louise to the drunks

"Yes find the cesspit, you were born in! And return to it"
charged Sophie,

The music was loud and the two blokes where both three
parts to the wind and full of their own arrogance... and
had not fully heard the insults....

Louise linked arms with Sophie; she knew she had had
one sniff of the bar maids apron too many and was a little
worse for wear and they headed back to Tommy....

The two morons oblivious to the severity of the insults
they had just incurred...carried on dancing by
themselves...
"Lesbians, lesbo's..."
"Dykes..."
They muttered as the girls walked away...

"Good dance ....." Smiled Tommy in control of his
emotions but burning up inside...
 .. All ok?"... He added raising his head in the direction
of the two twats.
"I think we used observations that were too intellectual
for them..." said Louise sarcastically....
"And how was your evening with your fan club...the
martini girls any time any place anywhere" she added
pointing toward the two preying mantis..

"I feel like I've just been metaphorically hung drawn and
quartered chewed up and spat out, devoured.... like those
chicken bones on the floor" quipped Tommy
 "Nice so have you... have you been devoured before...?"

"No I haven't! ... That's why I said metaphorically...."
and he smiled

"Good!"... "Keep it that way...!"

"I will...!"

And they stared at each other deep penetrating eyes slight nodding of the head and with wry smiles a knowing connection an understanding..............

What an understanding what a connection....... they both shivered....

Sophie was unable to join in the repartee.... although she didn't look to out of control she had indeed, had one sniff of the barmaid's apron to many.

... But she wasn't so far gone... not to pick up on the vibes and the significance of reading between the lines.

"Here we go again" she thought.

And her stomach churned.....

It was nearing the end of the evening by now and Tommy and Louise were so engrossed with each other and the connection re-ignited!

Chapter 30

Sophie looked around and saw the toilet sign... and staggered, off in that direction but before she could get there she knew, her stomach started churning from all the booze and she thought she was going to vomit so she dived behind one of the out buildings that was nearer.......

To her sheer horror she came face to face with the two blokes who had just finished urinating.... up the trees she swung an arm instinctively in his direction fist clenched hoping more than in knowing she would connect

Sophie didn't know whether to be sick or to run. She felt sick alright and her head was spinning, she was at a complete loss, but as she tried to turn back a powerful, forceful hand grabbed her arm.

Survival instinct came into play.... she tried to pull away again but his grip was too strong, so she took a swing in his direction hoping and praying she would hit her target, but she missed and her fist soared through the air.

She stumbled forward, losing her balance, she felt as if she was falling, but the second attacker grabbed her other arm and they both hurled her against the wall.

Trepidation spread through her mind and body......and the realisation of her situation quickly turned to horror.

"So you came to find us...?" slurred one

"Decided to come and play with the men..."

"And you like it rough..."

Yer she likes it rough..."

They both started to laugh....

And they started mauling Sophie... ripping at the buttons of her blouse, grabbing at her breasts.

Fortunately they were so pissed; they were both getting in each other's way. Fortunately, for Sophie, that is.

.... Then one of them began trying to lift her skirt...

"Get her on the floor..." one growled

She was fighting for all she was worth.... pushing them away using her elbows, her arms, her fists, her legs, punching and kicking out.... struggling for all she was worth, fending them off...... fighting for her own preservation.

With every last ounce of effort left in her body she fought them...

A battle she was rapidly losing: intoxicated, disorientated, helpless, hapless, terrified.......A HOPELESS SITUATION...!!!

"Come on you 'ore..."

"Come on you little tart... stop your fighting ..."

"You know you want to do it..."

"Yer... you know you want it..."

"Yer... That's why you came looking...for us"

"...Yer... you followed us..."

"...You're gagging for it..."

"...You're begging for it..."

Chapter 31

Louise and Tommy were in panic stations....

"Where has she gone...?" demanded Tommy into thin air
"I don't know... she must have wandered off..." Panic intensifying in her voice.
"Where...?"

It was only a minute they had taken their attention from her....

"God, one minute she's there standing with us, the next she's gone..." Tommy stated gesticulating with his outstretched hand.
They were scouring the vicinity with their eyes, frantically searching the area around them...
There was no sight of her....
"She could not have got far..." assured Louise
"Where is she then...?"
"The toilets..." Louise screamed, "The toilets...." pointing
They were sure she was not in the location where they had examined...
"The toilets..." affirmed Tommy.

They both started to run in the only direction she could have gone in because she hadn't, did not walk past them...
"It's got to be those ones... " pointing in the direction from where Sophie had been standing...

They headed toward the direction of the toilets, and as they approached the converted outbuilding........

At that very time Sophie summoned up one last surge of energy as she could feel herself losing consciousness...... and SCREAMED ... "Tommy help me... Louise!!!..."

On hearing Sophie's scream of " TOMMY HELP ME!'

Tommy changed in mid stride to his right; Louise was right there behind him....
 As they both darted in their new direction, manoeuvred and negotiated their course past the side of the building and reached the rear...

 To their relief and horror they saw Sophie pinned against the wall still fully clothed going into nothingness and her eyes were closing, she was limp and listless, there was no fight left in her...

   Louise screamed, "Stop it... Leave her alone..."
Both men looked in their direction....
One of the men move towards them with his arms out and his fists clenched...
"Fuck off ... she's ours..."

As he advanced, Tommy took three massive strides and launched himself leaping into mid-air straight at him; with his leg raised he delivered the full power of his six foot two inch frame directly penetrating into his would be attackers advancing chest.... at least two cracks were heard...

Tommy's actions sent his assailant flying backwards into mid air, crashing into his partner in crime sending them both sprawling, releasing Sophie from their immoral intentions.

As the second one started to clamber to his feet, now on all fours, Tommy followed through with a bicycle kick into his torso sending him spiralling backwards tumbling over and over.... into a tree... covered in his own urine.

The first assailant was staggering to his feet as he looked up to see where Tommy was. Tommy caught him flush on the chin with a right cross, no getting up from that one.

The second one started to try and get up; he looked at Tommy in a daze, who was now advancing towards him...

He fancied his chances with Tommy, because he looked so young and he tried to get up....

"...Is she your tart...? You ponce...!" He slandered... That was all Tommy needed to hear, Tommy caught the creep with a left upper cut; which sent him sprawling once more and he collapsed back onto the floor... "Na ... just a knockout which you can't have..."

Louise had got hold of Sophie cuddling her, holding her up, she was semi-conscious now but had witnessed all that had gone on with Tommy and her two attackers.
She was safe and with her friends.
"Please let us go back to the villa..." she begged.
"We have got to report this..." said Louise
"No take me back to the villa please we are in a foreign country and we don't need any more trouble..."
"Sophie we have got to report it..." affirmed Tommy.
"No Tommy, look what you have done to them. Do you think the Police are going to believe you ..."?

Tommy and Louise looked in the direction of the two semi-unconscious pieces of excrement laid out on the floor.

"Tommy you have kicked the shit out of two blokes... for trying it on with me... That's what those two are going to say... think about it?"
Tommy took a deep breath...
Louise touched his arm...
"....What are our parents going to say...?   ....Our first holiday away and this happens" she continued.
"It's not your fault what those animals tried to do..." countered Louise
"It's not our fault for trying to defend and save you..." stated Tommy ...then continuing... "....It's their problem which they have got to face up to..."
"They never got what they wanted ... thanks to you two ... please let's leave... please" pleaded Sophie.
"You also put up one hell of a fight girl..." said Louise comforting, assuring Sophie

"But fancy walking off in your state..." said Tommy angrily

"No recriminations ... not now... please..." pleaded Sophie starting to cry.....

Louise and Tommy got Sophie in between them and they linked arms; she managed to conceal her torn blouse, only a couple of buttons....... were missing.

They treaded the gravel path towards their coach; Tommy glanced occasionally over his shoulder, surreptitiously to check for any movement from behind the building, all clear.

They boarded the coach with the rest of the revellers who had all had an uneventful but enjoyable evening and no one was suspicious of any misgivings that may have occurred.

They sat at the back and being first ones on the coach nobody joined them as there were a few spaces spare. Louise was next to the window Sophie in the middle and Tommy facing down the aisle this was also to deter others from joining them, as his frame for a young man was quite formidable.

Sophie rested her head on Louise's shoulder and closed her eyes.

Louise surveyed and studied the grounds from the side window as the coach, one of the first to leave pulled away. Tommy knelt on the seat inspecting the area from the back window in the direction of the out building.

Chapter 32

As the coach approached the gate Tommy could make out two lonely sorrowful looking characters materialising from the side of the building.

Supporting each other, one arm around each other, they were just coming into view, one was grasping his chest, the other with a hand on his chin.

Both staggering along looking very worse for wear and still under the influence of too much drink......

"... They must have got drunk and fallen over hurting themselves, look at the state of them ..."

"... Or had a drunken brawl with each other...."

"...Wouldn't surprise me..."

"...They could cause an argument in a telephone box on their own... those two...!!!"

"...They are always inebriated...."

"...Upsetting people ever since they got here...."

"…No respect for anyone..."

These were the mutterings of their fellow holiday makers in the Hotel and around the pool that they were staying in, the following day....

"... No sympathy..."

"...Serves them right..."

"...They might sober up now..."

"....Been a pain in the butt since they got here..."

And they were not going to disagree with anyone with what they were hearing in and around the Hotel ... they were two very unpopular characters.

Indeed even when they went to the local hospital they sustained and endorsed the pretence

"...Ho I got drunk and fell over ... hitting my chin.... "

"...I ... err... tripped up and tumbled down a slope and crashed into a tree...."

They told the Hospital staff...

Who treated them with care, but total distain... they still stank of drink.....

and urine....

After all they could hardly divulge the truth... of the true proceedings, of the course of events from the previous night, or how they sustained their injuries.

.... The coach pulled out of the gates and started the journey down the hill, when they reach the town square they hailed a taxi back to the villa....

"...No disco tonight..." said Louise.

"You two can go... I want a very hot shower and my bed.... whispered Sophie.

"... Obragado..." said Tommy as he paid the driver.....

Bilingual now Tom...? ... Cockney and Portuguesa..." quipped Louise....

Tommy went into the kitchen and put the kettle on "anyone for a cuppa or a wassa..?"

"...Do you want one Sophie?" asked Louise sympathetically.

"...No thank you just a shower and bed..."

"Make yourself one Tommy ... I'm going to assist Sophie"

Louise and Sophie went in to Sophie's bedroom, Sophie stripped off throwing her clothing into the bin....

"I'm going to burn those tomorrow'

Louise didn't say a word but a lump came into her throat and tears welled up in her eyes. She placed her hand over her own mouth, "...look what you have done to my friends.... you bastards..." she thought.

Sophie it seemed was in the shower for an eternity.

... washing ... scrubbing ... dragging the dirt ... clawing ... the scum ... the mauling hands ... the violation ..., from her body ... her skin ... her hair...

And she sobbed her heart out...

Louise could hear her pain inside the tears as she wept....

And decided as hard as it was not to intervene and to let her grieve, to release the trauma she had endured by crying... sobbing...and screaming it all out...!

In the sanctuary of her shower she washed the filth from her....

She waited patiently until Sophie felt clean enough... free at least for now..............

Knowing then she would be able to console her dear friend....

Tears started to roll and drop down Louise's cheeks.

Knowing no words could express how Sophie must be feeling at this time as she herself had never experienced such an ordeal. *"I know how you feel"*. How could I possibly know how you feel...? How the bloody hell ... and ... it must have been hell, could I know how she feels...? How condescending and patronising it must be when someone says that...

Silence, comfort, strength, compassion, caring and kindness... Words only expressed in the right context, when they are the requisite, in answer of the seeker.

Sophie eventually emerged from the shower, wrapped in a big towel patting herself dry, her eyes were bloodshot from the tears and her skin was red raw and patchy from the scolding hot water, scratch marks from her attackers and where she had scraped vigorously with her own nails....

She laid down on her bed without saying a word; she slipped the towel from her and quickly pulled on her tee-shirt and cotton shorts.

Sophie pulled the thin sheet and summer duvet over her, pulling it tight into her sides and wrapping it around her face, she curled up into the foetal position.

Louise sat on the side of the bed stroking Sophie's hair and then snuggled up beside her, mimicking her position, spoons....

They stayed like this until Sophie slept... this did not take long.....

A combination of the alcohol, shock, hot shower and the two pain killers Louise had given her earlier.......

Louise waited until she knew Sophie was feeling safe and sound.... then left the room.

Tommy was sitting on the patio nursing his hand with a cold compress made of crushed ice wrapped inside a damp towel....

He had made a mug of coffee a "wassa" with brandy; he was looking up at the sky... "...Why...?"

Louise came out of the bedroom after making sure Sophie was settled. She saw the patio light was on and that the door was ajar.....

She went to the kitchen and made two drinks; coffee for Tommy and tea for herself... both "wassa's." She found the first aid box which fortunately had a bandage in it.........

Chapter 33

Standing by the patio doors without invading his space....... she had overheard his question.

"...You won't find the answers looking up there, star gazing Tom..."

"...Why not...?"

"...The powers above, do you think the powers above have all the answers? ... Divine intervention...?" she asked.

"... And why not...?"

"Because the answer is down here Tommy with us human beings... us people..." she answered thoughtfully

"So what's the answer...?" he quizzed

That is in the journey... the journey of our lives, we have just got to recognise it... as we travel along the way."

"...And in the meantime when we bull's up...?"

"...And we learn and we don't make the same mistakes again..." she added encouragingly.

"...and do we...?" he asked

"Some do..."

"...Make the same mistakes or learn...? He enquired.

"...Both...!" she confirmed

"It's the learning curve Tommy; the trouble is some of us don't want to learn...."

"Why...?"

"That's the 64,000.00$... question..."

"Can I have just a pound's worth....?" smirked Tommy

"You can have a hot coffee for a pound....

....and the conversation comes free of charge" Louise stepped forward and offered him the cup from the door way...

"... Want a hot one ...?"

"...Thanks...'he reached out his hand.

"....Want some company too...?" enquired Louise

"Always...!"

"How's your hand...?"

"Throbbing... I won't be playing the piano for a while"

"How are you...?"

"Confused..." confessed Tommy.

"I think we are all somewhat confused... with what's been going on..."

"Yes I think you are right ... it was so much easier when we were kids..."

"We are not kids any more Tom ... It's a part of growing up, physically, emotionally internally; inner growth Tommy and we are all getting bigger now"

"Yes I've noticed that..." he smiled...

"We should still have reported it Lou..." he added.

"We couldn't...!"... Remonstrated Louise.... and she continued...

"Sophie was protecting you... she was protecting me, she was protecting our parents and she was protecting herself...."

"Sophie said... I'd kicked the shit out of them two because they had tried it on with her" insisted Tommy.

"Any decent human being would have done what you did in protecting their family, their friends, their loved ones and another human being."

"Louise I've never hit a soul in my life, I've never wanted to...."

There was a pause.

"Sometimes we have to do things that we don't feel comfortable with but we have to do it, nonetheless... It can be easier to take the easy option sometimes. But is it really easier for us, easier for whom...?

...But the easier option is not always the right option, and that's growth mate..." she concluded.

"Surely they have got to be held responsible Lou ... or is she blaming me ...? It's my fault for interfering...? Am I responsible...?"

"NO...!

....As individuals, that's you, me, Sophie... that scum, everyone....

We must be aware that we are only responsible for our own action, that's our responsibility.... Yes?

...And other people are responsible only for their own action, that's their responsibility....

'Yes'

... Get it...? "

"Why do people do things like that Lou...?" he said nodding, understanding what she had said.

"Because they think they can.... and they believe they can ... and that no one will stop them...

...Do they have any morals, any principles, any ethics, any standards, any honesty, any truth, any transparency or compassion...? NO...!

...They think they can do what they like when they like, treat people how they like and they come in all forms of life Tommy....!"

"...Wow I never thought about it like that..." he said contemplating what Louise had said.

"....Tommy they are animals who have not grown and left the jungle... in fact that's a disservice, injustice and a slur to animals....

... For every action, there is a reaction. So people like you Tommy, whose shoulders are broad enough and have the courage of their convictions...!

... Others should be aware of the consequences of their actions..... Every action... creates a reaction....!"

"So what you're saying is those two had the courage of their convictions in attacking Sophie...?"

"NO... what I'm saying is you had the courage of your convictions to protect her ...
And they are suffering the consequences of their actions....." she said and smiled caringly at him.

"Don't try to analyze it Tommy... Don't break it down to the enth degree; so that you can't put it back together and make sense of it...... so don't beat yourself up for your actions..... Let it go......! You did what was needed to be done...."

"Wow Louise...that's a mouthful to take in."

".... I am proud of you Tommy Jackson I am proud that you are in my life and I feel safe when you are with me, protected secure....loved."

"I love it when you talk all that psychology stuff....... I can listen to you for hours... days even...." Tommy said seriously.

"Days...? Then you'll be bored of me ... with me...?

"Never Freud...." he sighed "Never...!"

"Come on show me that hand, I found a bandage in the box.   Oh, its really swollen, let me put a fresh cold compress and bandage round that... keep that swelling down......and hope it isn't broken....

 ... It was either your hand or his jaw that cracked; let's pray it was the latter..."

"I can move my fingers, just..."

"Apparently... that's a good sign..."

"Yes ... It looks like I will be able to play the piano after all' joked Tommy

 "Listen... and sniff up Tommy....!"

"What...! What did you say...?" questioned Tommy

"Listen, listen ... is that angel's singing...?   Are those harps playing...? "... She wrinkled her nose "Sniff, sniff or is that your bull shit...!"

 Tommy smiled at Louise.... and winked...

"....Do you think Sophie will be ok...?" quizzed Tommy

"She will, we will look after her.....

   .... I love you and I love Sophie...." said Louise

"...We will always look after each other, until we are old and grey" confirmed Tommy.

 ".... and now it's time for bed....!" Louise said caringly.

Tommy's head raised and he looked at Louise as she was fastening his bandage....

"Yes... I love Sophie..... And you aren't too bad either...."

They both rose from the table "make sure you take these pain killers I found"....

"Thanks..."

They walked in through the patio doors Tommy locking them behind him; they walked into the centre of the lounge looked at each other ... and smiled....

"Night Night Lou..."

"Good night Tom..."

They hesitated for a moment....

Then moved closer...

And then turned going into the separate doors leading into the corridors to the loneliness of their separate bedrooms.

Chapter 34

"I never learn..." Tommy said to himself as he slipped his shorts off.

"...I never learn...!" he repeated louder as he pulled his shirt over his head with his good hand, shaking his head...

"...why didn't I say I love you Louise...?"

He lay on his bed for a moment or two contemplating his lack of action and cowardice..........

"... Because you fancy her too much and you're frightened of letting the cat out the bag..."

"... I love you Louise. Do you fancy going out with me...?" Is that all a bit too much? I want to start seeing her, I want to go out with her, so now I can't say I love you Louise..."…. "... In case it comes over too heavy and frightens her away. She's going away to University soon enough, so I might lose her anyways..."

"It's a horrible thing to consider or think......

.... But I am so pleased it was not Louise... in that position... I don't know if I would have stopped........."

"...How am I going to handle this...?"

It had been a long day and a packed evening; he closed his eyes and slept.

Chapter 35

Louise walked slowly to her room. She popped her head around Sophie's door, and checked that she was ok. She looked like she was sleeping soundly.

Louise then continued on to her own room, pushing her hair back and stroking her chin..... She was in deep thought, contemplating the last few moments....

She undid her button up dress and hung it in the wardrobe....... she took off her underwear and slipped into her bed and placed her hands up behind her... She stared up at the ceiling....

"... Why didn't he say ... I love you Louise...?"

"... As a friend, I love you Louise..."

 "Ah Louise I love you as a friend...!"

"And you aren't too bad either....!"

"Oh thanks..."

        ... "I love Sophie ...."

"Well Whoopi..."

"Aren't I the lucky one......? I'm not too bad, don't you know!!!"

"Why does he look at me the way he does, all doe eyed... all gooey gooey..."

"...Or is that me, imagining it ...?"

"... He certainly did go to town tonight... sorting those two thugs out ... I've never seen him like that...!"

"... Perhaps he does care more than he knows about Sophie...?"

"STOP IT Louise .... After the ordeal Sophie has been through, you are whingeing on about...

"Not too bad either..."

"You should be ashamed of yourself ...'

'And if ... he does love Sophie...?'

...., Then I'll just have to handle it........... !"

She closed her eyes and slept.

Chapter 36

Tommy hadn't had a good night..... He rose from his bed, and sat on the edge, his hand was aching more now, but he managed to move his fingers tentatively at first and then clenching his fist..... He followed the same procedure clenching ... releasing a number of times.

"... That's sore, but hopefully it's not broken, time will tell..."

He pulled on a pair of shorts, and his flip flops, splashed his face with one hand and brushed his teeth. It was 8am, and already hot outside.

"Going to be a scorcher today..."

Tommy went into the kitchen; Louise had left the pain killers on the side with a cup, all ready prepared with coffee and a little note: "I'm sure you can manage the milk and kettle...! ... If not wake me..."

He smiled to himself and felt a little choked and emotional.

"... Bless her ..."

He went out onto the patio being as quiet as he could, not wanting to disturb them.

But he also wished Louise was with him! His thoughts went to Sophie "I wonder how she is? I'll wait until she comes out..."

"She may not want to talk about last night; I'll leave the lead to her, just treat her how I always do..."

Louise woke up, she had slept deeply "Let me check on Sophie! ... I wonder if Tom's awake...? I wonder how his hand is...?'

She quickly got dressed. "Wow it's a hot one" and she put her bikini on and pulled a long t-shirt over it.

She washed her face and brushed her teeth then she quietly opened Sophie's door and peered in.
 Sophie was huddled under the sheet, the duvet was on the floor and to all appearances she had not had a distressing night's sleep.

Louise wandered into the kitchen and saw the cup had gone but a tea cup was in its place... she smiled, leaning her head to one side as she approached the cup she noticed her note with an answer written on it... "Thanks". She popped her head around the door and saw the patio doors wide open; she made a cup of tea and a fresh coffee and on reaching the patio she could see Tommy sitting in the sunshine "Why didn't he say he loved me...?"... She wondered again.
"Morning...Want a fresh one? .... How's your hand? ... How did you sleep? ..." She spurted all in one breath...
"Morning... Yes please ... Painful but I can move it more freely ... Not too bad, no not good at all to be truthful..." he replied, impersonating her.
"... How did you sleep? ..." he added.
"Soundly and deeply eventually; I laid awake, I was thinking for a little while...!"
They were now sitting on the sides of the loungers by the pool facing each other with their backs to the doors...
"Penny for them...?"
"You and your penny..."
"To a poor man that's a lot of money..."

"Profound philosophy at this time in the morning... Tommy Jackson...!"

"That's my name don't wear it out..." Tommy said smiling.

"...Can I wear it ...? She whispered.

Not hearing her... "So come on spill the beans...?"

"Well now you ask..."

Louise took a deep breath ... pausing and collecting her thoughts.... *"Do I really want to go there? ... Do I want to open this can of worms...?" she wondered.*

"Do you like Sophie....?" she spurted out.

"... For an intelligent woman, what kind of a question is that...? countered Tommy slightly defending himself, not quite sure what was coming round the corner at him....

"Do you like Sophie...?" she demanded, now the ball was rolling...

"...Of course I like Sophie..." Tommy could feel the difference in mood... *"Shit where is this going?" he thought.*

"...Tommy Jackson... you know what I mean. Do you like Sophie...? ... Do you fancy Sophie...? ... Do you want to be with Sophie...? ... Do you want to have a relationship with Sophie...?" The interrogation had begun, the questions rolled off her tongue without her taking a breath, or a pause for a rational thought. She couldn't stop it once she opened up ... pent up frustration flowing.....

"Ho crumbs..." she thought to herself.... waiting in anticipation, on a knife's edge......

Just for a moment, a second... Tommy thought about saying something sarcastic or funny.... but he could feel Louise's sincerity and did not want to offend her dignity, or to muck up.... again.

Her words from the night before came flooding back to him ....rekindled and they resonated in his Heart and Mind

"And we learn and we don't make the same mistakes again..."

"... NO... I like Sophie very much... as a dear friend...

... Hum ... I love Sophie ... like the sister I never had....

... But I don't see her in that vein; I don't fancy her... in that way...

... I don't want a relationship with her... in that way...

... And I don't want to be with her... in that way....!"

Tommy expressed his feelings very softly, shaking his head from side to side demonstrating his intention *"...Don't muck this up..."* he thought never taking his eyes from Louise...

She sighed and with relief she released the tension, trepidation flowing from her mind and body....

And her words flowed once more....

"And how do ... How do you like me Tommy...?" she slightly lowered her voice and whispered... and was about to continue... "Could you...?

"It's now or never..." ... was his inner reflection ... "cut the crap Tom..."... "be honest..." '... dive in..." "Tell her straight" ... "how it is..."

Tommy lowered his head and took a deep breath, stopping her as she started....

"...Louise, I think about you all the time..."

She nodded her head... "Me to, I mean you....!"

"...You're always on my mind....'

"...Me too'

"...I can't stop looking at you.....'

"...Me too'

"...I miss you when you're not near me....'

"...Me too'

"...I long to see you....'

"...Me too'

"...I day dream about you....'

"...Me too'

"...I can't wait to talk to you.....'

"...Me too'

"...I love listening to your voice.....'

"...Me too'

"...What you have to say.....'

"...Me too'

"...I want you near me....'

"...Me too'

"...I want to share everything with you....'

"...Me too'

"...I want you next to me....'

"...Me too'

"...I want more with you....'

"...Me too'

"...I want a relationship with you....................'

"...Me toooooooo'

"... You too.....?' He murmured still unsure.

"... Me too…!" She exclaimed.

Louise had never taken her eyes from him....

Tommy raised his head....his mouth open...

"...You'll catch flies...." She whispered to him...

"...As long as I've caught you....?' He whispered back.

Her eyes moistened and tears rolled down her face...... in ecstatic relief...

"I have caught and landed..... Simply the best... in the world..." she said slightly resting, tilting her head to one side, with the most beautiful smile, aimed right at him...

"You too....!" Said Tommy... mimicking her movement. "Me too....!'

Tommy's eyes welled up and tears flowed down his cheeks... in joy.

Energy flowed between them ... giving and receiving ... freely... growing... flowing...

Their eyes connected ... inter locked, exchanging messages without words...

Like magnets they were drawn closer, no hesitation, spontaneously, without thought.

They leant towards each other and their lips brushed, met, touched in their first kiss. .... Gently, softly, then more passionately.... sensually, seductively, sexily, and time stood still......

They were cocooned in their own bubble of blissfulness, their own world, and their own time.

"That's the first time I've ever been kissed....!" Louise said softly, sweetly, sincerely....

"Me too'.... responded Tommy... mirroring Louise's tone.
"And it was soo worth waiting for....!" Louise whispered with a smile on her face.
"Me too...." replied Tommy genuinely.
"From the bottom of your heart...?"
"From the bottom of my heart..."

They paused... looking into each other's eyes.

"...These silly games we have played..."
"Everything happens at the right time, in its right time..." whispered Louise....

And they kissed again...
...And again....
 ...And once more....
...And yet again...

"I'm going to get used to this... as a past time ... It's better than eating" quipped Tommy.
"A past time.... a past time you saucy sod this isn't 90 minutes mate! ... This is for full time.....!" countered Louise and she continued ... "Found in a skeletal state... Lips stuck together ... kissed to death, they died together of malnutrition..." She giggled
"Do I take it you are hungry Mademoiselle.....? Can I interest you in ....Coffee and toast...?" Offered Tommy...
"You certainly do interest me ... Any advancement....?" Teased Louise... raises her eyebrows.
"....What you see darling ... is what you get ... it's all yours..." Said Tommy... with a wink and a smile...

"I'll remember that comment and you'd better be all mine.'

But for now... *Coffee...?* Said Tommy flippantly....

You know I drink tea...." mocked Louise.

"Ok tea and toast....?'

"Actually I'll try the coffee and toast....!' Louise said teasingly.

"You cantankerous....'

"Don't you dare....!' You get breakfast and I'll check in on Sophie" said Louise

"Yep good idea, I hope she's ok...."

"I hope she will be ok....' countered Louise

"Yes.... do you think she... has picked anything up...?'

"What like a bug...some sort of virus?" questioned Louise

"No not a bug... not a virus, nothing sickly...!"

"What then, When ...?" asked Louise slightly puzzled

"When we were in the kitchen...?" Tommy said quietly

"Hmm... She was a bit sarcastic for the rest of the day.... when she returned from town."

"But she shouted out, 'Hello where are you...? From outside...!" Tommy gestured with his thumb

They looked at each other questioningly, inquisitively...............................

"Well anything she had, had a notion about ... that in her eyes was happening"... started Louise and she paused..."When she eventually joins us....'

"That is.... if she ever joins us and comes out of hiding....!" cut in Tommy

"And we inform her of what has happened between us...." quipped Louise

"Then she will be certain of...."   finished off Tommy.

They paused smiled at each other wryly and looked pensively to the sky.

"... Are you certain....?" Queried Tommy

"Ho I am so certain...." confirmed Louise

"Are you certain...?" Enquired Louise

"Ho... I've never been more certain; of anything in my life ... does the Pope kiss tarmac? ... Do bees love honey? ... Do bears.......

"Enough enough" cut in Louise sternly... "We know what bears do in the woods....thank you very much..."

"...You're so bossy! So we both agree... We both know what bears do in the woods...?' Tommy was grinning and winked at her...

...And yes that's how certain I am..." concluded Tommy.

As Louise headed across the grassed lawn she glanced over her shoulder; she had a wicked smile that lit up a room... "Smart arse..."

Tommy gesticulated by nodding and pointing at Louise....

"No darling... that is a smart arse...." he smiled and winked.

"Tommy Jackson...!" she declared "take your eyes off my arse... well for now" and she winked back at him.

Chapter 37

Louise headed straight to Sophie's room...

Tommy made tracks to the kitchen, on went the kettle and the bread went under the toaster...

Louise tapped lightly on the bedroom door ... no answer ... so she opened the door tentatively and popped her head around it..... Sophie had the sheet wrapped up around her shoulders and head with her back to the door...

She waited, surveying the room and her friend... Louise bit into her bottom lip, a lump coming up into her throat, nauseated and her eyes welled, "You bastards! ...I should have been there for you ... I'm so sorry Sophie..." she whispered.

She closed the door gently.... and tears started to cascade down her pretty face.

 Louise checked the kitchen which was empty bar the smell of freshly toasted bread... her belly rumbled... what mixed emotions. "Who's to say I can't be sad and hungry...?" and she headed for the pool...

Tommy had prepared breakfast for them and set up the small pool table between the loungers....

He was smiling dreamily as he watched his beautiful lady, as Louise strolled across the patio area and then glided with the grass beneath her bare feet towards him.

His face changed dramatically; in an instant he was serious, straight-faced, concerned, when he recognised the distress on her face and the tears ... Tommy leapt to his feet. "Louise are you ok...? ... Is Sophie ok...?"

Louise nodded her head "she's sleeping ... Those bastards! What have they done to my... I'm sorry, our dear friend...?"

Tommy opened his strong arms taking a step toward her and she fell into them, placing her arms around his torso.... his strong young body.

"We should have been there Tom ... we could have stopped it happening..." tears were rolling uncontrollably down her face... "We were too wrapped up in us..."

"Without realising it Louise ... without realising it" ...

"We didn't tell her to get pissed, we didn't tell her to wander off without telling us...

Who told me about responsibility...? Baby, I feel as sorry as you do for her... and if we could turn back that clock we would..." he held her firmly in one arm and gently stroked her hair and face with the other....

"But I wouldn't turn back that clock in what's happened for us, no recriminations, no regrets on that one Louise... are there...?"

"...NO...!" and she hugged him tightly, "...please don't let anything like that ever happen to me..."

"...I won't. I will always protect you, I will always be there for you..." he held her firmly, confirming his words.

"She is strong and we will help her to get over this Tommy... Wont we...?" sniffled Louise

"...She is ...and we will..."

They had their cold toast and lukewarm coffee.....

They lay around the pool sharing the same lounger, chatting, cuddling, pecking, teasing ... kissing.....

They were becoming so familiar and very comfortable in each other's arms.

Enjoying their solitude....

Chapter 38

Sophie had been awake for some time but she stayed in bed all morning going over and over, remembering the events of the evening before, in fact the entire day before..... Reliving, re-enacting every traumatic second.

What she had witnessed in the kitchen and her feelings, her assumptions.... And then what had happened and could have happened at the BBQ.... She felt physically sick, she dashed to the bathroom, she was physically sick..... She felt betrayed, used, violated, angry... resentful....

"Those Two Bastards enjoying themselves at my expense"... using me...!

You think you can use me...!"... "You think you can use me and cast me aside"... "We've had our fun with you, you're no longer needed... bye bye"...

"One day... one day"... "My turn will come, and revenge will be sweet"... "On my terms"

"Stop it Sophie, stop this, you must deal with what has happened, come to terms with it and put it behind you..."

 "Just accept you cannot trust people…"

"If I have no expectations of others, then I cannot be let down by others…"

"People disappoint, so if I have no expectations of people, I won't be disappointed or let down, betrayed… look after numero uno…

That's my new motto…."

Chapter 39

"Sophie I'm doing some lunch; do you want something to eat?" asked Louise poking her head around the door after knocking and getting no answer....

No sign of Sophie but then she heard her... vomiting in the toilet...

"Sophie can I help you…? Can I get you something to drink…? Do you need anything…?"

"No I'm ok...." she said between retches

"Why not come outside and get some fresh air, get some sunshine…?"

"Please Lou I'm ok and yes I'm dealing with it.... I want to stay in here for now...

I'll call you if I need anything."

"OK! But I will pop my head in now and again that is either me or Tommy will, just to check in on you... just to make sure you're ok."

As Louise started to leave the room she glanced back....
"Sophie do you want to talk about it… you know, what happened...?'

"I don't want to talk about it...! You know what happened"... "I never want to talk about it..." growled Sophie

"Is there anything you want to talk about...?" asked Louise earnestly, caring for her friend.

"...Is there something else ... Is there something I should know...?" quizzed Sophie

"Well yes there is.... I don't know if this is the appropriate time given what happened, although there is no connection..."

"So what's going on...?"

"Strange terminology Sophie"... "Going on"... "Two friends of yours are very concerned and care about you" ... "but those two friends of yours, something has happened to them."

Sophie was sitting on the bed now.... watching Louise intently...

 "Like what has happened...?'

Tommy appeared at the door, "Are you decent, can I come in…?"

"Since when have men worried about if a girl is decent...?" snarled Sophie.

"That's not fair Sophie" ...defended Louise.

"Don't tar everyone with the same brush Sophie and I'm ...we are, sorry for what happened to you, but don't put me in the same category as those two pieces of garbage... those two pieces of shit… those POND LIFE" protested Tommy.

Sophie lowered her head... "I'm sorry Tommy; I know I can trust you"...

"... So what has happened to my two trusted friends...?" Sneered Sophie

"It sort of crept up on us from behind, we never saw it coming, a shot out of the blue" recollected Tommy with a monstrous smile of contentment on his face.

"You're right, it came up from behind and high jacked us, we were bush wacked" endorsed Louise.

Sophie stared at both of them.... "And just what are you saying...?"... "What are you getting at...?"... What are you jabbering on about...?"... "Speak English not double Dutch."

Louise and Tommy looked at each other perplexed, then at Sophie....

"You've done it again; you've taken the two of us fishing and landed us both", said Louise.
Tommy nodding his head in agreement "Caught us like a pair of kippers"
"I'm really not playing games... What are you saying to me...?" insisted Sophie.
"Did you take a bang on the head at anytime...?" Joked Tommy.
"Sophie my dear, it's quite simple. Something has happened and unfathomable feelings have grown, we were completely unaware of what was happening and suddenly we were struck by Cupids arrow"... "Is that English enough for you to comprehend?" stated Louise smiling

"You put it so elegantly my dear" added Tommy   ...
"Sophie we have fallen for each other, we have deeper feelings that are far more than just friends"
"But we will always be together"..."The Three Musketeers" reinforced, insisted, co-opted Louise

There was silence.... again. Louise and Tommy looked at each other and shrugged their shoulders. This was not the reaction they expected or hoped for; they then looked directly at Sophie, who was still sitting on the bed looking out of the window.

She must have gauged the atmosphere in the room and how the vibes had changed; tense, negative, low, flat; not a good energy... She regained her composure equilibrium, but inside....

Shock! Disbelief! ... Tommy was hers, Louise a dear friend.....

She turned and looked at them. "Wow when did this occur...? ... How did it progress..? Friendship to relationship ... friendship too deep and profound feelings *"cupid"*, she was being acerbically incongruous "What actually took place…?

God I'm sorry thirty questions."

"It's ok, take it easy... thirty questions, there are not thirty answers, it took its time as we say it crept up on us from behind and it enveloped us" Tommy simplified his answer

"Sophie we weren't even aware of what was developing between us, and then we were .... Bang, a shot out of the blue..." endorsed Louise.

 "I'm so pleased for you"…. "I'm sorry with what's gone on I'm a little self absorbed, possessed, I'm in a mess mentally, I'm in a mess emotionally.

Even though it's come as quite a shock, a jolt out of the blue, I wasn't expecting this news but Wow, I'm so pleased for you."

"Thanks Sophie that means so much to us, it's so important that you're there with us". "Do you need to sleep or you going to venture to the pool" asked Louise

"Come on Sophie, come and get some rays it will make you feel better"

"If it's alright with you two, do you mind if I stay here, at least until the sickness and vomiting stops?"

"We understand, call if you need anything" assured Tommy....

"Will do" answered Sophie nodding her head.

"And by the way as I first said, if you want to talk... if you need to talk, I'm only a shout away.... we are here for you Sophie" confirmed Louise.

"Don't forget it" added Tommy.

Sophie looked at them both...

"I'll deal with it... I'll deal with it all and at the moment I just feel so let down with people and their behaviour."

They both nodded in support and understanding.

Sophie remained in her room for the next two days only coming out for some fresh water she couldn't bear the thought of food.

Chapter 40

"You still up for lunch?"

"Prata do Dia"

Louise looked at Tommy... "Picking it up aren't we. Who's a clever boy?"

"Do you want to go down into town to eat?" enquired Tommy.

"Best we stay here today, just in case she comes out and we need to be here for her."

"Suits me; I've got you all to myself then and I don't have to share you with some waiter."

"Share me…! Never in a life time...! I'm all yours and you have no need to be jealous... of anyone ever" smiled Louise.

"Again that suits me."

"And likewise...." Louise smiled.

"But of course you'd never have the worry of sharing me with a waitress and definitely not a waiter... Cos I'm all yours honey child and you will never have to be jealous because I AM … I AM ALL YOURS MY BEAUTIUL LOUISE...!"

Louise smiled at him and they went into the kitchen where they grabbed the tray they had prepared earlier with some fresh rolls, butter, cheese, ham, tomatoes, onion and olives set out, they headed out to the patio...

"Grab the water."

It was a beautiful sunny, very warm day with a cool breeze and the smell of the ocean and the heady scent of the bougainvilleas circulating, swirling around them.

"Perfect'

 "It is just perfect"

They sat together enjoying their lunch and each other's company.

So happy together...

"I'm confused Louise, I realise Sophie has been through a traumatic episode and she may well be in shock, PTSD... post traumatic stress disorder isn't it... our psychologist at the club explained it...

Basically something stressful, traumatic or both can happen. You miss an open goal, make a bad pass or a bad tackle that causes a bad injury, someone gets hurt and it's your fault.

 Even if I get a bad injury and it can comes out of the body after the event. PTSD....

Even with what's gone on I thought she would be just a little bit more excited?"

"I know what it stands for Tommy. I did a course in psychology, but it can go a lot deeper than that, far deeper.

In fact this can affect people's behaviour.   Even something could be triggered by events from the past"

"So what are you saying.... where you going with this Freud...?"

"Give her time Tom; she is really stressed out at the moment although I'm confused as to the depth or the root cause of it...!

 This episode at the BBQ has obviously really triggered and compounded the stress and trauma levels she is feeling"

"In English not double Dutch please"

Louise swung him a look...

"Sorry what do you mean?"

"Ever since she returned from the shops and we were in the kitchen Sophie hasn't been the same: tetchy snarling, sarcastic and she went out of her way to get hammered at the BBQ...."..... "Then the episode with the morons didn't help and this may sound callous, but logically she got her self involved in a brawl. They didn't molest her, rape her, nor indeed get their hands or any other part of their anatomy inside her clothing."

Tommy looked puzzled and suddenly it dawned on him.

"Louise, it's US"

"It's US!" Confirmed Louise,

"I'm not diminishing or belittling, undermining what transpired.... Traumatic yes, but is that truly the root cause of her behaviour, I'm really not so sure"

"Best we keep a close eye on her then?" Tommy said questioningly

"I do hope it isn't us. I don't want this to spoil our friendship" replied Louise worriedly

"Would it, could it affect the two of us?" Asked Tommy.

"NO! Friendship is one thing, as close as it may be. But a relationship with feelings is something completely different"... "You know the old song: God help the sister that comes between me and my mister."

"And God help the mister...?"

"Only applies if there's a scorned sister."

"And is there a scorned sister...?"

"I don't know but one thing's for sure... never mix the grape and the grain."

"What?"

"Friendship and love"... "Love can grow from friendship and it does, it has, many times. But this should never be misconstrued and never confuse friendship for being *in love* and never take someone's feelings for granted, it may not be reciprocated."

"Mmmm deep"

"Then again not too deep, if there's no depth" Louise smiled.

"I need some sun" said Tommy shaking his head, he rose from the chair and headed for his sun lounger.

"Me too" and Louise followed him.

Chapter 41

The next two days passed quite uneventfully. Sophie stayed in her room only coming out for water and a snack.....

Without them being selfish this obviously didn't do Louise and Tommy any harm, it gave them quality time together...

Which they relished...

Walks down to town, coffee on the promenade, sitting on the cliffs overlooking the ocean, sauntering around the shops, people watching.., every time they always invited Sophie to join them...

"Sophie we are going to have a stroll maybe have a beer, a coke and some lunch, are you coming?"

"No I'm happy to stay here..."

"Do you need or want anything particular?"

"No I'm good thank you."

"Sophie we are going to go out tonight and have a meal."

"Sophie your favourite chicken piri piri come on it'll do you good!"

"No honestly, I'm fine."

"Over their evening meal Tommy said "this can't go on she's becoming a hermit!"

"We can't force her to come out with us."

"Then it is US! That's the real problem, isn't it...?"

"Who knows...?"

"And all this: 'I'm fine, it's all Crap!... Fucked up! Insecure! Neurotic! Emotional!" declared Tommy angrily

Louise threw him a glance and a wry smile ... "Freud's working then?

"Well Lou, if it is us let's all have a talk about it, honestly truthfully. A problem… share it… resolve it… move on ... I think the world of Sophie as you do ...but if this carries on what will happen when we get home?" Tommy was quite stern.

"Questions, questions, question I imagine." Said Louise

"Yes exactly.... and most of them coming from Sophie's parents. She decided to get pissed, put herself in a vulnerable bad situation and we will get the blame:...mainly from her parents, Great" exclaimed Tommy.

"And, where are you going with this?"

"Tactics my dear"

"Tactics...?" she enquires

"And to be truthful a little selfish"

"Tactics and selfish... tell me more?" enquired Louise very intrigued.

"Selfish as in when we go home I don't want what has happened between us, to be overshadowed by the events of the BBQ night if indeed that is the real problem…

...If it is US then Sophie and her parents will have to sort it out for themselves, whatever it is...."

Louise stroked her chin looking at Tommy curiously; there was a silence for a few moments...

"Well what do you think?" Queried Tommy impatiently....

"Remind me not to upset you too badly in the future ... Hmmm yes I concur and as for the tactics Ho Master...?" countered Louise continuing to stroke her chin with a smirk on her face, looking up to the gods.

"Cards on the table: Three card brag... call her bluff come clean... show your hand or back out... quit the game. Reverse psychology; I'm not living, walking on egg shells Lou" he paused for a second or two....

"...And we haven't done anything wrong so if it is the BBQ night then we will know... and it will have to be dealt with" he hesitated for a second more...

"...Tomorrow morning over breakfast..." finalised Tommy.

"Tactics, selfish, Freud and so assertive... ho Master" she smiled at him lovingly.

"Finish your dinner Grasshopper" he closed his eyes and raised his eyebrows.

The Following morning Tommy prepared some croissants, cheese, ham and olives, pots of coffee and tea, plus a jug of fresh orange.

"Sophie we need to talk to you. Can you please join us on the patio" Louise asked Sophie through the bedroom door.

"Do I have to...?" answered Sophie dismissively.

"It's important, relevant to what will happen when we return to England" responded Louise mischievously, promptly expecting Sophie's nonchalant response.

"How do you mean...?" retorted Sophie suspiciously.

Louise opened the door and walked in…

"Well if you continue to be an agoraphobic! Or is it depression, and that's stopping you from coming out and joining us? Or indeed.... this is the case…

....Then you will need to seek medical help, inform your parents… and if this all stems from the BBQ night then it will have to be shared, out in the open, as we will be asked what happened and we won't lie and we cannot lie and that is for your benefit"

"I'm not depressed and I'm not agoraphobic and no I don't need psychological help" declared Sophie quite resentfully, turning her nose up and narrowing her eyes at her....

"I'm very pleased to hear that. So no trauma from the BBQ night then...? quipped Louise drolly, wittily trying to defuse the tension.

"No!" stipulated Sophie.

Tommy's head popped round the door, and with big smile on his face...

"Then if that's not the issue which I'm relieved to hear and you have no deep rooted traumatic psychological phobias which I'm also pleased to hear... yet on another level ... also very sad!... You see that leaves only one other conclusion. The only other remaining factor, glaringly obvious is...

　　　...It must be the company that you are keeping, that you are here with! ...

... Both of US... Is it US being an US or US individually....? In which case do you want to divulge the problem, issue or what has so suddenly turned you against us. From stopping you sharing a dinner table, a swimming pool or THE AIR THAT WE BREATH...! Hmmmm?" finished Tommy indignantly, winking at Sophie.

There was silence....

"It's not you two individually ... or you two being a ... US...! ...in a relationship." Sophie responded quickly, although somewhat defensively of her actions and words, deflecting the blame and the responsibility, protecting herself as she felt vulnerable, and exposed.
She hated to be proved wrong and in feeling she had been caught out... it showed her own insecurities.

The truth being declared...! It was out in the open and she was no longer in control. She hated that.

"... It just takes some getting used to; adapting to... it was always US...! Us three...!" shared Sophie sombrely, deviously.
"Sophie it will always be US" reiterated Louise.
"The Three Musketeers..." Tommy chorused.
"You said it would always be US" enforced Sophie
"Sophie it could have happened the other way. What if it was You and Tommy that had fallen for each other... I would have had to cope with it and I would have been happy for you both" said Louise... lying through her teeth.
"Liar liar pants on fire" Tommy was singing in his head.

"YES what if that had have happened...? Would you have been pleased....?" enquired Sophie, puzzled awaiting the answer with baited breath.

"Of course...!" she looked at Tommy pleadingly

Tommy decided it was time to bring things to a conclusion....

"Ifs... Buts and wherefores... OK we can go over and over and over this, we can go on and on forever. The thing is... what is this really all about...? It is what it is...! What is the problem...?

...Sophie the main fact is it's not the events of BBQ night, thank God...

So surely what has happened between Louise an me, is good...isn't it...! It is for Louise and me, why isn't it easy for you to accept it and be happy about it... Be pleased for us...!"

"Please Sophie" echoed Louise.

"Lou and I never saw this coming. It came straight round the corner at us like a juggernaut... hit us on our blind side... it may as well have come from behind and slay us . But it's happened and we are so pleased it has and we both want you to be a part of it..."

Sophie looked at Tommy accusingly "You Always said we would be together"

"And we will" chorused Louise "we will!!!"

Sophie took a deep breath and glanced down at the floor, contemplating all that had been said and the possible consequences... having to accept the relationship between Louise and Tommy and admit to herself ... yes she was jealous and was acting like a petulant, spoilt little madam, who could not have her own way… She breathed out....

"OK! Let me take a shower and I'll meet you by the pool I need to top up this tan" she said rubbing her arm with her fingertips.

Chapter 42

They closed the door behind them, they danced into the lounge, turned to face each other and did a high five....

"Yes…! I love it when a plan comes together" declared Tommy pretty smug and pleased with himself.

"Yes, well done, good tactics and you were very precise and masterful", praised Louise.

"Teamwork my dear you prepared the ground work and I followed your lead, we make a good team." not wanting to take all the glory and being magnanimous.

"Premiership... watch out... you will make a good manager one day." said Louise laughing.

"But there's one down side Lou..."

"I know what you're going to say; at least I think I know what you're going to say..."

"Together then!" he said smiling.

"3 ... 2 ... 1..."

"SORRY"

"The word SORRY"

They said simultaneously

They walked outside onto the patio in silence.... the mood had suddenly changed.

"Do you not think Sophie could just have just used that word....? SORRY and meant it, considering what she has put us through and the way she has behaved"... I was so worried that the BBQ night had affected her badly" said Tommy clearly unhappy.

"Yes I do and I'm as disappointed as you obviously are, I'm not taking away the enormity of the events of BBQ night. That was a horrendous situation for any human to go through, but that is not the fundamental issue that has propelled her into her actions....! yes sorry would have gone a long way" confirmed Louise

"Disappointed, yes disappointed is right...!" highlighted Tommy.

"Tommy, I've just remembered something we were taught in philosophy... tucked away in the back of my brain.... she paused.

"... Never have any expectations of anyone, those you know, even those you love,

Expect nothing... So when they let you down... you won't be disappointed" she sighed.

"Wow Lou, you know so much ..." Tommy said in respect and admiration... metaphorically looking up to her.

"Tommy always try to keep in mind what the Buddha said..."

 "The one thing I do know for certain is....

... I know nothing!" She smiled and lowered her head in respect, high regard and approbation.

There was a moment of supreme silence....

She then emphasised in an exaggerated Spanish tone using her hands as props...

"I know nothing...Tommy!"... "I know nothing...!"

They smiled at each other... then burst out laughing and hugged each other ardently.

"Don't give up your day job... babe" Tommy said earnestly.

Sophie wandered on to the patio and eyed up Louise and Tommy hugging and laughing....
"Woops I haven't interrupted anything... have I ...?" she inferred sarcastically.
"No Sophie you haven't" brushed off Louise... smiling and winking at Tommy.
Tommy raised his eye brows.... mockingly "you haven't seen anything ... yet...!" and smiled and winked back at Louise.

"Well now I certainly need to pick up some sun rays to catch up with you two" Sophie smiled.
Louise and Tommy smiled back.....

Chapter 43

"Ok let's tuck in"

"I thought you already had" smirked Sophie.

"Now now Sophie... don't get tacky" pleaded Louise.

"Sarcasm Sophie...? Would have thought better of you...!" moaned Tommy disappointedly.

"Lowest form of wit..."

"So sorry I will try not to lower the tone, you two really have become quite a team...!"

"Give it a rest Sophie or go back to hibernating, Miss Irritable."

"Ho we are touchy... whoops sorry no pun intended."

"Sophie... please…!"

"What I'm playing, only messing about, Christ is this what happens when you get involved... lose your sense of humour... you know your sense of fun.

They proceeded to devour the breakfast Tommy had put together in relevant silence.

"Hmmm shall we stay around the pool or venture down town and onto the beach for the day" suggested Louise.

"Yes let's get out for the day" enthused Tommy.

They both looked at Sophie.

"Sounds good to me let's go...."

"Away we go ... One for all..." chanted Tommy looking at the girls for a response.

"All for one..." responded the girls....

And so the day was spent down the beach....

"Lunch anyone?"
"Ho yes..."
"Bifanas..."
"Definitely..."
"Bifana and a Sagres..."

The next few days passed by quite uneventfully the tension and terseness disappeared.
"I like sharing valuable times together."
"Sophie fancy going shopping in the market and around the shops...?" asked Louise.
"I'm staying at the villa give you girl's some quality time together" Tommy quipped.
"Tommy, Louise why don't you go for a walks along the cliffs edge" offered Sophie.
"Give you two time together" Sophie would be discreet.

Sophie and Tommy would be frolicking around in the pool.
All seemed peaceful on the western front…..

"So my lovely friends it's our last full day and evening." exclaimed Sophie as she prepared breakfast.
"It's flown by too quickly." said Louise sadly.
Tommy sat looking at the two girls across the table....

"So let this be the perfect day for the Three Musketeers." said Tommy sincerely.
"To town or not to town to the beach or not the beach they are the questions...?" quizzed Sophie.

"I'd prefer to stay around the pool as it's our last day" said Louise earnestly.

"And catch as many Rays as possible...?" quipped Sophie.

"I'm not looking for Rays ... I've got a Tommy" said Louise gazing at her man.

"Ho excuse me, while I throw up!" said Sophie sarcastically pretending to stick her fingers down her throat.

They both looked at Sophie slightly concerned and then she burst out laughing...

"Only joking" confirmed Sophie.

They both smiled broadly.

"And your man is going down to the shop for a paper anyone want anything...?"

"No thanks."

"Don't be long."

All three were sun bathing around the edge of the pool on the loungers...

Sophie ... Tommy ... Louise ... side by side

The girls were topless and Tommy had just his shorts on.

Tommy and Louise would be holding hands swing their arms to and fro.

Then they would start up.... *"da da dada da...."*....

"You can keep the Algarve..... I'd rather be in Yarmouth with all the family"...

"I don't think so ... chicken piri-piri ... a garraffa of vino - verdi and fourteen days of sun"

Singing in harmony....

"You can keep the Algarve..... I'd rather be in Yarmouth with all the family"...
  "I don't think so ... chicken piri-piri ... a garraffa of vino - verdi and fourteen days of sun"
"The Three amigos...!" Introduced Louise
"The three degrees...! Roared Tommy
"103 bloody degrees" yelled Sophie

"Wow it's a hot one."
"Let's take a dip in the pool."
"All for one ... one for all." they bellowed out.

And they rose as one taking a few strides and plunging into the warm water, plunging deep and then submerging, rising out of the water like phoenixes from the fire...

They floated on top of the water on their backs, mimicking the movements of synchronised swimmers, diving bombing, teasing and tormenting each other treading the water, all was well...just as it had when they were kids...

"You can keep the Algarve..... I'd rather be in Yarmouth with all the family"...
  "I don't think so ... chicken piri-piri ... a garraffa of vino - verdi and fourteen days of sun",

"Ah bless I'm with my two best friends that I love to pieces ... simmering away in a massive pot of

DUMPLING STEW...!" ogling and pointing at their boobs Tommy roared out laughing.
And the girls joined in....

"You can be a mongrel at times Tommy Jackson but I love you so much...!" said Louise in between laughing and talking as the water was splashing about.

"You can only love him really can't you... incorrigible... but a dog nonetheless..." laughed Sophie.

They dozed away the day lounging, swimming, dipping, and bathing; enjoying each other's company... soaking up the sun...

"So are we eating out tonight" enquired Sophie open armed
"Glad to hear it", smiled Tommy and winked at her.
"Piri piri...please"   pleaded Louise

"Chicken piri-piri ... a garraffa of vino, we think so".
Sang Sophie and Tommy

"It's our favourite meal so it was no hardship especially on our last night"... endorsed Sophie
"I'll order a taxi and arrange some transport to our favourite piri piri house, even though its half way up the Monchique Mountain...!" Tommy pointed towards the mountain acting out the scene like an exploring pioneer...
It's near to the venue of BBQ venue... he added concerned.

"Are you sure Sophie" asked Louise concerned.

"Yes ... no problem it's our favourite and nothing will spoil our last night...!" demonstrated Sophie...

"Cool lets go" encouraged Tommy.

They ventured up the mountain and enjoyed a beautiful meal whilst sitting overlooking the Algarve and the ocean.

"This is bonito... I could live here one day." Tommy divulged opening his heart up and tentatively seeking encouragement and confirmation in that direction... from Louise.

"Bonito, Beautiful, yes Tommy it is a very beautiful place, you could quite easily settle here one day"
Concurred Louise.... smiling at him...

Sophie injected "Yes I could live here too."

They returned to the villa very content...

"I'm tired guys I'm going to hit the sack goodnight" Sophie decided she didn't want to play gooseberry on their last night..... And so she retired.

Chapter 44

"Ho it's such a lovely warm barmy night, a wonderful cool breeze and clear skies; so peaceful and so quiet." sighed Louise.

"Could I ask for anything more...."

She was sitting on the edge of the pool in her bikini with her feet dangling in the warm water, she was milling the time away looking up at the stars swinging her feet gently side by side, to and fro creating a ripple of a wave ebbing and flowing side to side.

She began to daydream; she smiled to herself... evening dreaming...

"Whatever, it's a dream come true she thought, who would ever have imagined the outcome of this holiday"...

"What a perfect end to my holiday, our last night in Portugal, with a future to look forward to with Tommy. We came as best friends and we are leaving as a couple."

Tommy in his swim shorts and flip flops was watching Louise from the patio; he stood by the marble pillar supporting the pagoda.

He stood there in silence smiling, watching, and admiring his beautiful lady...

"What a holiday this has turned out to be." he thought to himself "How close we were as friends, now how close we have grown" ... "and we are going to grow together as a couple with a future... what a lucky man I am and I know it"

Tommy wandered slowly down to the water's edge, he crouched down behind her and kissed her neck... she sighed.

He then took his weight on to the palms of his hands, supported by his powerful arms, lowering his legs down into the water, moving his legs in tune with Louise's... swinging slowly side by side, mimicking her movement, creating more of a ripple and a wave.

Tommy wrapped his powerful arms around her waist, holding her tenderly, she melted into his muscular frame and snuggled her head into his neck. Timeless...!

"Tommy what do you want from a relationship... in a relationship...?" tentatively probed Louise.

"ALL OF IT...! THE WHOLE CUBBUDLE... Tommy charged flamboyantly... then mellowed with frankness and sincerity;

Honesty, truth, respect, morals, principles, ethics, standards, consideration, Ho yer.... care, kindness, monogamy, magnanimous, loyalty, communication, laughter, fun, to be proud of, to be wanted, to be needed, to miss, to be loved.... to be in love..." "...HO YER..... WONDERFUL SEX....!"

"Wow Tommy that's deep, very profound, clarity, sincere and from the heart, ingrained... In to the very fabric of your being.... so true... so you..."

"It's what my Mum and Dad have... it's what they gave me, nurtured in to me, and shared with me.... showed me....to have the best, it's what I need, it's what I want... the best... I'm worth it"

"Me too... I'm worth it..."

"I never asked you.... this is my dream...!" teased Tommy....

"Then ask me.....? I want it to be my dream as well..."

"Louise what do you want from a relationship... in a relationship...?"

"Ditto... all that you said... and something even more...!"

"What... more is there...?"

"An abundance of Contentment, Peace, Happiness, entwined with Health, Wealth and even more Looovee...!!!... because I'm also worthy of that..."she said humbly.

Tommy nodded his head.... "ME TOO.... we are both worthy of that...."

Louise turned her head sideways toward Tommy's face; Tommy stretched a little upward and turned his head sideways to face Louise.......

Looking into each other's eyes, in a moment of silence, perusing each other without prompting they said in unison........

"Our dream..."

   ...And kissed gently, brushing each other's lips: teasing, tasting, and tantalising....... probing...

"Louise I have something I need to ask your advice on something I want to share with you..."

"Ok it sounds important...?"

"I know this girl; I meet her and have known her for some time"

"Ho yes"

"Yes and I've grown quite fond of her"

"Only quite fond of her...?"

"Well actually far more than fond..."

"Ho yes"

"Yes do you think I should tell her...?"

"Yes I do...."

"Do you think she would want me to tell her how I feel...?

"Ho Yes....! She would"

"Are you sure...?

"Yes I'm sure"

"You don't think it would frighten her...?"

"No it wouldn't, not at all"

"Not even if I tell her how I truly feel...?"

"I know she would want you to tell her how you truly feel"

"Do you think she might feel the same way...?"

"I am certain she would feel the same way"

"Would you want to know?"

"Yes I would by the way... how fond...?

"Ho very fond... more than fond in fact... I..."

"I think you should share with her.... immediately now in fact... this moment in fact!"

"I love you Louise I'm in love with you Louise"

"Me tooooo...!"

"You too...?"

"I love you too Tommy...!"

Tommy pushed himself upward and backward out of the water and stood upright looking down at Louise, he held out his arm, she responded and he took her hand in his.

Louise pulled her legs from the water, their eyes were locked into each other and as she rose from the pool side, they stood face to face, locked into each other....

Louise gently squeezed Tommy's hand, more for comfort and security than anything else and a shiver resonated through her.

Tommy smiled at her caringly "are you cold?"
... "No"...

He lovingly squeezed her hand...

They stood motionless gazing into each other's eyes, transfixed as one....

There was positive energy flowing between them, it was electrifying, excitement, tension, pulsating, tingling..... Not a word was spoken.

Tommy turned toward the patio doors and took a tentative step ... Louise without hesitation took the same step....

They walked slowly across the grass lawn bare footed onto the patio area through the doors....

They stopped momentarily and then proceeded through the lounge until they reached the door of Tommy's room.....

Once more they looked into each other's eyes and they could see there was radiance, warmth and trust.... the windows to their souls.....

They could truly see and feel beyond time and space.... their love for each other was boundless no perimeters....

Chapter 45

They entered the bedroom together, they turned and faced each other there was nothing more to say they fell into each other's arms, cocooned in their own energy and love for each other....   nothing else mattered at this moment, their dividing line in their space of time.... from humanity….

They kissed softy tenderly, passionately, ravenously, caring, considering, each other's feelings connecting, understanding...

As they kissed their bodies gradually moved to the bottom of the bed their legs touching the mattress... Tommy stopped and edged slightly backward from Louise looking her square in the eye...
"Lou ... I want to kiss every inch of your body I want to lick every segment of your body...!"
"Tommy! ... I want you to kiss every inch and lick every segment of my body...!"

Their own motion allowing them unconsciously... in slow motion to gracefully glide down onto their bed......
They continued to kiss; their mouth's probing, teasing, nibbling, their tongues touching, entering, searching, moist, tender.... there was no compunction in either's actions, comfortable, lovingly, seductively, sensually ...Wanting, needing and desiring each other.

 They kissed; their hands sensitively exploring each other's bodies, smoothly, soothing, a gentle silk like touch.... stroking each other, caressing each other, zealously...

They stopped... and looked at each other... deeply, tentatively, softly...... electrifyingly, tingling, pulsing.... throbbing....

Lou ... I want every single inch... fragment, of your beautiful gorgeous body..."

"Me too...!"

"You too...?"

Tommy I want every inch ... every particle of your muscular firm luscious body..."

Tommy subtly took the tie up of Louise's bikini top between his fingers and pulled on it slowly, until the bow was undone.....

Louise never flinched; she slipped it to the side and dropped it by the side of the bed.

Tommy could feel Louise's firm breasts against his chest as they continued caressing, kissing each other's lips.

Tommy's mouth began to move down to her neck kissing her gently, down to her shoulders stroking his tongue over her soft skin, touching, fondling her breasts with his finger tips, his open mouth manoeuvring down her body kissing her tentatively, his tongue licking her rigid nipples, she sighed in ecstasy, her body shaking, she had her hands around his head cradling him in place...........

Tommy slipped his shorts off and dropped them by the bed, he then lowered himself slowly down her beautiful firm body, caressing her body with his tongue, licking her body tenderly until he reached her navel.... probing, gently, gliding across the soft texture of her moist skin to her hips... he undid the ties on the sides of her bikini with his teeth...

Louise raised her buttocks just enough to allow him to remove her bottoms.....

Tommy's tongue was like a man exploring an adventure playground for the first time...

Louise's body quivered and shook with delight... as the tip of Tommy's tongue ventured forth and found every curvature of Louise's slender firm succulent body...

His tongue sampled the soft texture of her skin and the moisture of her... that was flowing ... she yelped with desire...

He started to re-explore her body, edging upward, the tip of his tongue and warm breath hovering over her navel and then her trim tummy...

... Upward until ... he was on top of her.... he pecked her slightly on the lips...

Tommy then pushed himself up with his strong arms holding himself above Louise...

They looked into each other's eyes ... knowingly, there was no going back and Tommy smiled and nodded... Louise smiled and nodded back.... she mouthed the word "yes"

He lowered himself until their bodies connected effortlessly...gently, slowly melting into each other, their bodies became one. Louise gulped and groaned.... their legs, their arms, weaved, plaited, intertwined, swathed, sensitively, intimately, seductively…. a beautiful interaction, energetically... they complemented each other in perfect rhythm never missing a beat, blissful harmony in motion.

They rode each other on the crest of a wave; they excelled every fibre and feeling of their very being....

They took each other to the very edge…. to places they had never been, then beyond the limits of their boundaries, catapulted into a realm of altered dimensions.... until they ignited and exploded with passion....

Louise sighed in rapture, blissfully…. and Tommy sighed in seventh heaven....

They lay drenched in their own perspiration, cuddled up holding on to each other like there was no tomorrow...

They looked at each other with tenderness; the lottery jackpot could not buy!

"Louise"

"Tommy"

"Louise"

"Tommy"

They started to giggle....

"Wow"

"Wow to you as well"

"Tommy"

"Louise"

"That was...! The first time I've ever made love"... Louise smiled serenely, looking adoringly into his eyes...

"And it was worth waiting for..." she continued sincerely.

A tear started to roll down her face.

"Me too... my gorgeous Lady" Tommy said nodding his head in agreement "me too"

As he wiped the tear away...

"Where did you learn to do what you did to me?" she asked candidly

"Did you not enjoy what we did...?"

"Enjoy... Ho Yes... I enjoyed...!"

"Me Too...!"

"Well?"

"Lou ... it just seemed so natural to do what we did... I wanted to kiss, lick, eat every part of you... and make love to you...!"

"I like natural" she smiled...

"And I loved what you did to me. So where did you learn...?"

"I followed your lead, Ho Master... I had a good teacher and I want to learn...more...!"

"Good, remember that... for when the Student is ready the Master will appear... and I accept I'm a Student too, Ho Master Lou.... So it's a ditto situation."

"I like Ditto... So will it always be that good...?" She said with a wink.

"I'll let you know, I haven't read the second half of the Football Manual" he started to laugh

"Let's hope the second half is as good as the first!!!" she giggled

They rolled around the bed play fighting... then snuggled up...

You ready for the second half...? Whispered Tommy

"You read the Manual...?" whispered Louise

"I'll wing it..."

"You're a Centre Forward.... so get on and score... once more....!"

And then devoured each other again and again and again.....

They continued to explore erotically, intimately, kissing, licking, sucking and seducing individually every part of their bodies... Melting, flowing, exploding until...

Until they were exhausted and fell off to sleep peacefully wrapped in each other's arms enveloped in Angel's wings ... dreaming sweetly the night away.

 In the morning Louise was awake early, she lay next to Tommy gazing at him sheepishly, smiling happier than she had ever been, ever considered she could be and she loved this emotion, this sensation, this sentiment.....

Louise slipped out of the bed grabbing one of Tommy's tee-shirt that swamped her. She crept out of the bedroom and into the kitchen; she started to make them a drink... coffee for Tommy and tea for herself, two glasses of fresh orange. As she waited for the kettle to boil Louise pulled Tommy's tee-shirt up to her nose she could smell him and she smiled the broadest smile and sighed contently "God I love you Tommy Jackson!"

Louise thought she heard a noise coming from the lounge; she popped her around the doorway... nothing.

Then she came back to earth with a bump, "ho God Sophie" she thought. "Ho well... no harms done, we love each other that I know and that comes first..."

Louise went back to the kitchen and gathered the drinks; as she headed back to the bedroom she looked at the door leading to Sophie's room.... and quickened her step. "I don't want to rub salt in the wound…. as I'm sure she likes Tommy." "But he loves me and I'm never going to give him up!"
She put the drinks beside the bed and slipped back under the sheet into bed, removing his tee-shirt...

She stroked his face with her finger tips until he stirred, opening his eyes and a beam extended across his face...
"Good morning beautiful…!"
"Good morning handsome…!"
"I can smell coffee ... wake up and smell the coffee" Tommy decreed with a Yankee accent.
"It's beside you" she answered in a Southern droll.
"I must have gone to heaven to wake up with my beautiful Lady and a mug of hot strong coffee..."
With that Tommy rolled over and grabbed his…. mug.
"Hmmm just how I like it" he winked at her ... and then kissed her tenderly… "Thank you..."
"Smooth talker" she whispered.

They drank their drinks and snuggled back down...
.

He started to stoke her hair and touch her face; Tommy kissed his middle finger and placed it onto Louise's lips….

This action proceeded to start a frenzy of activity in the bed; they started where they had finished the night before.....

"Replay"

"Replay"

"Tommy…!   Tommy…!   TOMMY...! Ho….my….God....!!! Ho…Ho…....Ho Wowwieeeee...!"

"Hooooo Ho Yes… yes… YES….!!! Louiiissseee.....!"

Chapter 46

They cuddled up and dozed off exhausted....

 Louise woke suddenly...

"Tommy, wake up….please."
"What's wrong...?" he was startled.
"Wake up" she said tenderly.
"Ho great...! Are we going again....?   Can we have another coffee first...? He teased and grinned...

"Do you think we should get up before Sophie does..?"
"Why?"
"Because we don't need to cause any unnecessary upset..."
"Who's upset Louise...? ... Are you regretting what's happened…? Are you regretting last night...? Are you regretting it now...?" Tommy looked sad and concerned.
 "No never... I have never felt so loved, so wanted, so needed...   Amazingly magic and very different... contented and fulfilled" she confirmed.
"Then Sophie is going to have to learn to cope with us..."
"Ok you're right."
"What time is it Lou...?"
"8.15."
"8.15…! I'm on holiday in Portugal ... there's not two 8.15's in the same day... crazy woman."
"We have to leave the villa by 12 noon, we have to book into the airport by ... latest 2.00pm and our flight is 4.15pm."

"I love it when you're so assertive, so commanding, so organised, sooo bossy...! still you make a good mug of coffee." He said trying to keep a straight face, turning into a wry smile, eventually giggling and laughing to himself..."

She also started to laugh.
"I suppose your right, we should get up, and he swung his legs out of bed, in the same manoeuvre he leant back and puckered his lips toward Louise...

Louise responded diligently leaning forward and meeting him smack on...

 "Lou how do you think your parents will take to this…?"
"This!" She exclaimed.
"Sorry... you know what I mean, us...? Assuming there is a... us...?" he looked up at the ceiling looking forlorn.

"You know Jackson for someone with an inkling of intelligence... to assume! Makes an ASS/ out of / U and / ME... So is there an US....? Or have you had your wicked way, and now discarding me...?" Louise turned her head away from him... her voice cracked with emotion.
"There'll always be an US Louise! I will always... I would never discard you… I will always love you." said Tommy.

Louise could hold it in no longer facing him she started to giggle "I love you too and my parents will be over the bloody moon... Jackson" then she started to laugh.
"You COW...! You landed me good and proper."

"And you landed me big boy, don't forget it... how do you think your parents will be...? Quizzed Louise...

"Well, Mum can be a bit bossy and lets Dad think he wears the trousers, which suits both of them. As Dad thinks he does and lets Mum think she does, so I guess you'll fit in perfectly Louise, they will be happy as pigs in SH.."
"STOP right there, we know where pigs are happy" cut in Louise before he could finish.

They both smiled and hugged each other

On a serious note said Tommy "how do you think Sophie's parents will react...?"
"Why should they be concerned unless they had hidden aspirations of you and Sophie, as an item...?" Remonstrated Louise "and that has never been obvious, I think they all thought we would end up sharing a home together?"
"Hmmm bit kinky." Smirked Tommy...
"You're a mongrel at times" retorted Louise "and don't even think about it, otherwise you'll be a Footballer with no balls to play with!!"
"Ouch! That means not scoring!"
"Exactly and there is only one net your scoring in ... and that's if you keep last nights and this morning's performance up." Smirked Louise surprised at her own flamboyance, compared to her normal shyness ... demeanour.

"Wow get hold of you tiger, bit bold aren't we, last night's released a wild cat...!"

Louise started to blush a little embarrassed of her own brazenness.

Tommy took her in his arms "you're my wild cat and I love it, my little pussy"
Louise hugged him so tightly "and I love you and I will never make you ashamed of me."
I'll never be ashamed of you Louise, never in a million years, I love you to pieces."
 "So do you think everyone will be happy for us...?"
"Everyone in the whole wide world will be, why not...? Why wouldn't they be...?" enquired Tommy.
"No reason I guess... but you know people get jealous... it's in some people's nature... they want what you have... instead of being pleased and happy for you. Those individuals; their character, their personality, is to envy, resent, be angry, be jealous, and let's hope it doesn't happen or affect us ever...!

 "I love it when you do that entire deep and meaningful profound Freud stuff, even at 8.30 in the morning on the last day of our holiday... wicked...!" stated Tommy.
"Are you extracting the urine out of me...?"
"My love I'm not taking the pi.. I mean it and I love it because I listen, hear what you say and learn."
Louise gave him an enquiring, squinted eye look.
"I mean it...."
"Ok get dressed and we can go and have some breakfast by the pool....."

"Yes captain." he smiled.

"I'll go and prepare your coffee and meet you on the patio" Louise smiled back at him and disappeared through the door.

She went to the kitchen and noticed the breakfast plates had been laid out she shrugged her shoulders "mmm"

Louise placed the plates laced with Croissants ham cheese and olives on the tray; she made a fresh pot of coffee and tea.... "I'll put these on the patio and go and wake Sophie."

Chapter 47

As Louise walked onto the patio to her surprise Sophie was sitting there...
"Ho ... morning Sophie" Sophie smiled at Louise "Morning Louise......"

Sophie had woken early "the last day today, we leave for home" she had already packed most of her things the night before....

"Could do with a drink... I'll make Lou and Tommy one"

She slipped her sun dress on over her bikini and headed for the kitchen, stopping she knocked softly on Louise's door opened it and popped her head around it, no Louise and the bed was made "already up!" She opened the door to the lounge area and saw in the reflection in the mirror Louise in the kitchen...... in Tommy's Tee-shirt, Jackson No.9... on the back!
She closed the door and returned to her bedroom.
"I wonder where Louise slept...?
"I wonder if she will make me a drink too...?"...
"Perhaps she's taking him an early morning coffee" she raised her eye brows, puzzled.
Sophie waited long enough, composing herself....
"Tommy may have lent it to Louise last night...!!!"
Clutching at straws...

She went to the kitchen and made herself a drink, then headed to the patio area half hoping they would be sitting drinking. Her hopes were dashed as she sat on the lounger, she saw two sets of flip-flops one pink, one black, then realised the dirty marks she had seen in the lounge, they were footprints made from damp feet, two sets leading into Tommy's bedroom area.

"She has slept with him!
She has made love to him...!
Has she had sex with him...?"

"We will always be together Sophie...!   .... That's what he told me."

"For how close they have been, I suppose it was inevitable, if not here, then back home"

"I've made some breakfast; I was coming to wake you...." stuttered Louise
"That's nice did you sleep well...?"
Louise regained her composure *"I have nothing to be ashamed of"* she thought to herself.... *"Eventually..."*
She smiled at Sophie..."Yes thanks I had an extremely wonderful night, educational, and enlightening. I stayed with Tommy last night." she countered strongly, confidently, raising her eyes brows and smiling broadly.

"Louise... I'm only asking are you rushing things..? Are you taking things too far..? Too soon...?" Interrogated Sophie...
"Thanks for your concerns Sophie; I know you mean well, but what has happened between Tommy and me, we believe has been(developing) festering, growing for some time. The recipe is gourmet, the ingredients are the exact

preparation, perfect, and the coming together, left us breathless... Moorish...!"

She smiled trying to alleviate Sophie's concerns, and to let her know, they knew what they were doing and she had had the most wonderful experience.
And she didn't want anything or anyone to diminish what had happened or to rubbish it...

"I see... for some time, well I never noticed it" defended Sophie

"Neither did we out in the open, but inside it was growing like a hidden time bomb waiting to explode, I guess we needed to be in the right place for things to flow, shot out of the blue you might say..." Louise countered not trying to do battle but to justify she wanted to be happy... she smiled.

"I'm only asking because I don't want either one of you to get hurt..."
Hurt...! Why would we get hurt...? Sophie we are in love this isn't a game or some holiday fling some fun in the sun..." declared Louise passionately.

Tommy had been standing out of sight but within earshot leaving and enjoying what Louise was saying and leaving her to deal with the situation... until...

"HURT... who's going to get HURT...? Tommy said loudly, moving into sight and joining in the conversation ... "Sophie you heard what Louise has said and I personally could not have put it any better myself, very well portrayed." Tommy finished lowering his voice and was smiling at Louise he then leant down and kissed her on the lips. He then proceeded to kiss Sophie on the cheek...

"...Good morning by the way"

"Morning... look guys I am genuinely pleased for you both but we leave England as friends, we are in Portugal for two weeks and we are going back with you two in love. Is there something in the air out here…? Well fast or what...! Did someone press fast forward...? You know wait a second what's the rush...?" defended Sophie.

"Sophie there isn't any rush; it has happened whatever you want to call it. Why should we deny what we feel for each other…? We are in love Sophie, and for me I could stand on the top of the Empire State building and share it with the world...!"
 Tommy was standing now with his arms extended, stretched out wide speaking in a Churchill manner
Louise blushed, then stood and applauded him admiringly... "That's my boy...."

"Ok ...ok I hear where you're coming from; I'm only saying before you go in all guns blazing, think about how the families are going to react....?
    .... I am just being Devil's advocate. Are you rushing events… are you rushing into a situation... without considering the consequences of your actions...?"

"Consequences of our action...! Questioned Louise stunned and bewildered.

What consequences...? Demanded Tommy.

"You have slept with each other so there's no going back from that one...

No shame it happens when people get carried away...." interjected Sophie derisively.

"NO!"

"NO!"

"What about your football career...? What about your place at university...? Remember you're going away! ...! "

   "... I'm just thinking logically..." concluded Sophie

They both looked at her then at each other at a complete loss for words, and then Louise said softly

"Sophie, we are in Love. It's not Fantasy Island, it's not some infatuation, we are not playing... when the cats away the mice will play" Louise stated sincerely with moisture building up in her eyes, and tears rolling down her cheeks.

"I'm sorry; I don't want to upset you. I'm trying to be open and honest. How are you going to deal with all the admirers, football fans who see him as their hero? How are you going to deal with the press? You're going away; he's out with team mates… pictures, pictures and more pictures in all the papers.... all the little girlies trying to snare him...?"

"Sophie, stop this right now, you're trying to destroy us before we have even had a chance to have a life together." raged Tommy.

"And you…!" Sophie said challengingly, pointing at Tommy, "she will be away at university surrounded by intellectual, clever, affluent family men... you'll be able to cope with that week in week out, will you…?"

"Sophie stop it... stop this now. I would never cheat on him... And I don't believe Tommy would ever cheat on me. We trust each other, I thought you were our friend...?" sobbed Louise sadly with tears running down her face.

Tommy jumped in "Sophie we are in love and we will cope with whatever is thrown at us by jealous, resentful, spiteful, and nasty, small minded, little brained prats... sorry people...!"

"I'm trying to show you the facts that you will have to deal with when we get back to England and real life" said Sophie feigning innocence.

"Really…? Feels and sounds more like a Rottweiler gnawing at the Gregory Peck, ripping our jugular veins out and enjoying it in the process" Tommy replied angrily.

"What's your motive behind this Sophie...? What's the agenda behind all this negative deluge of wilful, destructive, distrustful accusations...?" Declared Louise, now becoming as irate as Tommy...

"While you're at it Sophie don't worry about our happiness... rip our souls out.... in the process of destroying us" fumed Tommy

"No... You have me all wrong, as I said, Devil's Advocate, if you can survive me then you can survive the media and peer pressure, as well as people who don't want you to be together..." sympathised Sophie

"Devil's Advocate...! Sounds like you have tried us, judged us, found us guilty and sentenced us to failure... Sophie" growled Tommy unconvinced.
"No Tommy I'm on your side" defended Sophie feeling under pressure.
"Yes... is that right...! What about my side Sophie, are you on my side as well...?" charged Louise her temper flaring and getting the better of her again.

"You seriously have me all wrong, I'm your best friend" said Sophie feeling threatened. "I'm trying to show you how it might be and you have passed the test with flying colours" and she started to laugh... "Well done you are truly in love"

"Testing...? You're testing us...?" queried Louise still unconvinced, sniffing and glaring at Sophie.

"Testing...? Fucking testing... You made Louise cry and you made us both fucking angry" accused Tommy.

"Yes I'm sorry… but if I can get under your skin imagine what the media will do" stated Sophie cockily.

"But Sophie if there isn't any fire... and there isn't, and there won't be...! Then there isn't any smoke... if there is nothing to write about what can they say...? We have nothing to hide"   professed Tommy.

"Who do you think will be interested in us...? We keep ourselves to ourselves, get on with what we have to do and mind our own business" asked Louise shaking her head.

"I'm sorry I thought I was helping." apologised Sophie.

"I can't believe you have just put us through all that." Louise said glaring at Sophie.

"Helping who Sophie...?" Tommy slandered, still angry getting up and walking down to the pools edge.

"I think you took it a massive step too far... shooting from the hip Sophie" affirmed Louise walking away from her, finding solitude and solace in the garden.

Chapter 48

"Tommy we have got to prepare, the taxi will be here in 30 minutes..."
"Ok I'm coming"

The journey to the airport was made in stony silence.

"We are boarding at gate number Twelve and we can book in now, so let's queue." organised Louise.

They made their way through customs and into departure still in silence.

"Coffee anyone...?" Invited Sophie sheepishly, trying to break the ice.
"Yes please" replied Louise coolly.
"Tommy do you want one...?" echoed Sophie.
Louise threw him a glance and mouthed the word *"please"*
"Yes please Sophie...."

She handed Tommy and Louise their coffees.

"I'm sorry... so sorry.... I apologise I didn't mean to hurt you... please forgive me"
She said mournfully
"You went too far Sophie... but apology accepted" said Louise graciously.
"Sophie I love you to bits, but don't ever pull a stroke like that again, we are supposed to support and protect

each other, we like our knee caps where they are… not you of all people… taking our legs from under us...!" Tommy accused… pointing at her. Then taking a deep breath….. "But apology acknowledged and now we will put it to bed" he ended open-handedly.

There were cuddles all round and tears from Sophie and Louise.

Tommy hugged the two of them firmly pulling them together, into him.

Louise rested her head on Tommy's shoulder, her eyes closed;
Sophie looked straight ahead, a distant look in her eyes.

Chapter 49

They boarded the plane and seat belted up...

"Cabin crew prepare for landing" was the voice coming out of the speakers...

Ladies and Gentlemen we will be landing in 15 minutes we hope you have enjoyed your holidays and going home with good memories. Sadly it isn't quite as warm as in Portugal, thank you for flying with us."

As they waited for the cases on the luggage carrousel Louise was getting very excited "I can tell my parents about us Tommy... can I...?"

"Mmmm" he smiled "can I tell mine about the beautiful woman I've fallen in love with...?"

"Yes yes yes together or individually...?"

"Louise I couldn't stop you even if I wanted to... you tell yours and I'll tell mine....and I'm sure at some point we will come together...?" he winked raised his eyebrows and smiled at her...

"Animal... I'm sure we will... now be good...!"

"Grrrr..."... "Go tell them...!"

"And Sophie will tell hers."

"I really do hope she can be happy for us."

As they walked through "Nothing to Declare" and into Arrivals their parents were waiting to ferry them back home, eager to hear of the exploits of their adventures...

Louise made a bee line for her parents as soon as she spotted them and hugged them so tightly; at first they thought something was amiss. "What's wrong Louise...?" asked her father sternly, concerned.

"It's Tommy...!"

"Tommy...! What's wrong with Tommy...?" he enquired compassionately, at no time was he suspicious of any wrong doing.
"I have fallen in love with him.... We have fallen in love with each other"... "It's so wonderful... I'm so happy." she spurted out, tears flowing down her face in happiness.

"I would never have guessed darling" said her Dad sarcastically but overwhelmed.

"I am so pleased for you and Tommy, ho Louise I'm so pleased" Joan started to cry with Louise.

"You will make a fine couple" said her Dad also starting to get emotional and smiling.

Sophie made for her parents also crying.... "What's wrong Sophie...?"
"Louise and Tommy have fallen in love whilst we were away, it's been growing and it came out on holiday."
"Ho I see"
"They are now a couple..."

Her parents could tell they were not tears of happiness and joy...

"Come come darling, things will be alright, you'll see...." said her mother caringly, sympathetically, hugging her tightly, knowing Sophie had always had a soft spot for Tommy and looking at her husband for support.
"....We must be strong at times like these Sophie and stay dignified my dear"

"We must be pleased for them Sophie we must show support for them; they are our dearest friends." affirmed Fred.

"Mummy, I'm broken hearted!" confessed Sophie
"I know you are darling, I know you are, but we must show solidarity and joy."
"You'll get over it Sophie, there's more fish in the sea.." confirmed her father.

"We went away as friends... they have come back in love.... my love... it should have been me......"

Tommy's Mum and Dad were aware of all the commotion going on; the pandemonium, the hugging and the tears… but not the reason....

"What's going on Martha...?"
"I don't know...! Where's Tommy...?"

Tommy was last through the door pushing the trolley with three suitcases and three pieces of hand luggage stashed on it.

The smile on his face as wide as the Grand Canyon…

Louise, her Mum and Dad were looking at him... smiling.

Sophie, her mum and dad were looking at him... smiling.

Sophie the best she could muster...

He made in the direction of his parents, big hugs all round…

"What's all this palaver and fuss about son...?" enquired his Dad who hadn't missed a thing.

"Is everything alright love, why all the tears...? You haven't fallen out have you...?" asked Martha

"Tommy everything OK...?" asked Tommy snr nodding at him.... then in the direction of the others.... "This entire hullabaloo... what's the SP...?"

"Ho dear how am I going to tell you this..." Tommy said hesitantly with a straight face.

"Whatever it is son, spit it out, we will deal with it" confirmed Tommy snr

"Tommy what's happened...?" His mum said almost in tears.

"Well... mmm... well, it happened after a few days, but I guess it's been going on for some time, only no one was aware... I certainly wasn't…. but then again I must have had my suspicions..."

His mum and dad looked at each other wide eyed, then glanced over at Louise and then at Sophie without catching their parent's eyes....

"What do you mean... like... the two girls are....?"
"No... He doesn't... do you....?" his Mum interrupted.
"What...?" he asked innocently.
"WHAT IS GOING ON...? Tommy snr insisted impatiently.
"Tommy please tell us now...? Demanded his mother....

"Mum Dad... I love you both so much, so please accept it, please be happy for me... us...!"

They both looked puzzled... What...?

"Suddenly life has new meaning to me, suddenly you're in love" he sang out at the top of his voice...

"Louise and I have fallen in love and I have never known a feeling like it. I'm so happy and a bit like a trifle all mixed up and fruity... seriously though, I love her with all my heart.
"YES YES YES... ho son I couldn't be happier for you... for you both" Tommy hugged Tommy
"I don't know whether to hug you or slap you... trifle indeed... you have some respect for that young lady... now come here and give your mum a big hug, I love you boy.
I know Louise will make you happy" tears were rolling down her face and his dads.....

All the families huddled together shaking hands cuddling and crying....

"So back to ours to have a drink to celebrate" said Louise's dad.
"Sounds a great idea." endorsed Tommy snr
"Well, we will have to have a full run down of events, how the holiday went" suggested Sophie's dad.

So back to the house they all trudged and the drink flowed until the early hours of the morning; telling the families the whole story from airport thongs, topless, the flight.

"Watch the Loo Sophie…"
The reverse psychology, wind ups all around...
The kitchen... their wall…
The meals out and the trips.....
The BBQ…!
Minus the incident that went on....

The blossoming of their romance…
The blooming of the buds into the beautiful roses....
The beach trips and days around the pool…

Minus Sophie's; hibernation….
Minus the; tension, the stress and the terse conversations.... between them...!
Minus; Inquisitions…
Minus; Prosecution and defence…
Minus; Conclusions….

Minus; No man's land and the treaty of the end of hostilities and peace....

Now for future plans....
Enjoy your time....

And so they all wandered off in different directions slightly inebriated, jolly and mellow.
Happy in their own time.... And back to their beautiful, content filled homes.

Chapter 50

As soon as Tommy got into his bedroom he looked out of his window across the grass common and pond; he could see Louise's bedroom light go on, seconds later Sophie's bedroom light came on, they all had their rooms at the front of the house...

Tommy dialled Louise's Mobile number....
"Hello my darling... missed me all ready...?" Answered and questioned Louise softly.

"Yes I have gorgeous all ready... Lou I must speak to you on a very serious note. I've given what I want to say a lot of thought and consideration on the flight home and during our interrogation of the holiday..."
Tommy stated his intention without a hint of humour in his voice.

"Ho dear this sounds serious; you haven't changed your mind regarding us...! Have you...? She asked fretfully..
"NO! Not at all, God woman I love you and want to be with you for the rest of my time."
"HO GOOD... ME TOOO...! So what's wrong...? What's so important...?"
"I have never lied to my Mum and Dad… ever in my life and it isn't going to start now....! It's like a claw in my throat Lou; I know what we said to Sophie.... Not to tell what happened on BBQ night, but I can't look myself in the mirror without wanting to throw up....."

"I know it doesn't resonate with me either, I was wondering how you would react."

I don't lie and I don't take to liars... it doesn't feel good inside, so what's your intentions Tommy...?"

"I'm going to sit my Mum and Dad down, ask them to keep it between us, as I don't want to betray Sophie's confidence. But I can't lie and I can justify my actions to myself. I'm going to divulge the facts of what transpired that evening; come clean if

You like. We did nothing wrong we have nothing to hide and I don't want it coming back at a later date and biting us on the arse... *"You never told us"* do you agree...?"

"I agree.... "Louise confirmed.

"Good because it wasn't up for conjecture or debate..." and Tommy giggled.

"Do you want to get both sets of parents together and we tell them at the same time or individually...?" inquired Louise enjoying Tommy's strength in taking decisive action.

"Together, do you think that's best...?"

"Yes that should be arranged ASAP."

She also appreciated the fact he asked her opinion whilst still taking the lead...

"ASAP.... please my precious!"

Two days later the meeting was arranged clandestine style, so as not to bring suspicion from Sophie or her parents....

Louise and Tommy explained in detail how the BBQ evening commenced from the afternoon, *our wall... Sophie's attitude and actions on the night and then after,* without missing a single detail.....

"...And so the coach pulled out with Sophie between us, and the sight of the two morons staggering from behind the building.... and we returned to the villa...."

Tommy concluded without swagger or bragging and Louise held his hand throughout; which was not missed by their parents.

"At which point we had heated words with regard as to what we should do... how we should deal with this..... Police... family...!"

...We were then told in no uncertain terms it had to be a secret between us, but our consciences won't allow that to take place, so we feel the need to share with you in confidence." added Louise.

"Which sounds two faced but we don't see it like that. You all need to know, plus it takes a weight off our minds and shoulders" finalised Tommy.

They both sat looking at their parents in anticipation.... their relief was evident....

Geoffrey, Louise's Dad was the first to speak, in his legal voice...

"You were both right and correct in your decision to share the events of the said evening of the BBQ and the aftermath of the decisions taken out of your hands; the burden of secrecy, placed upon you, a burden that one day could hold serious consequences..."

Tommy snr was no slouch in coming forward but he respected Geoffrey when it came to legal matters...

"Geoffrey are we all clear of any aftermath with our son's future...?" he asked diligently.

"We are indeed Thomas; I have written every detail, exactly as it was spoken... this will be kept in abeyance in the event it should be called upon in evidence....
... As this misdemeanour happened in another country and no action was taken at the time it would be inconceivable to think these two rogues would dare to make noises in the corridors of law....
.... Given their surly, dishonourable, insidious, actions and young Thomas giving the two blighters a thorough and deservedly good thrashing, I cannot foresee any repercussions. Case closed."

"And what about Louise's involvement ...?" Questioned Martha caringly...

"Bystander and reputable witness; to Thomas's chivalrous actions, in defending the young lady's honour...." Geoffrey replied without blinking an eyelid....
"A text book case..."

"And what do we do about Sophie...?"   Queried Joan looking inquisitively at the others...

"Good question and accordingly so... what do we do about Chloe and Fred...? They are our good friends as well" pointed out Martha.

"Dilemma indeed" stated Geoffrey...

"I don't like this, Fred and Chloe deserve to be informed of what happened. What happens if we watch Sophie.... and there's a change of pattern in the way she acts....?

Do we then inform Fred and Chloe, *ho by the way your daughter was attacked on holiday, we knew but we didn't tell you… but we have seen a change in her, so we think now you should know....!"* Tommy snr laid it on the line.

Silence prevailed....

"Those one eyed fucking mongrel interbred cow-sons they want their Boll...."

"Tommy... Don't lose your temper we all feel the same way as you do." Martha cut him off short.

"Worse than a dilemma it's an impossible task." confessed Geoffrey.

"Kids what are your feelings...?" asked Martha.

"Yes you are in the middle of this dilemma." added Joan.

"Is it possible for Fred and Chloe to be informed and asked for their consideration and judicious understanding of the position we are in with regard of Sophie's magnitude of trust in us...?" proposed Louise...

.. And asked for their deliberation and discretion: because Tommy and I have been put in such an awkward position with regard to our promise to Sophie to keep quiet about the entire incident.

"Also for the trust of others in the future.... if she can't trust in us who will she feel she can confide in, in the future... should she need to...! Isn't it enough for them to know so they are aware of what went on...? I'm not being callous but she wasn't actually touched intimately, if maybe it can be described in that fashion?" shared Tommy.

"I like the direction you are heading; if this is handled carefully and diligently and dealt with in a sympathetic and compassionate manner the outcome can be extremely positive and with no ill-feeling. A positive conclusion" summed up Geoffrey.

"They will know, no one else needs to know and Sophie holds onto her dignity." Tommy snr was nodding his head.

"My suggestion is that we four take Fred and Chloe out for a meal and tell them diplomatically, so no ripping bollocks off, Tom." suggested Joan.

"Understood, calm personified." smiled Tommy.

Tommy however did grab hold of his son "I'm so proud of you, protecting the girls."

Chapter 51

The meal was arranged and Geoffrey had the opening gambit; the unpleasant task of opening the conversation they were all dreading.

"Chloe, Fred, it's come to our attention that whilst the brood were on holiday there was an incident that took place; it appears that two opportunists tried...to get to amorous with Sophie....

"Two opportunists..! Amorous..! What the fuck happened...! I'll kill the bas.....!" Raged Fred...

"Please Frederick allow me to continue" cut in Geoffrey, cutting Fred off....

"...They did not understand the word NO...! Nor would they listen to the phrase: I am not interested in either of you. Sophie tried her very best to defend herself, but there were two of them and they flatly refused to take no for answer...

...Fortunately young Thomas and Louise were on hand to rectify this unpleasant state of affairs.... Thomas gave the two rogues a thoroughly good thrashing and Louise was there to pacify, console and look after Sophie. No sexual impropriety took place, so her honour is intact".

"I'll kill them...! ...Who are they...? ... What are their names...? ... Where do they live...?"
"Get in the queue, not before me...!" stormed Chloe.

"And this reaction is the very reason Sophie didn't want you to be informed" countered Geoffrey.... "This reaction...! This is exactly how she thought you would react." he said trying to calm the situation.

"She insisted that they were not to take any further action in Portugal, plus they were not to let you know about It." said Tommy.

"She asked Louise and Tommy not to say anything". Repeated Joan... "But on their return they were really uncomfortable about this and decided it was best to tell us" added Joan

"And we all thought you should know" added Martha

"We all felt the same as you two do; kill the fu..... Mongrels...! That would have been our reaction as well" confirmed Tommy... "But Sophie made her mind up and doesn't want you to go searching for them."

"Can you respect her point of view... her feelings...?" begged Geoffrey

Fred and Chloe looked at all of their friends....
"Thank you all for confiding in us; we do appreciate it..."
"Nothing untoward happened...?" demanded Chloe...
"Nothing happened to my baby"

"No...!" they all said at once.

"Then we must honour her wishes... yes Chloe...?"
"Yes Fred..."

"Then this matter is concluded and never to be spoken of again." declared Geoffrey.

"Thank God the wigs on our side." muttered Tommy snr

When Fred and Chloe saw Louise and Tommy in private, they hugged them very sincerely and said "Thank You.... for saving and protecting our baby... we will always be in your debt."

And the subject was never broached again

Chapter 52

In the blink of an eye... time drifted by.....

They were always together with the girls going to watch Tommy play football; as often as possible.

On the rare occasion when Tommy was playing and Sophie was in a competition on the same day Louise would alternate between going to watch Tommy and Sophie. Although she admitted to herself going to see Tommy on her own was her preference; not having to share him.

She would travel with him to home games, watch him from the stand and meet up with him afterwards. To be with him at the away games, she secretly looked forward to this, After all he was her man.

But she hated the thought of deceiving her friend and they always made a point of meeting up with Sophie later in the evening.

Sophie would ask twenty questions....

"How had the day gone...?"

"How had he played...?"

"Did he score...?"

"Had they won....?"

"Where had they been...?"

As much as she really didn't like not being there with them she tried not to let her jealousy shine through.

It never entered her mind that they could see straight through her act; her jealousy was so transparent, so palpable, they could feel it. The repeated interrogations, it was like walking on broken glass.

They would make such a great fuss of her; Tommy would ask...

"How was the journey...?"

"What was the venue like...?"

"Was anyone nice there...?"

"Did you win"...?"

"Did you shoot well...?"

... And if she had not won they would console her.

Louise also went to watch her shoot on her own trying to spend quality time with her best friend and with regard of the questioning; she tried hard to diminish it put it down to the concerns of a great friend.

Louise and Tommy had spoken of this....

"Tommy I feel like I'm under scrutiny as if I've done something wrong, in the spot light, divulging the information.... prodding prod, prod....prod...!"

"I know Lou, it's like walking on egg shells... questioning, probing... trying to make us feel guilty..."

It's making me feeling uneasy and she's our best friend... I don't want to feel like this, I feel terrible even speaking of it..." confessed Louise.

"Isn't that the idea reverse psychology...? .... She is our best friend but she is not actually acting in that way... is she...?"

Louise looked at Tommy.

"No she is not...! What do you suggest...?"

"Continue to support her but in the same respect make her aware of her failings... toward us... like true friends would"... concluded Tommy.

"You think she is doing this sub-consciously or deliberately, trying to cause pressure on our relationship for her own ends. You believe she as an agenda...?" questioned Louise.

"I don't know Lou I only know what I see and feel... there is always an undercurrent and I don't care for the way she speaks to us, undermining, patronising and diminishing.... it's my intuition... my gut feeling..."

"Always trying to put us down...?" summed up Louise

"Yes but I think that comes from her own insecurity...."

"So we support her and let her know she has nothing to fear...."

"That is the best we can do...!"

Tommy and Louise would go and watch Sophie representing her Club, County and Country as often as they could.

At Club and County she was formidable.

As yet she had not won any medals for her country but it wouldn't be long, so in winning or losing they would cheer her or console her.

Sophie had also gained promotion at work and she was doing incredibly well.

Deep down Sophie knew that when Louise went to university Tommy would be staying behind and she would have him all to herself. She liked that that idea very much indeed.

Louise had accepted that she would have to go to University after her eighteenth birthday to enable her to achieve and fulfil her potential and ambitions.

Tommy was making great progress but still had not made his full debut.

Tommy had the world at his feet; if he achieved half of what the expectations were, he would be a superstar.

Collectively they had grown; now on their individual pathways, the world was there for the taking.

Chapter 53

The party had been organised and it was four weeks away.

Tommy and Louise's emotions and feelings had grown and they both knew it but tried to keep it in check, well at least in front of their family.

The party had been set for the Saturday that his team where playing a big game away from home.

Tommy had been playing for the reserves and scoring lots of goals on a regular basis for them, the reserves were playing at home that day.

It had been planned that way, looking in advance at the fixture list so it would not be too much of a problem for him, so he could attend.

The two girls had pre-booked appointments at the hairdressers on the day and had planned in going out to buy new dresses for the occasion.

First stop though was the beauty parlour... *"Bits and Bobs"*... *"for pruning and priming"*: hot stone massage, full body spray, manicure, pedicure, and finally the make-up artist... not forgetting the lashes...!

All the parents had helped out to prepare the food and the drink

A bar had been erected and the dads would take charge of that.

The ladies knew exactly how they were going to lay out the fare with the cake in prime position

The house had been beautifully decorated balloons and banners in abundance.

Then the surprise came out of the blue the night before the big event... Tommy arrived home from training,

 "Mum, Dad I need to speak to you both..."

"What's wrong son...?"

"That is if there is anything wrong son...?"

"Wrong no not really wrong..." he paused

            ".... I think I'm going to upset Louise...." Tommy said sheepishly

"Why...?" Questioned his dad

"Why would you do that...?" Asked his mum

"It's not my doing Mum I wouldn't do it for the world..." he answered looking at the floor shaking his head

"Who would...? What's going on Tom...?" Queried his Father concerned for his son

"Tommy please come to the point; explain this to me ... please!" Implored his Mother

"Who...? What...? Why...? It's all rather irrelevant" Tommy shared softly.

"Irrelevant" cried out Martha Jackson.

"What's happened son...?

"It's out of my hands dad, mum I've got to go away"

What...! Exclaimed Martha....

"I'm leaving tonight; I need to pack a bag..." Tommy said so calmly.

"Leaving, why you leaving...? Asked Louise softly, she had entered the room at the end of the conversation.

"Tell me what's happened Tommy I'll sort it" said his father commandingly

 "Sort what out...? ... Tommy sort what out...? Louise asked sincerely, anxiously and inquisitively...

Tommy looked at all three of them individually rubbing his chin he had to come clean and he could not keep the pretence going on any longer, he had to tell the truth...

"I'm going travelling.." he said ever so calmly, nonchalantly... he paused, then he screamed out at the top of his voice... ..."up to Manchester...!" he said with the biggest smile on his face clenching his fists and punching them into the air....

Relief hit all three of them ... at the same time as anger... They all realised they had been had...

"You Bastard I'll kill him..." declared Martha, as she glanced at Louise and her husband, whilst taking a step forward...

"Kill him, ho no you won't that's too quick I'll break the little fuckers Legs first ...one at a time... slowly...!" growled Tommy snr ... distorting his face ... "Then you can kill him Martha dearest..." he scowled, winking at her at the same time.

Louise's eyes filled with tears... "That wasn't funny Tom" she whispered mournfully... "I thought you were leaving me..."

"I will never leave you Lou... I swear to God..."

".....I'm Sorry I couldn't resist it..." he said apologetically knowing he had taken the wind up too far... looking at his parents.

"Resist it, can I resist punching you straight in the Gregory peck and making you gag..." growled Tommy Snr again.

"You have upset all of us when we should be having a celebration..." said Martha sincerely.

"Tommy you went too far...." Louise said sternly pointing a finger at him

"I'm sorry I had great teachers...!" his head tilted slightly a truly sorrowful look on his sad face and he opened his hands out begging for clemency.

They all looked at each other... then at Tommy.

And in unison made a beeline for him hugging him, kissing him, cursing him....

Tommy had been picked for the first team squad due to injury and was selected to travel away up to Manchester.....

"Mum Dad Lou I've been picked for the first team squad...!" He exclaimed...

It was such short notice it wasn't possible to get tickets for the gang but they also did not want to spoil Louise's big day.

Tommy would be there but he would be a bit late.

The party was prepared, the hair was done, and the dresses were bought and everybody; Martha, Tommy, Louise, Sophie, Geoffrey, Joan, Fred and Chloe were huddled around the television set 16:40 pm, results time....

It ended in a 3-3 draw.

The commentator announced.....

"Little Tommy Jackson all 6' 2" of him on his league debut has scored three goals – a hat trick....!"

They heard no more.....

There was bedlam in the house all hugging, dancing, cheering, tears and chants of....

"He scores when he wants, he scores when he wants, Little Tommy Jackson he scores when he wants...."

"He's Six foot Two, eyes of blue little Tommy Jackson belongs to you....."

And they all began holding their arms aloft and bowing to Martha and Tommy, who in turn pulled Louise into the middle of them...

This was before the party even started.

At the final whistle, Tommy retrieved the ball and handed it to the referee, who in turn shook his hand. "Great game, great goals Tom and I think this belongs to you.."
And handed the match ball back to him....

In true tradition all the players from both sides had signed the ball and his manager presented it to Tommy in the changing room congratulating him on a great achievement.....

His captain and team mates had made a great fuss of him at the final whistle...
The opposing team members slapped him on the back and some shook his hand...

Many sentiments where passed...
"Well done son..."

"Great game kid..."

"Next time boy I'll remember you... "

To which his skipper shouted out "yer next time Tom... put your scoring boots on..." and winked at Tommy.

And now for the long journey home.

The party had started and was well underway, great music, loads of food and drink.

All of the family friends and work colleagues were there but for Louise it wasn't complete – no Tommy.

Chapter 54

On the journey home Tommy hung on to the ball tightly with both hands, like the opposing goalkeeper... hadn't been able to...!

There was only one destination for that ball; it was for Louise with an inscription on it "To Louise – In Your Hands Forever Love Tommy".

The party was in full swing when Tommy arrived at around 11.30pm. Louise, Sophie and their parents were first to the door.

They all made a great fuss of him.

"Ah hat trick man...." the chorus went up....

"He scores when he wants, he scores when he wants, Little Tommy Jackson he scores when he wants...."
"He's Six foot Two, eyes of blue, little Tommy Jackson belongs to you....."

Tommy smiled, "Thanks, Thank you all..."and he nodded his head modestly.

He hugged his Mum and Dad so tightly....

"Well done son, well done my boy..."

"Thanks I would never have been there and done it without you two..." he whispered in their ears and they all started to let the tears flow down their faces.

This inspired another great cheer and whooping.

Tommy then turned and looked at Louise he tenderly tossed the ball to her and she caught it easily and then read the inscription...

They took a few strides toward each other and then kissed full on the lips...

.....It lasted a couple of seconds, too long and a great roar went up, whistling and cheering from all.

They just gazed into each other's eyes and everyone in the room knew.

Martha smiled.... "I don't know who he takes after..." and looked at Tommy snr... adoringly who shrugged his shoulders and smiled. "Come here you big lummox..." she said and they hugged.

"I think he takes after me..." Tommy said in his "DUKE" accent shrugging his shoulders.... "But with your looks and brains"

"Geoffrey she takes after me..." bragged Joan

"Yes dear she does, so beautiful a true catch..." praised Geoffrey blowing his own trumpet in the mean time.

"Would one be singing one's own praises... dear...?"

"One must take credit when it's due dearest..."

"I love you".... she smiled and snuggled into his arms.

"I concur and second that emotion..."

"I think I might be buying a new hat dear..."

"Ho dear... how dear....?"

"Could be very dear....!"

"Mmmm" his bottom lip quivered "do you think so....?"

"On the evidence so far... overwhelmingly conclusively.... dear"

Geoffrey looked at Joan raised his eyes brows and smiled....

".... She looks overwhelmingly happy it could be an extremely dear hat... my dear..."

Fred and Chloe where standing admiring the happiness and contentment they could see on their friends faces....

"Isn't it lovely Fred...?"

"Yes my darling it is."

"Ha Fred, young love...."

"And not so young love" he said nodding in the direction of their friends closeness and smiling at his wife.

"Do you remember when we met... love at first sight?" She said all gooey eyed.

"You were trying to stick a needle 6 inches long into me" he winced closing his eyes.

"You pussy it was your backside, fleshy... mind you; you had a cute butt..."

"And then I rolled over and then we fell in love at first sight" raising his eye brows and puckering up his lips.

She manoeuvred took aim and bulls eye... Direct hit....

"Ho don't Louise and Tommy look so good together...?"

"Yes they do..." He nodded in agreement ... "very much in love, that boy is off the market, he reminds me of me when I met you."

"How do you think Sophie will deal with it...?"

"As in life we don't always get what we want, we deal with the hand we are dealt... adapt and improvise" said Fred talking from his military training.

"Overcome adversity; she is strong enough, she as the will power to achieve her desired goal"... "She'll be a winner..." affirmed Chloe.

"Sophie darling come and join us" beckoned Fred... then continued....

"...They look so happy together Sophie, don't they...?

"I have a feeling.... This is for life; signing up for the duration and you my darling; you're going to be a beautiful bridesmaid; the maid of honour...." Chloe whispered sincerely.

Sophie smiled but her stomach churned.

The pangs of jealousy she had felt before, now in her life... forever more.

The party went off with a great bang into the early hours of the morning; dancing, singing, drinking, eating... chatting, leg pulling.... the night away with so much fun...

Drinking and dancing, and the music played on:

"*No matter what they say, no matter what they do, Believe in what you know, what is right for you, Don't let them put you down, ignore that silly frown, Smile back, and keep on track, Just smile back, wink and keep on track...*"

"*I'm looking pretty hot; I'm not kidding myself, let's hit the floor adding up the score, if you're pretty hot and you hit my spot, We can close the door, I'm not saying no more... Think what you want, Think what you like, Where gonna party... right through the night..."*

"Whenever *we met, always in a crowd, never on our own didn't seem allowed... The banter would begin, the verbal would flow, Giving everybody... a fabulous show, But deep inside...I really wanted you....! To know..."*

"But *we were put together For a reason bigger than we know, Could it be... just maybe... possibly...? To help each other grow, Let each other go...! Remembering the good times, forgiving the bad.... I don't hate you...."*

"A *differences to the world I thought I'd make, But swimming upstream without a break, Give us a helping hand for heaven's sake...Open a door let me in, to give someone a Chance is not a sin, could you begin...."*

"At *this moment in my life, how long is a moment? Have you found your moment? I'm going to... enjoy my life; I know My soul mates out there...!. Yes I know you're... out there...! To share our true love... eternally. Could it be you...? Could it be true...?"*

Tommy and Louise spent most of the evening together seldom out of each other's sight, dancing the night away with family and friends, interrupted by slow smooches, talking about their feelings for each other and about Sophie.

"Louise I'm so pleased our parents sent us on that holiday....."

"So am I...."

"Just think if we hadn't gone and I hadn't made lunch that day...."

"I know... And I hadn't got cramp....."

They both giggled and cuddled, remembering.

"Do you think it would have grown, cultivated within and then exposed itself anyway...? Asked Tommy...

"Hmmm sounds disgusting when you put it like that, you'd get 18 months for that...act...! Giggled Louise then her face change...... IT...!" Emphasised Louise

"Ha ha ha...! You know our feelings for each other..." credited Tommy.

"Divulged it's self...? Yes... IT! Would have come to the forefront.... developing, maturing, nurturing, lying dormant and concealed, then exploded like the big bang" she articulated.

Tommy's eyes lit up "Winner takes all...?

"Love conquers all... love will always win...!" genuinely affirmed Louise.

"The masquerade would have continued and then out of the blue.... Crash Bang Wallop Wham...! Exploded, erupted a passion of love..." he proclaimed like the Town Crier with his arms open wide, exaggerating every movement.

Everyone startled by Tommy's outburst looked in his direction and then started to laugh, clap and cheer.... *Tommy Tommy Tommy.*

Louise was shaking her head looking at him her eyes radiant, indulgently, "He's irredeemable..." She conveyed publicly pointing at him with both hands.

"Yes Tommy something like that...!"

"Ha Sophie, come here.... I want a hug."

"Come on Sophie let's dance..."

They never wanted to hurt Sophie so when she joined them they would be discreet, caring and loving toward her as they always had been with no change on their part.

Everybody was so happy that Tommy and Louise had truly found each other before she went away.

Sophie was joining in the fun but the pangs in her belly tightened.

They made long term plans to go and see Louise when her term got underway and she would come home whenever it was possible.

Tommy would phone her every night without fail.

Not too long to wait on this occasion as she would be back in a fortnight for Sophie's 18th party.

The timing of Louise's departure to University, could not be more untimely, but unavoidable due to the sequence of events in life. The dates were set for her orientation and induction.

Louise left the following morning cuddles kisses and tears were in abundance as she boarded the train.

The families discreetly gave them some space...or tried to...

"Move aside, move aside, come on now some privacy for these two love birds" bellowed Tommy snr getting a dig in the ribs from Martha

"Stop embarrassing them and think of Joan and Geoffrey"... "God you have an inappropriate North and South at times."

"Aren't you going to kiss me goodbye....?" Louise's voice croaked and with tears running down her face.

"I never ever want to kiss you goodbye...!" solemnly replied Tommy, his voice choked and broke with emotion.

Tommy phoned Louise every night chatting and laughing, then the tears of sadness and missing....

Making plans for when she was home and the future, although somewhat tentatively, sounding one and other out, reading between the lines, although they both knew deep inside what they wanted.

"Louise Louise Louise, please you have to talk to me....?" Tommy pleaded down the phone.

"Tommy.... What's wrong...? She answered alarmed.

"I need a fix...!"

"What....!" She screeched... She was shocked

"A fix... I need a shot... a fix... a main liner" he said sorrowfully

"So my understanding is that you have withdrawal symptoms....? My poor baby" she responded sarcastically, sympathetically.

"Yes... I need to hear your voice... my gorgeous girl." He said softly.

"And now you've heard from your dealer...?" She replied mocking him.

"Ha I'm in seventh heaven floating on a cloud.... all mellow and fulfilled.... for now...!"

He would more often than not meet up with Sophie who began to enjoy this close union more and more.

"Hi ya...

"Good to see you you're looking fitter...!"

"How was training...?"

"Who you playing next....?"

"Why aren't you in the first team after scoring a hat trick?"

"Are you sure you picked the right team?"

I bet one of the big teams would buy you...!

This is nice spending time together.... cosy nights...!

"Have you heard from Louise...?"

"Is she happy at University......?"

"I suppose she's studying into the early hours, she must get lonely...?"

"Do they group study...?"

"Or is it buddy studying...?"

"Once she graduates ... I wonder what she will want to do where she will work...?

"Tommy took it all with a pinch of salt.....

"Mind games Sophie mind games" he would think...

"I'm doing ok Sophie."

"I'm good where I am."

"Good to spend time together."

"I'm enjoying my life."

"I so badly miss Louise, do you...?"

"Whatever she decides to do, I would support her..."

"I can ask her for you, who she studies with...!"

"Have you phoned her recently...?"

"I can't wait for you to come home darling, even if it's only for the weekend"

"Me too, is everything ok...?

"Sophie; she keeps playing innuendo, her games again"

"Take no notice Tommy I'll be home and we will be together it's just her insecurities; she'll get over it and everything will be back to normal"

Over the next two weeks Tommy continued his training and playing.... missing Louise so badly...

Sophie went about her job and practised her shooting.... when she wasn't meeting up with Tommy....!

Louise settled into University quite quickly...... studying, and meeting new class mates....

She missed Tommy and Sophie so much and longed for the party.

Chapter 55

Friday night and Tommy was waiting at the railway station: Alone.

"Tommy Tommy, ho darling come here big boy it's great to be home it's even greater to see you...!"
"Louise I'm so pleased to see you give me one of those special hugs..." he winked
Louise gave him one of those looks "Not in public you mongrel, you wait 'til we are on our own..."
"Hmmm heaven...!"
Resulting in a rapture of giggles....

That evening they spent together with Lots of Loving and Intimacy....!

Chapter 56

Tommy was playing for the reserves at home so there would be no glory hat tricks and ball presentations.

The girls booked into their regular hairdressers and went shopping for new clothes to wear.

First stop though was the beauty parlour... *"Bits and Bobs"*... *"for pruning and priming"*: hot stone massage, full body spray, manicure, pedicure, and finally the make-up artist... and not forgetting the lashes...! Old habits...

This gave Louise time with Sophie...

All the parents helped with the food and decorations, bunting balloons and a cake...

The bar was set up and the music was ready to rock.

The party was going well when Tommy and Louise arrived together.

Sophie was none too impressed with this but didn't let it show, she thought they would have been there earlier.

Dancing, drinking, eating, frolicking, banter, and the party was in full flow...

Drinking and dancing, and the music played on:

*"**There** are so many nights that I lay awake, All on my own, Ho my heart does ache, Thinking of you, dreaming of you, Just wanting you, just me and you, And of what might have been...."*

*"**Love** can be so spiteful, but never more than hate, A dividing line in the space of time, I'm afraid I' can't relate, There must be reasons I don't know why, We meet we love we grow, we let each other go, Remembering the good times, Please don't say you hate me, I don't hate you..."*

*"**Seeing** my existence pass me by, Swimming upstream without a break, Knock on many doors give us a chance, we won't give in We won't go away, We'll eventually win, we'll eventually win..."*

*"**No** matter what they say, no matter what they do, Believe in what you know, what is right for you, Don't let them put you down, ignore that silly frown, Smile back, and keep on track, Just smile back, wink and keep on track..."*

*"**Party** tonight, lets party tonight, Those on their own, No one in sight, Let's party tonight, Let's Party tonight, Come on everybody, lets party tonight, Party tonight, lets party tonight....!"*

It had been pre-planned by the conspirators for the music to slow down, the volume to be turned down and then a presentation all timed to perfection so that Sophie would be the centre of attention.

.... Her Birthday Cake... the candles were lit and she was encouraged to blow them out.

To which she frowned a little "I'm Eighteen.... not eight...! She muttered under her breath.

This was deliberately arranged so that Louise and Tommy could present their best friend a gift... they wanted this to be a special day, to make Sophie feel special and loved....

Everyone was singing to her... With Louise and Tommy leading the barbershop group, Arms aloft swaying to and fro...

"Happy birthday to you ... Happy Birthday to you ... happy birthday dear Sophie, oh we all Love You....!"

.... She scores when she wants ... She scores when she wants ...   Dead Shot Sophie ... she hits the bull's-eye ... SHE SCORES WHEN SHE WANTS.....!"

A big cheer went up and the crowd began to Bowe, *"Sophie ... Sophie ... Sophie ..."*

Tommy and Louise then presented Sophie with a beautifully wrapped package... Gold Embossed paper and ribbon... she looked at them perplexed, slightly squinting her eyes and tilting her head...

Louise and Tommy were eagerly urging her on "Unwrap it... Unwrap it"...

The party dwellers egged Sophie on louder, "Unwrap it...! ... Unwrap it...!"

She looked at them quite taken aback, so much attention...

She carefully dissected the wrapping with great aplomb...

Before her eyes was a mahogany wooden case 12 x 6 inches, magnificently inscribed in Gold Leaf... *"All for One" ..."One for All..."*

She opened the box slightly; tentatively, diligently aware that all eyes were focused on her, she shivered...
She glanced around the room... optimistically... pensive... enthused... mixed emotions...

Her attention came back to Louise and Tommy who were grinning like Cheshire Cats, glowing with pleasure.
Their attention was solely on her, beaming with delight at their friend whom they loved so much.
She smiled; nodding her head at the audience she had before her.... and opened the hinged lid fully.
Her face told a million stories....

Inside was a... Double-Barrelled Silver Sterling Ivory Handled, Derringer.... and a row of bullets.
Sophie gave out such a shriek; you would think she'd been shot by it.

She was thrilled with her present *"How could I have ever doubted their friendship and love for me..."*
She placed the case down carefully, turned and threw herself at them, together they cuddled and hugged, trying to put aside her own feelings and be happy for both of them.
"Thank you, ho thanks you for being my best friends, I love you both so much..."
"And we love you Sophie we will always be friends... forever..."
"We certainly do and we certainly will...!" Confirmed Tommy.... "Despite all the crap we have had to put up with from you...!"

She looked at Tommy then Louise, they smiled and they all began to laugh.

"I know I've been a prat and a right little diva... I'm sorry, I'm sorry, I'm sorry it will never happen again..." she whispered to them..." ... "Have I really been that bad, so much crap...?"

"So diplomatic so much North and South just like your Dad; it's her birthday...!" scolded Louise.

She looked at them sombrely "Have I...?"

Instantly, simultaneously they yelled "YES...!!!!"

And they pulled her toward them enveloping her with hugs and kisses.

The party was a great success; Rocking and rolling, drink was flowing and the food... exquisite....

Tommy danced with Sophie on quite a few occasions, making her feel very special, it was her night.

"Ho Tommy how lucky we are..." said Sophie whilst they had a slow dance.

"We certainly are Lou... sorry Sophie, sorry Sophie it's so natural to say Lou an innocent ... mistake"   "*If only the ground could open up...*" he thought.

"No problem it must be easy to make that mistake...!" she said smiling at him.

Louise was never jealous, just happy they were all backing each other again, back together and her "sister" was having a great... great night.

"Louise dance with me" asked Tommy and proceeded to tell her of his mistake and Sophie's response....!"

"Diplomatic as a nuclear missile..." she sniggered... "You should join the diplomatic core Tom" ... "You could cause an upset in a telephone box on your own...!"

"All right girlie take a breath have you grown vipers' gills on that Gregory Peck...?"

And as always in their satirical banter they laughed... so happy, so content, so in tune with each other's feelings....

"Louise looks very joyful, ecstatic even" said Geoffrey, watching her dancing a slow dance with Tommy.

"Yes, she looks so pleased with herself... so blissfully happy... in such high spirits..." responded Joan, she paused......

"... Blissfully happy my love... as I am" she looked at Geoffrey adoringly.

"Very Conducive my dear... very well said" he countered. Geoffrey found it hard to be romantic. To show his feelings and emotions; a bit of a stiff collar but loved his *Joanie* as he called her in private, so very much...

"I concur with you" she re-countered

"Furthermore... I second that emotion" over ruled Geoffrey.

"Changing the subject" Joan said slyly, looking up at him through her lashes "Louise and Tommy look euphoric, so perfect together" Joan said, countering him again, and throwing him a curve bull...

"Objection my dear that's below the belt, no Queensbury rules applied there...!"

"I've seen such a perfect hat, beautiful, for a special occasion" she whispered in is ear, and then blew softly...

"You Mercenary...! ... You sniper, that's Assassin tactics...!" he declared.

"Love you too..." she breathed in his ear.

Geoffrey gazed admiringly, tenderly, lovingly, adoringly at Joan

"I love you more..." he mouthed the words

"My boy is growing into a man, Tom do you think I'm going to lose him.... he looks so happy and besotted with Louise.... don't get me wrong I love Louise..."

"Your never lose him Martha; a boy grows into a man and meets partners, he may fall in love and be happy.... but he only ever as one Mum... no one can ever replace that connection and no one ever should... love for your mum is different for love of a partner."

"Ho love, this has been such a wonderful night; shared with good friends and our Sophie as the best friends ever...." said Chloe sentimentally.

"Yes love it as... and we are all so lucky to have such close friends..."

"I do wish Sophie would meet someone and find happiness Fred..."

"She will Chloe but she has to let go first...!" Fred put an arm around his wife and hugged her.

And the party went on... and on... and on....

Louise prepared to go back to University the following evening after making her plans with Tommy.
After all it was Tommy's birthday in two months time.
After all the goodbyes' tears and hugs they left...

Tommy took her to the railway station
"No goodbyes my darling..."
"No, no goodbyes..."
They kissed and held each other tightly
As she boarded the train Tommy said ... "I miss you already..."
A tear rolled down her cheek and she blew him a kiss that he caught... and placed it on his heart...

Chapter 57

Over the next two months Tommy saw Louise as often as he could visiting her at university, going for walks, boating, picnics, and phoning on every occasion.
They were falling deeper and deeper in love.

Tommy also spent time with Sophie, has often as he could, he would introduce her to some of his teammates that he thought she would be interested in and he trusted, sadly to no avail.

He invited her out to events that Louise could not attend with him due to her commitment to her studies at university.
Introducing her to an array of different friends, some outside of football, after exchanging a few words and encouraging the conversation, he then politely made excuses to excuse himself on some pretence, leaving her in there company.
Hoping that she would be attracted to one of them and it might lead to something, but she never took up the offers of dates.

"Louise I can't fathom that girl out, she baffles me... she just doesn't seem interested in the slightest in any bloke I introduce her to...."
"And some of them I have to say..." pointing a finger in her direction and a wry smile on his face... "If I was a bird or that way inclined ...Id fancy's them....!"

"....Take Freddy my best mate, good looking feller... not as handsome as me... But none the less a tasty geezer..." he paused slightly

"... Now it doesn't bother me and I'm not being judgemental... as you know I'm not sexist, homophobic or detrimental toward.... any ones favourable sexual preferences. But you don't think that maybe Sophie bats for the other side...?"

"Take a breath Tom; one would think you had grown gills..."

"Tommy you've known her long enough... Ask her....!" suggested Louise.

"What...! She'd most likely shoot me..."

"Why would she shoot you... perhaps she wants you to... ask her that is...!" smiled Louise.

You don't think she has the Quasimodo about us....do you...? Because she as the fancies for you... Lou...? Quizzed Tommy winking...

"It might be you...she fancies Tommy boy...!" winked Louise back.

"No... I'm sure I'd know... I don't think she likes blokes..." he assured himself.... grinning.

"What will be, will be....let us wait and see...?"

"Your right of course.... now I think about it...!"

"What...?"

"It must be me she fancies, God's gift to women and all that, how could she not...!" he said with a glow... smirking at the same time.

"One of these days you'll shoot your big head.... woops mouth off to many times"

"I only have eyes for you... Lou, and no one will mix your head up or steel your heart..."

"Tommy you're an incorrigible tart...... with a heart...... that's why I love you, so much and my eyes are set on you... too..."

Chapter 58

Tommy's birthday party had been arranged.....

He was playing away but was expected back early enough to greet his guests...

The same procedures took place...

The mums had arranged and prepared the food, set up the tables and placed his cake in prime position.

The dads had put up the decorations, under the supervision of their better halves...

Then they had the job of setting up the bar, more in tune with their way of thinking and the stage was set, ready to roll and roll....

The girls went out shopping "I'm going to buy something really special for him."

"A nice mini dress perhaps...!" Giggled Sophie....

"Actually he's got the legs for it..." Louise joined in the banter.

"Suspender belt and Silky pair of stockings...?"

"Sophie what a great idea the Full Monty... Brilliant, thank you, yes the full kit and caboodle for him, it's his birthday present... me...!"

First stop though was the beauty parlour... *"Bits and Bobs"... "for pruning and priming"*: hot stone massage, full body spray, manicure, pedicure, and finally the make-up artist... and not forgetting the lashes...!

Then into the hairdressers, Old habits... die hard.

Tommy had played for the first team and to his credit scored the only goal in a 1-0 win, so he was in high spirits when he got home.

The party was in full swing... Friends and family arriving and being greeted "come on in, get a drink..."... "Foods over there... please help your selves..."

The music had them bopping around the floor and the drink was flowing...
The party was in full swing...
Drinking and dancing, and the music played on:

*"**I'm** gonna spend some time pampering myself, Pulled a little black number right off the shelf,*
I slipped it on and admired myself,
Took another glance, now I wanna dance,
Let's hit the town and make it a night..."

*"**There** are so many nights that I lay awake, All on my own, Ho my heart does ache, Thinking of you, dreaming of you, Just wanting you, just me and you, And of what might have been..."*

*"**Hate** is such a spiteful word, when you put it next to love, and love is what you used to say In that kind and caring way, I love you...."*

*"**Then** eventually, we find out who we are, Then eventually, we find out what we want, We become.., cocooned.., in a sea of love, We have peace.., in each and every way, We have peace.... in each and every day...".*

"At *this moment in my life, I didn't want no attachment, I didn't know what love was, Now I've found my.... inner peace, Now I know....what love is, Have I found my.... moment...? Could you be my.... moment...? Could it be true? Could it be....You...? Could....it....be YOUuuu....!"*

"Can you believe it... he's 18, my boy... is 18 and going to...." sighed Martha...

"Yep... do you remember when you took advantage of me, I was an innocent man, virginal...!" Tommy cut in.

"Virginal, virgin on the ridiculous more like, and Innocent, you've never been innocent.... you were born 25...! And a scoundrel....! And took advantage of me, as I recall it...!" Martha blushed and snuggled into Tommy's large frame....

"He's done us proud lover..." Tommy's eyes welled up...

"He is going to make us even prouder love..." and two tears rolled from the corners of Martha's eyes.

"Geoffrey dear you know that new hat; well I'VE found it...."

"Ho I am so pleased and I suppose you've found some where nice to wear it..."

"Yes Geoffrey dear..."

"No doubt that will be extremely dear ... dear...?"

"Reasonably Dear....!"

"Ho dear, I thought you may say that.... If that makes you happy my Dearest ... she who must be obeyed..."

"Thank you Geoffrey Dearest... it's for the best... it's for your daughter...!"

"Do you know something I might like to be aware of... some privy inside information, dear...?"

"Nothing concrete... just women's intuition...." nodded Martha...

"Ho Dear..."

"Fred I do believe Tommy's friend Freddie, he's a nice boy, is rather taken with our Sophie and she is looking a bit flustered..." smiled Chloe in suspense, hoping...

"Chloe it's possibly because he's all over her like a rash..." grinned Fred.

"Fred do you think she's taken to him....?"

"She's taken to him.... like the Devil takes to holy water..." Fred shook his head from side to side.... "I'm worried about our daughter...."

"Fred she's just fussy..." defended Chloe.

"You're the one trying to get her hitched..."

"She will find someone... won't she Fred, she's only 18...?"

"She will have to Chloe.... because who she wanted ... isn't available.... he's off the market.... lock, stock, and two smoking barrels... in love with Louise..."

"Ho my poor Sophie.... The Three Musketeers will be separating; she will be broken hearted..."

"She will survive, she will come out fighting, shooting from the hip... said Fred with a stern upper lip, "she's got over worse..."

Tommy knew they would try to embarrass him and do the candle on the cake stunt... and they did... "Tommy ...Tommy..."

The music was stopped dead and everyone's attention was asked for, the cake was lit... Tommy blew them out and the songs kicked off...

"Happy birthday to you ... Happy birthday to you ... happy birthday dear Tommy... happy birthday to you...."
"He scores when he wants ... he scores when he wants ... little Tommy Jackson he scores when he wants."..."6'2" eyes of blue ... little Tommy Jackson ...we love you..."

Then Tommy sprung a big surprise...
He called Louise to the middle of the floor and from his pocket he took a gold ring with a centre sapphire surrounded by a cluster of diamonds.

Going down on one knee Tommy said...
"Louise you are a beautiful and gorgeous person...
... Louise you are the beat in my heart....
...... You are the blood in my veins....
.....You are the air in my lungs....
 ....You make my soul as one....
...Would you please Marry Me....?
......And make me the happiest man in the whole wide universe".

 There was a loud silence as a tear rolled down Louise's face, and she said...

"ME TO..."
"...I mean I feel the same..."

"...I mean you make me feel the same way..."
"I mean....

     ....HO YES, ho yes yes yes ... and you have taken long enough to ask me....!

... Yes yes yes, I love you so much Tommy Jackson..."... a smile etched on her face as wide as the Grand Canyon Louise joined Tommy down on one knee... holding his hand tightly....

"Tommy Will you please marry me too...?
"Me too.... Yes I will marry you... Louise....."

They kissed to the sound of a rip-roaring cheer.
It was a double celebration and the party continued into the night.
Sophie was in torment but she joined in the congratulations and celebrations.

"Sophie Sophie" Louise and Tommy held out their spare arms to Sophie....
"Come here ... come here..." beckoning her to join them. They hugged...
Louise showed Sophie her ring... with sheer delight
"Sophie I'm so happy I'm going to be Mrs Louise Jackson ... and we want you to be my only bridesmaid..... Maid of honour...
She looked at Tommy who nodded instinctively...
"An old maid..." Sophie thought.
  ...And when we have children will you be a God Parent"
"Children...?" Exclaimed Tommy... "Gorgeous.... Is there something you need to tell me...?"

Silence erupted... you could hear a pin drop.... anticipation filled the room....

"Children...! Ho my God I'm going to be a grandfather and I'm only getting my head around the cost of The New Hat... Joan.... *Joanie*...!" Geoffrey pleaded.

Joan's mouth opened and her jaw hit the floor...

"My women's Intuition ah... my, my, I never saw any evidence of that one being sprung...."

Martha looked at Tommy snr who shrugged his shoulders..... "I know nothing..." and he was serious.

"My innocent little boy isn't such an innocent man now...." Martha was wide eyed and gob smacked.

"Is this why they are getting hitched...?"

"They love each other; we will deal with this.... no problem.... Grand Dad..." Martha smiled.

"Yes we will.... Granny..." Tommy nodded and winked...

Sophie's eyes rose from the ring and looked at Louise.... "Louise....

Chloe and Fred looked at each other, then at their friends....

"Shotgun wedding...? Fred whispered sounding disappointed... "No I can't believe it...!"

"Who's your money on... for who's shooting who...? ... "I don't want to believe it...!"

"Does it matter Chloe, you can see how much they love each other, and what would we say if it was Sophie... in Louise's place?"

"I love your logical mind Fred, I love you Fred, we, I don't have any doubt would be over the moon.... as so would have Sophie..."

"If I was to hazard a guess, I believe Sophie would love to be standing in Louise's shoes right now..."

"Two blasts in one evening...."

The party patrons ...... where startled and.... waiting in anticipation of her answer.....

Everyone's eyes focused on Louise....

"NO I'M NOT...! ... Slow down...! Calm down....!"

"Looks like multiple coronaries are imminent.... No I'm not..!. Definitely Not...!" she Stated.

"Mums pick your chins up off the floor dears...and have a drink"

"Dads do have a large brandy, you look like you need it"

"Tommy when that time is right, you'll be the first to know my darling...!" She looked around and smiled at them all, and then she winked at Tommy clutching his arm...

"Now I think I need a brandy...!"... "And let's celebrate... our engagement for the right reasons ... we love each other...!" she orated with an air of supreme conviction

"Me to... I need a brandy...."

And the roar erupted and the party swung into full bloom....

Chapter 59

Tommy in true tradition had visited Geoffrey and Joan prior to the party...

"Is everything OK with you young Tommy...?" Geoffrey enquired.
Joan waited impatiently, intuitively....
Tommy had planed what he was going to say over and over... and over...Calmly, assertively, and respectfully.

"Mr and Mrs Childs... I would like to ask your permission to ask your beautiful daughter Louise to be my wife... to marry me..." he blurted out without taking a breath.

Joan looked at Geoffrey.... Geoffrey looked at Joan... They both looked at Tommy who was shaking...
"Get him a drink Dear, whiskey I think..."
"In fact Dear get a round in, I think we can all do with one..."

Geoffrey poured three large whiskeys and handed them out...Joanie first.

"Bottoms up..." Joan showed her pronouncement with a very satisfied beam on her face, and clinked glasses.
"You better buy your hat my Dearest...!"
"What...? I mean pardon...?" Tommy asked gingerly.
"I mean young Tommy you have known us long enough to call us Joan and Geoffrey"
"Yes sir...!"

"Now it's sir... I like it..."

"Geoffrey put Tommy out of his misery, please" Joan sympathised.

"Of course my Dearest, you knew all alone didn't you I'm sure there's gypsy blood in your veins, and your crystal ball... all that spookiness... hocused pocuse...?"

Tommy looked at them puzzled.....

"I mean young Tommy you better call us mum and dad in due course"

"Ho yes...! Thank you...! I promise I will look after her and love her, although I don't know if I can love her any more than I do now, but I'm sure I will, Ho Yes yes yes"

And he hugged Joan who by now was crying....

"You're marrying my daughter not the wife, so put her down" and Geoffrey started to giggle....

"Come here you old tyrant" chastised Joan and pulled Geoffrey into the hug "His bark is worse than his bite Tommy, your get used to him..."

"Not so much of the old please my dearest, welcome to the family Tommy, with any luck your dad might buy a drink now... ho ho ho".... "I must tell him that one...!" and he wiped his moist eyes, as tears rolled down his cheeks.

Before Tommy visited Joan and Geoffrey he told his Mum and Dad of his proposed intention of proposing to Louise after asking her parents for their permission...

"I think that is very honourable Tommy, now come here and give your Mum a big hug, I love you son, I'm proud of you son and I'm so happy for you, you will always be my baby..." and she started to sob...

"Tommy you go for it my boy and if that little Gail makes you half as happy as ya ma's made me, you'll be king of the prairie...!"... He said in his "Duke" accent.

"Ho My God...! We'll be in-laws with the Wig..."

He took Tommie's hand into his and pulled him close, as he hugged him with the other arm, he sniffed up and his eyes welled up, then tears began to roll down his face. Tommy responded in the same fashion.... hugging his Dad, tears flowing...

They pulled Martha into them, and hugged tightly... she was sobbing, they where all sobbing....

"Thank you for being my Mum and Dad, I love you both so much..."

"We love you son....

..... We are so proud of you, as our son...."

And more tears flowed.

The following morning hangover's where a plenty....

Tommy took Louise to the railway station, only this time travelling with her into London... Then on to the university...

He stayed a few hours with her in her room.

"Fair well is a lonely sound when told to someone you love" Louise crooned lovingly.

"You're in my heart; you're in my soul" Tommy sang softly to her as he cuddled her.

Louse studied extremely hard at University, completing courses and passing tests with ease.

 "A unique talent" her Masters called her.

"She as a gift" the principle had affirmed.

 "A future Master if she so chooses..."

Tommy was making great strides and He became a regular in the first team.   He made his debut for the England's under 21's gaining a number of caps, as captain...

 "A very mature young man with his feet firmly on the ground, he as a gift" his Manager was quoted as saying in a national newspaper, which Louise had cut out and put in her scrap book.

So did Sophie.

Sophie had buried herself into her work gaining promotion after promotion "a gift" this lady will go far" her directors had said in discussion.

"The young lady as No Nerves..."

She was earning herself a reputation as a competitor in the shooting competitions, for club and England.

"Gifted indeed", "Dead shot Sophie", "No Nerves Sophie" the media claimed.

Louise couldn't always make the tournaments, but she would be there if at all possible, which was the way Sophie liked it, so long as Tommy was there....

Chapter 60

The wedding date was set.
It was like it was meant to be....

There had been a cancellation at the church that they had wanted; a small country church dating back to the 18th century in the local parish that they lived.
The reception was to be held at a local hotel with beautiful lush gardens and grounds.
They had met the Rev Smythson and sorted out dates, times and the taking of the banns.

The bridal suite was booked; and the menus had been picked.

The wedding had been set for two weeks after the football season had ended; this had to be sanction by Tommy's Manager.
This dispensation was granted as no promotional tour had been booked by the club in going abroad to play games.
His Manager, who along with his team mates, would be attending the wedding.
This also allowed them to fly off on their honeymoon to Portugal, Carvoiero... where else...

Joan and Geoffrey had insisted that they would pick up the bill in the old traditional style, it had to be said they could afford it.
"How dear is that new hat dear...?" he asked her.
"Not as dear as it could be...."

"Money is no object, not for our Louise's big day and I know how proud you will be, my dear...."

"And you won't be proud of her...!" she teased.

"But of course...!"

"So you should be, after all you will be walking her down the aisle...."

"Quite so ... tip top..." and a grin turning into a smile grew across Geoffrey's face, looking so proud.

Joan smiled "you old fraud ... no doubt you'll be peeling an onion... that old chest nut again... and a frozen brussel sprout stuck in your throat...!"

She pre-empted his excuses he always used whenever he got emotional, he ridiculed himself in humour, and to cover up is emotions.

He cleared his throat and raised his head... "Now now dearest ... allow one to remain with some dignity...."

"You old fraud everyone's aware of what you do, and everyone loves you for it..."

"Loves me, Loves me, ho...! I say ... is that so....?" he said quite taken aback.

"Yes... and I love you the most....!"

"Ho I say... how jolly good is that..." and Geoffrey wiped his eyes.

Joan gave him a big hug.

"Tommy, Louise, Tommy and Martha... it would be our honour and privilege to pay for this wonderful, momentous event. Being the proud parents of... May I say the most beautiful bride...to be" announced Geoffrey;

they had gone with them when they had picked the hotel....

"... And that is not up for Debate...!" demonstrated Joan.

"Geoffrey I know I always accuse you of being a dry lunch, short arms, long pockets.... so tight you wake up in the middle of the night, to ensure you have lost no sleep.....! Ha-ha ...

"And Joan, the lovely Joan, it is such a generous offer but we cannot accept it...!" said Tommy.

"We appreciate the tradition of the bride's parent's role, and how proud you are, and honourable you both are." Added Martha.... "But so are we...!"

"We would hope we could share the cost and pay half...." stated Tommy.

"Joan and Geoffrey, it's a truly magnanimous, generous, gesture from you both ....but please, allow us to share the cost, after all we're not going to fall out before the wedding ... over the wedding... are we...!" Martha said sternly but composed.

Tommy and Martha being of good stock from the East End... and proud had to pay their way.

Geoffrey glanced at Joan who nodded approvingly and smiled

"Joanie and I can surely see the merits of your candour and accept your proposal...in good heart"

"He means let's have a drink on it, cheers...!!!"

Louise and Tommy sat in the bar with their parents whilst they placed in their tenders on who will pay for what....
"Is it settled...?" asked Louise bashfully...
"The Covenant is sealed..." pronounced Geoffrey
"This could be the start of a beautiful friendship...." Young Tommy said flippantly.

"Now can we have our say...? Good....It is a wonderful, generous, magnanimous offer, gesture, indeed by both parties but we are paying for it...!" He glanced at Louise.
"the wedding and the reception...."
"And that is not up for conjecture or debates... comprehend" endorsed Louise.
She and Tommy where holding hands... waiting for the reaction and response, tentatively...

Geoffrey and Joan looked horrified ... Martha and Tommy looked shocked.

Louise and Tommy looked pensively at each other....
"Ho dear, we have truly upset you..."
"We didn't mean to offend you...."

Silence....

"We have discussed this and you have paid out for us all our lives and we want to pay for the wedding and the reception, as a thank you, to you all" shared Louise.
"For you to enjoy it as much as we will" added Tommy.

Silence...

"The best thank you.... you have bestowed on us... is who you have become..." granted Geoffrey, Joan placed her hand on his forearm lovingly.

"And to accept gracefully, in giving us the pleasure of this deed for you both....!" said Tommy emotionally Martha squeezes Tommy's hand.

Eyes moistened and tears rolled, uncontrollably.... as they sat at the table holding each other's hand in circle form.

Chapter 61

Over the next six months every weekend they would go house hunting, until they found the one they wanted; a lovely cottage in the country. Not remote, just on the edge of civilisation.

They always took Sophie with them, so as not to leave her out, to include her.

Tommy spent as much time with Sophie whilst Louise was at university.

Going to the cinema, to dinner, talking about the future with Louise and how she would meet someone and be just as happy as they were.

All the preparations were falling nicely into place.

Louise and Sophie had the wedding dress and bride's maid dresses made.

They were like Angelic Angels.

"Ho... they are beautiful dresses and complement each other so perfectly..."

Glowed Joan....

Martha and Chloe where in attendance... they were all in good spirits...

"I remember my wedding day..."

"That long ago..."

"My my... she does have a good memory...."

"Sophie this is so wonderful us being here together, picking out our dresses, trying them on, I'm so excited..."

"I could never ever imagine being on my wedding day without you being there, you are so special to Tommy and me"

Portrayed Louise to Sophie in the dressing room

"How could there be a wedding day without Hum Wah being present" teased Sophie

Tommy had picked his best man, his best mate Freddie who he played Football with. They had hit it off as soon as they met on the training field.... Freddie also came from East London. They had the same sense of humour and complemented each other off the pitch as well as on the pitch; Freddie played in midfield and created a lot of Tommy's goals...

"Now Fred there's something I've got to say you, now we both know... I'm the main man, but you're just as important because you're the creator....." Tommy had that incorrigible persona about him, with a massive twinkle in his eye and immense smile.

"You're a legend in your own lifetime... Come on big head what do you want..." mimicked Freddie

"Fred you know you're my best mate..."

"No...! whatever it is NO...! You're being too nice to me; I'm not use to it, stop otherwise I'll think I'm hallucinating.... and definitely No...! I won't go out on a date with your mate Sophie. I tried it once, it was like walking on hot coals ... and drinking bleach, sticking needles in my eyes, she doesn't like me.... I'm not sure see like blokes..."

"Finished...? Jesus take a breath...!"

"It is it... I knew it... if you want me to do something for you... anything mate, I mean it, except that Sophie... that is a bridge to far, a bunny boiler and I am not for the cooking pot ...?"

"She isn't that bad..."

"NO...!"

"I'm getting married as you know and I want you to create a speech..."

"To be my best man, you are my best mate... although sometimes I wonder why...?" Tommy lowered his eyes.

"Ho mate... Tom you only had to ask....." He smiled... "It will be my pleasure; I'm over the moon that you asked me..."

"I need you to be there for me... I want you to be there for me...? Affirmed Tommy

"I'm there Tom...!"

"One last thing Fred..." Tommy said sincerely.

"What's that...?" Freddy said concerned... "Whatever you need I'm there..."

"Good I'm so relieved you said that..." still being sincere... "You'll have to walk down the aisle with Sophie on the way out, escort her and dance the second dance with her... and spend a bit of time with her through the night..."

"You done me... how low can you get... you could sliver under a snakes belly.... so you ask me to be your best man ... just so I escort and dance with Sophie..."

They stood eyeballing each other... then embraced
"No Probs...!"
"Thanks mate"
Their morning suits and top hats were hired out from an exclusive men's ware outfit, as was Geoffrey's, Fred's and Tommy snrs...

"We look like the Wise Guys...!" said Tommy snr...
"The Good fellows..." Fred echoed.
"Ho dear I'll have to defend you... not guilty no doubt..." announced Geoffrey.

Whenever it was possible Louise came home, spending as much time as she could with Tommy – so much in love... the perfect couple.

Sophie would join them whenever she was invited, which was quite often, Tommy would bring along a teammate but nothing would ever develop from this.

"Do you think Sophie will ever find joy and happiness in her life Louise...?"

"The Joy of life begins.... With happiness from within..." pronounced Louise

Chapter 62

Whenever Tommy and Louise: were holding hands, touching each other, teasing, bantering or messing about.
Sophie would look at them through the side of her eyes and her stomach would churn.

On one occasion when Louise was home from university the three of them went out for a meal at a plush restaurant.
They were sitting around the table, giggling and joking about.
Enjoying vast quantities of red wine, copious amounts without realising it, quite at ease... getting pleasantly inebriated, considering none of them where familiar with an heavy, big intake of alcohol, they had devoured plenty...
When Louise said quite out of the blue...

"I wonder what the weather will be like on our wedding day...."
"It will be a bright warm sunny day, with a slight light breeze to freshen your hair, bird's will be singing and the aroma of carnation's and honey suckle will waft through the air" replied Sophie.

Both Tommy and Louise sat looking at Sophie; so profound, so beautiful... so unexpected...
Louise clasped her hands around her friends and said "Sophie that is so beautiful"
"Yer" said Tommy "It'll most likely rain" with a grin on his face.

"If it does" said Sophie "They will be angels crying with happy tears..."

"Ho Sophie that is so romantic" exclaimed Louise...

"And as for you" said Louise standing up and shackling Tommy's hands as she slipped out of the booth... "As for you you're terrible and so unromantic..." "I'm off to the lady's room" and she slipped away.

"And you call me unromantic" roared Tommy.

Louise took the two steps down out of the booth and walked along the aisle, between the booths on the other side.... slightly swaying.

She did a right turn heading towards the lady's room; Tommy's eye's never left Louise once. She was in his radar, locked on; He focused on her, following her every step adoringly....

"Terrible and unromantic am I... so you think so...?" he said in no more than a whisper to himself.

"You're not terrible Tommy and you are so romantic" said Sophie, her elbows on the table, her chin cradling into the palms of her hands, never once taking her eyes from Tommy's lips as he talked.

At that precise moment Louise looked directly at Tommy, their eyes met, she was smiling and mouthed the words....

"I LOVE YOU SO MUCH....!"

"ME TOO...!"... Mouthed Tommy "And you are the most beautiful girl in the world,

I LOVE YOU SO MUCH...!"

Louise disappeared behind the draped curtains in front of the lady's room.

Sophie smiled at him, the broadest smile.

" Ho Sophie, I am the luckiest man in the world" said Tommy "I am so in love"

"So am I Tommy, so am I, SO IN LOVE..." said Sophie.

Tommy's eyes had never once left the curtain, scrutinising, transfixed, hypnotised.

Sophie's eyes had never once left Tommy's lips, scrutinising, transfixed, mesmerised.

"Really Sophie... that's a result, I did wonder if you batted for the other side... not that I'm sexist or homophobic in any sense... I did ask Louise... I wasn't sure you fancied blokes." his eyes had not wandered from the curtain.... engrossed.

Sophie was under her own spell... her mouth moved without her brain being in gear...

"Ho...! is that right... well you should have asked, why didn't you... give us a chance, were you never aware...? you should have found out for yourself... you should have tried... you would have been pleasantly surprised... you'd have lit up like a pin ball machine... maybe you picked the wrong one... I am so in love.... I love... " she slurred and the words rolled....

"Wow... I wasn't... yes give it a chance... should have tried.... pin ball... surprised.....!"

"Come on Lou...." his attention and eyes immersed on the curtain and then Louise's appearance.

Louise reappeared, still smiling, their eyes locked and they watched each other all the way as she walked back to the booth.
Immersed in their own time and space

"So what have I missed...?" Mused Louise as she rejoined the table.
"Well it looks like Sophie's been holding out on us Lou" Tommy said sitting back in his chair, putting on a serious face, still absorbed in looking at Louise....
"What do you mean...?" quizzed Louise looking first at Tommy then at Sophie.
"Come on tell me the gossip, no secrets, tell me... tell tell... come on" she was looking at both of them at the same time ... smiling.

Sophie was now sitting upright her head no longer resting on her hands, she looked at Louise, she looked at Tommy and she didn't know whether to smile, laugh or cry.
What is Tommy going to say...? She thought realising what had happened; he was never referring to her, but she revealed all to him

"Come on tell me... it can't be that bad" demanded Louise noticing that both of them where no longer smiling.
"SOPHIE TELL ME WHAT'S WRONG...!"..."Sophie tell me" she said in a more caring voice, taking her

friends hands in hers, she was becoming concerned, she looked at Tommy "Tommy."

Tommy couldn't hold out any longer, he burst out laughing...
"She's in love... SOPHIES IN LOVE...! I don't know who to, but she's just told me she's in love, she don't know whether to give him a chance, she's not sure she's picked the right one, but wants to find out, Ho yer... he lights up pin ball machines, by the way it's a him... she doesn't bat for the other side....It's definitely a HIM....!
... I'm sorry Lou I couldn't resist it....!" He slurred

"It sounds like theirs more than one ... you dark horse ... you hussy ... no one, then Two, Three ......"

The relief that Sophie felt was incredible, she sank back into her chair, a wry smile appeared on her face, and her hiccup had been accompanied by Louise and Tommy's. Her true feelings for Tommy had not been revealed. She would not be upsetting her two best friends.
Instead she began to laugh and play along with Tommy's wind-up... bulls up...!
He had misconstrued everything she had spurted out...!
He had taken everything out of context.

"You bastards"... "You... you BASTARDS...! I thought something was…" she looked straight at Sophie,
"Who...? Where..? When...? SOPHIE...! I'm so pleased for….
Who is he...? Who are they...? Where did you meet him, them...?

When did you meet him...?

Them...! What's his name...? Their names...? How long...?

Sophie I'm so pleased for you...!" She slurred

"Hold on a minute....! How comes you haven't said anything, I thought we shared everything, Sophie tell me" by now Louise was cuddling Sophie.

 "If you give her time to breath and answer she might tell us" said Tommy.

"OH I've over reacted, there's a bloke at work... I'm not in love with him... I've had too much to drink and got carried away with the atmosphere" said Sophie as the red glow began to disappear from her cheeks.

"One bloke ... two...! How many...? No wonder you don't know if you're in love with him ... them, which onc do you fancy the most...?"

"Mmm One I suppose... yes just the one..."

"Why don't you want to give him a chance... give him the chance and let him take the chance... if you like him that much... tell him...!" emphasised Louise.

"If you like him that much, make a move on him.... fair maiden and all that...!

.....Is he the one who lights up the pin ball machine...!" Tommy raised his eyebrows, recalling some of Sophie's words.

Sophie lowered her eyes

"Lighting up like a pin ball machine Sophie..." Louise raised her eyebrows and grinned, shrugging her shoulders and winking. Delighted for her friend.... *She has found someone" she thought.*

"Louise please...! Not in front of him...!" said Sophie shocked, but trying to deflect her words, their words...
"Also there's no way she could have heard what I had said and Tommy never mentioned that bit...!" she thought...

"I know the mongrel is rubbing off on me...." she said innocently.

They looked at each other and busted a gut rolling about laughing.

The fuse had been left dormant... embers without memory...!

"What a big fuss about nothing then, blimey I thought we had cracked it and you'd met someone... handsome, suave, sophisticate, debonair and modest... ho yer funny" he pulled his shoulders back and glanced upwards.
"I thought you'd met a bloke and fallen in love... Louise God knows how you would act if she was getting married" chuckled Tommy.

"Someone like you... you mean..." Louise was trying to bring him down to earth but she adored him.
"If you say so... thank you for the complement..."

Sophie raised her eyes and glanced at Tommy... "If only you knew, how true your words are... she contemplated

"Oh Sophie we could have had a double wedding, you never know there's still time"
"I don't think so..." she repelled
"And as for you, I told you, you are unromantic...!" giggled Louise.

"Pin ball machine.....!" Tommy reflected.

Chapter 63

The girls had gone out on Louise's hen party two nights prior to a club with friends. The night went well: dancing, drinking, laughing, crying, laughing, dancing and drinking.

The two girls were sitting in a corner quite drunk chatting when Sophie let slip....

"I wish it was me Louise" Sophie slurred.

"Ho Sophie it will happen...."

"I wish it was me getting married..."

"Sophie you will find someone so special, who deserves you, someone who loves you, like Tommy...!" Louise endorsed sincerely

"Someone special ... who's like Tommy...!"

"Yes just like Tommy, who loves you..." she repeated.

"It should have been me....!" said Sophie adherently.

"It will be..."

"It should have been Louise... Tommy and me... I love Tommy...!" Sophie confessed slurring.

Louise giggled "you can't have my Tommy; you'll have to find your own Tommy..."

The following day Louise had some Hangover; Sophie had spent the night with her in Louise's bed, at her mum and dad's house.

They were drinking black coffee and oodles of water when it dawned on Sophie what she had said.

Louise had been in a tentative mood, very quiet, deep in her own thoughts... racking her brains....

Sophie hesitantly asked Louise "can you remember much about the night before"

Louise was not a good drinker and said "I can remember the beginning, but not the end, it was a total blur".

"Ha Lou that club was so good, the music... it was brilliant"

"I don't know about that, but I certainly drank too much... my poor head and my throat feels like a falcon's crutch..."

"Nice... do you remember getting home...?

"Nope"

"Do you remember sitting in the club....?"

"Nope"

"Don't you remember chatting...?"

"Who too...?"

"Us..."

"No..... Do you...?"

"No...! It's a blur... a blank... only the beginning, I thought you might have remembered... to tell me we had a great night" Sophie smiled sarcastically, then laughed falsely... Sophie was so relieved.

That evening they spent the night pruning and prepping... They were still very tender.

"I'm never drinking again" declared Louise "what's frightening is I can't remember too much"

"Me neither" insisted Sophie

They settled down to sleep.....

"It should have been me....!" came flooding into Louise's head.

"I want to tell Tommy what Sophie as said, but I can't, it will spoil our wedding day."

Chapter 64

The two girls were up early...

Louise had found it hard to sleep.... that thought kept springing back into her mind ... memory box... *"...It should have been me ...Tommy and me... I ....!"*

Both mums where fluffing about, "come on now a good breakfast will sort everyone out, settle us down..." this was quite normal practice so no complaints.

"We have a long day, so we need some substance...." Chloe affirmed.

"Bacon, 2 sausage, egg, toms and beans..."

"... Bread and butter ... tea or coffee... fresh orange"

They all tucked into a plentiful feast and then rested....

Both the girls' disappeared upstairs....

"What did you mean Sophie...?"

"What..." she answered innocently, appearing confused.

"In the club... what did you mean...?

"What...?" she said dismissively, nonchalantly.

"You said it should have been me...!"

"Did I...?"

"Yes ... what did you mean...?" she questioned.

"Only that.... I wish it was me; it should have been me..." she answered defensively.

"To Tommy...?" quizzed Louise.

"You said I should get married to someone like Tommy, who loves me, so yes I want to get married, so it should have been me.... Don't you remember...?"

"No... I don't...! You're telling me I told you that Tommy loves you and you should be getting married...?"

"Yes Louise...!"

"God I must have been pissed Sophie, Tommy does love you and he loves you as a friend... but we are in love, a massive difference, and we are getting married today...!" Louise affirmed definitely.

"I know that..."

Chapter 65

Both the dads were very nervous....

Mr Childs was practising his speech, time and time again, driving everyone crazy.

"Geoffrey now please put a stop to it... you will be eloquent, articulate, and fluent my precious, my dearest...!" Encouraged and confirmed Joan.

"Yes *Joanie* ... thank you dear..." mellowed Geoffrey.

"Come along sweetheart, let's get dressed....

"I'm going up..."

Their hairdresser and a beautician, from *"Bibs n Bobs"* had come to the house for the girls, doing their makeup and styling their hair to match the tiaras.

They started to get ready; they dressed in matching under ware, stockings and a garter to boot...! Classy, sensual and sexy...! Stunning....

They put on their elegant gowns and looked ho so beautiful, Louise's wedding dress and Sophie's bridesmaid dress complementing each other, yet individually debonair...

Louise looked over at Sophie.... *"I'm not sure I want you to be my bridesmaid, something doesn't resonate with me, truthfully regarding that conversation.*

I would never tell Sophie she should be marrying Tommy, that's been concocted to suit her agenda... fabricated, she's tainted our relationship" she deliberated, *"I want*

to tell Tommy now..!. Everything she has said... Sophie you're a Hypocrite...!
"How can I, it will ruin the whole day, I will tell him when we are on honeymoon..."

Joan looked exquisite in her new attire.... elegant and graceful.
Geoffrey looked very distinguished in his morning suit... and top hat.

"My *Joanie,* you still look like my passion flower, blooming and beautiful..."
"And you my darling are still my knight in shining armour, and I know the soft heart you have inside..." she kissed him on the cheek.

And then Louise and Sophie paraded down the stairs.... Louise leading the way...

Joan got very emotional "My darling, my darling girl, you look so stunningly breathtaking...!"

Geoffrey cleared his throat, twice... "My darling daughter, no father could be more proud than I am of you... now and always... I love you my darling, with all my heart..."

"Ho dad you'll have me crying and I'll have to do my mascara again" sniffed Louise.
"I am already, Ho Geoffrey, come here you big lummox..." sobbed Joan grabbing Geoffrey.

"Ho Sophie you look striking... darling... arresting..." praised Joan.

"Sophie sweetheart you look breathtaking, stupendous my dear..." confirmed Geoffrey.

Fred and Chloe had returned to their house...

"Come on Fred let's go and get suited and booted..."

"Isn't it wonderful Fred, such a happy time... for everyone and their dresses, so beautiful..."

"It's as wonderful my love as the day we got married, as for the dresses, I'll have to wait and see, but I will take your word for it..."

"Do you think Sophie will be ok...?"

"Sophie will cope and take appropriate action, all Millers do and she'll be grand..."

Chloe looked stylish and chic in her attire.

Fred stood straight and upright in his morning suit, his forces stance...

Fred was to be giving out flowers and to be an usher at the church.

So he and Chloe left before Louise and Geoffrey taking Joan with them in their car...

They left directly they saw Tommy and Freddie leave.

Leaving Louise and Geoffrey to take a slow drive to the church....

And make a grand entrance....

Chapter 66

Tommy Jackson snr, Geoffrey Childs, Fred Miller, Young Tommy and Freddie,
Their Granddads, a few Uncles, close friends and team mates, had arranged to go out on Tommy's Stag night.

"Ok let's all meet down the local and have a few beers' there..."
"Then we can move on into town...!"
"Good idea...."
"That's for those with stamina...."
"Don't worry about all that old tosh; we are out for the duration...!"
"Quite so, we will show these lads how to drink...."
Geoffrey put down the gauntlet.

The crowd hit the town like a tornado...

The following morning Tommy and Freddie came down the stairs looking very worse for wear.....
Tommy snr was sitting at the table with Martha....
"Good morning boys...." said Martha sprightly...
"Is it..."
"What day is it...?"
"I think I'm dying...!"
"I think I died.... and went to heaven..."
"They sent you back for being drunk in charge of your wings..."

"Lovely, come on now, nothing better to put ya right after a good night on the tiles, bacon, sausage, bubble, egg and beans couple of door steps and a mug of Rosie Lee."

"Dad do you mind...."

"God I feel ill...I've got a throat like an Arabs armpit"

"Good night then boys...?" asked Martha sarcastically.

"Come on get a breakfast down you... sort you both out" insisted Tommy snr

"Yer good idea, please mum"

"So did you have enough to drink, a little worse for wear are we...?

"Enough to drink, Freddie was that drunk; he tucked his trousers in to bed and threw himself over the chair...!

"Anyone for a livener, air of the dog... a bit later we'll nip down the local...!" teased Tommy snr.

"Do you have no conscience father... really, another drink...!"

The family had a very low key day and early night....

Tommy was lying in his bed unable to drop off, going over and over in his mind:

"You might have been surprised..."

"You should have found out...!"

It came flooding back into his mind.

"... Your loss, then you should have found out, maybe you picked the wrong one, you may have been pleasantly surprised in the response, and you may have lit up like a pin ball machine..."

"Ho my God ..... Shit...!

                .....I must tell Louise...

      .....Freddie, are you awake...?"

"I am now...! What's so important that you must tell Louise at 11.35, the night before you're marrying her...?"

Tommy unfolded the full scenario of that night to Freddie, who listened intently not once interrupting, taking it all in... all what Sophie had said.

"And now you want to unload all this on to Louise, the night before you marry her, come on mate so the girls infatuated with you and was pissed, mangled out of her skull, jealous..."

"Louise needs to know..."

"And she's your bridesmaid... and you want to substitute her now!"

"So you would think she would know better..."

"Tomorrow you are going to Marry Louise; Sophie won't have any axe to grind after that...."

"She shouldn't be coming on to me Fred; we are all supposed to be friends..."

"A women scorned mate...!"

"I've never led her on; I never encouraged her or tried it on with her..."

"We pertain to want what we cannot have, and we want it even more if we are rebuked... or so they say..."

"I never rebuked her...!"

"In her mind you said we will always be together and now you're Marrying Louise"

"Freddie I meant that as friends *"The Three Musketeer"'s* one for all, all for one and all that, but I'm in love with Louise... I need to see her"

"You can't mate its bad luck to see the bride before the wedding day or something like that..."

"I need to bring Louise up to speed..."

"You need to sleep, you've shared it with me and we will deal with it tomorrow, I can tell Louise tomorrow if you feel the same way, although not a good start to her wedding day... or tell her when you're away on the beach, on your honeymoon"

"She shouldn't be our bridesmaid; she can't be our bridesmaid.... she's supposed to be our friend, bloody Judas... she's treacherous... two faced bitch...."

"Tommy take it like a tackle from behind, your legs have been taken.....cut from under you... What do you do...? You get up, you know... but you don't let them know they've hurt you; you keep your friends close, your enemies' closer, treat her with the contempt she deserves..... Now you're aware of what to expect....!"

Tommy looked at Freddie admiringly then smiled "that's why you're the team's captain....!" "That's why I couldn't have picked a better friend and best man"

"Play the 90 minutes, play the game, win the game...! then cut her out of your lives forever, she lost...."

Chapter 67

Tommy and his best man Freddie were up early; Tommy had struggled to sleep as he was full of mixed emotions ... so excited and wanting to marry Louise, yet something was nagging in his head *"...You should have tried.. You should have given me the chance".... "how could she, she is supposed to be our best friend... I must tell Louise."*

They had breakfast cooked by his mum and then went for a good long walk to clear the cob-webs and monkey mind.....

"Logical thinking Tom, joint up thinking, joint up talking.... no emotion... clarity of thought" emphasised Freddie.

"Picked the right one..."... "I picked the right one all right, I can't ruin Louise's day and cause havoc now, but it will never be the same with Sophie in our lives, she as stained that relationship... our closeness and trust... in her....

.......I'll tell Lou when we are away.... it would blow her away if I told her this morning ... wouldn't it...?"

"Your decision mate, you tell me what you want me to do and I'll do it, in saying that, it seems logical in what you're saying..."

Tommy's mum was fussing after them "come here boys... sit down have a cuppa and settle your nerves...!"

"Martha you have a cuppa and settle your nerves and why you're at it my gorgeous, pour us all a brandy with that cuppa, make it a wassa...!" Tommy winked at his wife.

"A wassa Mr Jackson...?"   Quizzed Freddie

"Call me Tommy Fred, yes son a wassa..."

"Wassa...?"

"Cuppa tea or coffee with a brandy or whiskey mixed in it.... it WASSA...! Cup of tea or coffee...!" explained Tommy snr.

"Hence Wassa" exclaimed Tommy.

"You sure he's an East Ender...!" smiled Martha.

 "Time to get ready lads, up you go... don't be late, you can't be late for the church, not today" said Martha emotionally.

"Come on you, let us go up and get ready as well..." Tommy cuddled his wife...

Mr Jackson was in his morning suit looking very dapper, he was helping the boys with their cravats, adding the finishing touch.

Mrs Jackson had bought a new dress, shoes, hat and gloves, she looked stunning...

Martha took the red roses and placed it on Tommy's left lapel.

"I love you son..."

"I love you mum..." He said sniffing.

"You look very smart Freddie... let me put your buttonhole on"

"Thank you Mrs Jackson"

"And you my love are as lovely as the day we married..." complemented Tommy to his wife...

"What you after you Smooth talker....?

"You... you ravenous creature.... I want you..."

"Tut tut... you mongrel... not now... not here... well just not now...!" She raised her eye brows and winked.

Tommy looked at Freddie who was grinning... "Mum, Dad, not in front of the children..." he said pointing at Freddie.
"You carry on Mr and Mrs Jackson, no harm done there, smooth action, a death man would like to hear it and a blind man would like to see it..." replied Freddie.

"I hope Lou and I have the same fire, passion, and love for each other that you two have, after so many years together... to grow old together with the same intensity, for each other, that's magic"
"Not so much of the old...!" Martha and Tommy chanted in unison...

"Me too...!" blurted Freddie.
"But you're not with anyone yet..."
"I know, but whatever it is your mum and dad drink, I want some...."

"I believe you will son, I see in you two what your mum and I found...."
"Soul mates with a passion for each other.... a fire that continues to burn..." inserted Martha.

"Wow...!" said Freddie "I'll have a double shot please...!"

Eventually it was time to leave for the church....

They left in two cars and arrived at the church.... in plenty of time.

There was a small police attendance, although the supporters were very courteous and stood at a respectful distance from the church....

Tommy and Freddie waved at them and said hello to the early birds, they did some autographs and entered the church.

Martha and Tommy did the dutiful welcomes outside the church and the "how are you...?" to all and sundry.

They eventually entered the church and sauntered down the aisle, arm in arm, finding their seats at the front.... waiting patiently for the big event to start.

Chapter 68

Tommy and his best man Freddie were standing patiently, if somewhat nervously at the altar.

Tommy had confided in Freddy "I could play at Wembley in front of 100,000 people Fred and never be as nervous as I am today..."
"...I hope I don't cock-up my lines"...
"...I hope she isn't late it will make me worse..."
"You do think she'll come Fred, don't ya...?"
"Tommy", said Freddy....
"What...?"
"....will you shut up and give it a rest, you're driving me crazy..."
"... Of course she will turn up, she loves you mate, she loves you...
...and in any case you're making me bleeding nervous and I've only played at the old-rec in front of 10 people" he smiled at Tommy.

Tommy smiled back and then began to grin "Thanks Freddy... 10 people indeed, you make me look good on the pitch, you make most of my goals and I couldn't have picked a better best man or best mate".

All the family and friends were in the pews.
The church was full to the brim.
Mr. Childs and Louise where standing in the doorway of the beautiful old church, the bells had been ringing all day and carried on as the ceremony began to proceed.

They stood arm in arm, the two big wooden doors pushed firmly back against the walls, Sophie was standing just behind them holding the train which had been folded up nicely, as she had been shown and would unfold as Louise led off.

Directly out in front of them the floor had been laid with mosaic tiles depicting the last supper.
At the far end was a full length window, of blue, red, gold and purple stained glass. in the middle was clear glass with a lead surround in the shape of the cross.
There were twelve stone carved pillars, six either side of them, with Angels carved into them overlooking the aisle and pews.
The six to the left were blended from the ceiling into the floor creating six pews, the six to the right where parallel creating a further six pews, with a centre aisle leading to the altar.

The first chimes of the wedding march began; ding ding da ding, ding ding da ding. They had chosen chime bells and a gospel choir to sing the hymns and to hum the wedding march in harmony with the chime bells. Ding ding da ding, ding ding da ding, Mm Mm Mm Mm.
It all came together in perfect harmony.

Slowly Mr Childs and Louise walked forwards towards the centre aisle; on reaching it they turned to their right and stopped.
Sophie had followed behind, moving round to her left so as to be behind them, but slightly to the right of Louise creating an angle, they stood very still.

The idle chitchat of the congregation had been going on...
to everyone's enjoyment....

"Love your hat."

"Your suit look's lovely."

"Where did you buy that dress...?"

"How's the kid's...?"

"Haven't seen you for so long...!"

"I thought you were dead...! haha"

"Aren't they a lovely couple...?"

"Shame about Sophie..."

"It had to happen..."

....It began to quieten from the first chimes and humming, there was now a complete silence.

Mm Mm MmMm, Mm Mm MmMm Ding Ding Da Ding, Ding Ding Da Ding.....

Mr. Childs and Louise set off up the aisle towards the Alter, arm in arm, step by step, her train unfolding behind her.

The Vicar was facing them as they approach, waiting patiently; both the bridegroom and best man stood to his right and had their backs toward them, standing quite still and erect.

Tommy's nerves where ebbing away and then a calm assurance came over him, he could no longer resist temptation.

He had to see his bride to be, walking towards him.

Louise was beside her dad, holding on to his arm, with Sophie just behind in full view.

They where half way down the centre of the aisle when Tommy turned sideways to his left and there they were in full view, he smiled.

Mr. Childs had donned traditional morning suit, grey-pinned striped trousers, grey waistcoat, and white shirt with cravat and black jacket with tails.

Louise wore a white full-length silk gown that swept the floor, satin and lace embroidery with a scatter of pearl's, a lace veil, complemented by a diamond tiara headdress.

Attached was a full length satin train, with an overlay of lace which swept from her waist down to the floor.

Sophie who was following on a few steps behind and was just to the right of Louise, she was holding the train with one hand and a bouquet and small satin bag with the other.

Sophie wore a full length cream satin dress with silk and lace motifs, a lace train from the waist to the floor, a silk and lace headdress with a tiara and a lace veil, exposing her eyes.

Tommy was filled with emotion and pride at the wonderful sight set out before him; his smile was so broad it filled the church; in turn Mr. Childs was smiling at Tommy, a very proud father.

Louise could feel Tommy's eyes on her, her head had been slightly bowed and she raised it, their eyes met and she smiled, as did Sophie.

They all moved slowly towards the altar Step by step, closer...

Tommy's smile was getting broader, unable to take his eyes away from his bride to be....

In his periphery he could see Geoffrey Childs, smiling and so swollen with pride.

Behind he could see Sophie, she looked stunning... one glance and he bit his bottom lip....
"Judas..." he thought

Then he only had eyes for his beautiful Louise....
He mouthed the words "I LOVE YOU....!"

"Louise's face lit-up, her body began to tingle, her mouth went dry and her eyes moistened, she was so overjoyed and in love "I LOVE YOU TOO" she mouthed back to him.

The smile on Sophie's face erupted, her eyes turned to beams of light, her eyes transfixed on Tommy, her body erupted with passion and she mouthed the words, "and I love you....!"

There was silence; you could hear a pin drop...

Louise came side by side with Tommy...
Geoffrey stood back as did Freddie...

The ceremony began; the verse flowed from the Vicar's mouth.

Tommy and Louise gazed into each other's eyes and at last the Vicar announced: "With the power invested in me, I pronounce you Man and ….."

When Sophie had heard the words, "Does anybody here find just cause" she heard no more...!

Sophie's mind had drifted into a deep trance....

Chapter 69

"NO...!!!"... "No...!" ..."What the fuck is going on...!!!"

"It's a fucking nightmare...!"

"What is she doing marrying my Tommy...?"

"Everyone knows Tommy is mine, he's always been mine...!"

"If anyone is marrying him, it will be me...!"

"I'm marrying Tommy, not Louise...!"

"Who does she thinks she is...?"

Sophie was beside herself, hysterical...

"Are you out of your tiny fucking mind Louise...!"

"Who the fuck do you think you are, trying to steal my Tommy....!"

"Sophie, Sophie, are you ok...?"

"What is all that screaming about...?"

"What are you shouting about...?"

Sophie's mum had heard the bellowing coming from upstairs...

"And mind that language, please madam...!"

"... Well have no more of that language in this house... thank you...!"

Sophie had woken up very distraught, disturbed by what she had dreamt, sitting upright in her bed, shaking her head and wiping her eyes all in the same movement.

"It was a nightmare, just a bloody nightmare, to dam real though... for my liking...!"

"...It was a dream, just a dream...!" she began to laugh.

"Just a silly... Silly dream...!" She quickly found a football programme.

"Let's see... On the date of Louise's party... yes... Tommy had played for the reserves a 1-1 draw... Tommy never even scored... ha"

"They won't be getting married ever, not even engaged....

    ... In fact it's my birthday today and my party tonight...!"

Sophie went down the stairs to the kitchen

"Coffee...?"

"Please... Sorry mum had a bad dream, a bloody nightmare come to think of it..."

"Sounded like it... do you need to talk about it, do you want to share it...?"

"Louise got married..!"

"That's nice dear who to...? Anyone we know...?"

"To Tommy...!"

"Ho dear...! That won't do will it" a wry smile came on to Chloe's face.

Sophie glanced at her mum smiling

"Why's that...?

"Well dear we all know who Tommy has eyes for, don't we...?"

Sophie blushed...

"Mum...!"

"Are you looking forward to your party tonight...?" and she starts blows kisses into the air....

"Who are you blowing kisses at...?" quizzed Fred walking into the kitchen... "You sound like tweety bird...?"

"Sophie's party tonight... two little love birds.... tweet tweet tweet..." teased Chloe.

"Ho, Don Juan... *Tommy you mean...?*"

"Mum Dad...!"

"Six Foot Two, eyes of blue, little Tommy Jacksons.... in love with you..." Chloe and Fred began to serenade.

Sophie blushed again *"I don't think so..."* she responded.

"Louise's party was good wasn't it..?"She interrupted their serenading.

"Yes dear" Chloe satirically answered.

"And Tommy danced with her a lot...?"

"Yes dear" Fred copied his wife.

"Well then...!"

"And everyone knows Louise is going away to University..."

"And...?"

"And won't be here much of the time...!"

"And...!"

"And leaves you a clear pathway"

"What...?"

"Take the blinkers off dear..."

"Wake up and smell the coffee dear..."

"He's six foot tall, eyes of blue, little Tommy Jacksons in love with you... dear....!"

"He's six foot tall, eyes of blue, little Tommy Jackson... is head over hills for you... dear...!"

Sophie looked timidly, naively, at her parents and shook her head.

"What...?"

"She would never have made a Comanche scout... don't smell the scent"

"Or SAS... can't follow the track...!"

Fred indicated over his shoulder with his thumb....

"She's come from University; don't leave her at the door..." Fred began to sing.

Sophie looked at her Dad suspiciously, and the door bell rang..... She ran to the door...

"What were you in, in the army....?" Sophie shouted.

"Ha... that would be telling... but I'm in the know.... *Sophie and Tommy....*"

"How did you know...?" asked Chloe.

"I saw her taxi pull up..." he smiled at Chloe.

"Louise"

"Sophie"

They hugged...

"Come in..." shouted Fred from the kitchen...

"Hello Louise... how are you...? How's University Dear...?" inquired Chloe.

"How was the journey...? Added Fred...

"I'm great thank you, good journey and University is fun lots of fun...!"

"Fun...!"

Louise smiled "So where's Tommy, I thought he would be here helping you...?"

Sophie looked at Louise puzzled... "Why...?"

"I thought he would be here on your birthday..."

"Tommy's playing for the reserves... away but he will be here later"

"What's the plan...?"

"Bibs and Bobs" is booked for 10.30 – 1.30..."

"....The hairdresser is booked for 2.30..."

"So we will we have time to go shopping, I need to get a new mini skirt and top, stay ups and boots..."

"Wow...! University as done you the power of good..."

"Very good, dress to thrill girl, if you've got it... flaunt it..."

"And.... so spill the beans...?

"I'll tell you all about it in due course, the worlds my oyster Sophie..." Louise opened her arms being very flamboyant.

The house had been beautifully decorated balloons and banners in abundance.

"Ok ladies lets prepare the food and get it ready to put out..."

"If we put the bar by that wall..."

"All sorted...

"Is the music set up....?

"All ready to rock and roll...

The party was in full swing... Friends and family arriving and being greeted, "come on in... get a drink...".. "Foods over there... please go and help your selves ..."

"Where's the birthday girl...?"

"Sophie is in the living room, she and Louise are in great form laughing and joking... catching up..."

Tommy arrived, bringing along a teammate with him, Freddie....

He gives Louise a big hug as he hasn't seen her for a while.

"Ha Lou... you look great, give us a cuddle then"

She hugs him "You don't look to bad yourself, who's your mate..?"

"Freddie... Freddie this is Louise, Louise this is Freddie..."

"Hello gorgeous, charmed I'm sure" Freddie smiles....

"Hello big boy...!" Louise raises her eye brows.

Tommy then turns to Sophie with a big smile.

"Wow you look stunning...!"

"Ho Tommy, stop it....!" she replied timidly and blushed

"Come here and give me a proper cuddle and a kiss" he flirted.

"You love embarrassing me don't you...? Your habitual she said.

"Mmmm, Love..."

He gives her a cuddle and bides his time....

The party was in full swing...

Drinking and dancing, and the music played:

"No matter what they say, no matter what they do, believe in what you know, what is right for you, Don't let them put you down, ignore that silly frown, Smile back, and keep on track, Just smile back, wink, and keep on track..."

*"**I'm** gonna spend some time pampering myself, Pulled a little black number right off the shelf, I slipped it on and admired myself,   Took another glance, now I wanna dance, Let's hit the town, and make it a night.*

Let's party tonight, let's party tonight, Come on everybody, let's party tonight, Party tonight, and let's party tonight.
I'm looking pretty hot; I'm not kidding myself, Let's hit the floor adding up the score, If you're pretty hot and you hit my spot, We can close the door, I'm not saying no more, Think what you want, Think what you like, Where gonna party... right through the night...."

Right on cue, outcomes the cake... as planned.
Happy birthday to you, happy birthday, happy birthday to you....
Happy birthday to you, happy birthday, happy birthday to you...
Sophie was embarrassed, but did the dutiful thing and blew out the candles....

"Sophie please can you open my present first..." insisted Louise.
This had been arranged.....

"Ok"
 She started to unwrap it, then she opened the box…
Inside there was a jet black leather, shooting jacket, with "No.1" emblazoned on the back in gold.
Sophie was thrilled.

"Ho Louise thank you..."she said, pulling it on "it's beautiful and it fits perfectly...ho thank you....!"
Sophie hugged Louise.

"My turn...!" Tommy stated stepping forward...
"Just for you birthday girl..." he handed her a package with purple and gold wrapping paper....
Sophie looked at Tommy with adoring eyes.

"Ho my God..." she said aware she was blushing and everyone was watching her intently
"No... It's just from me darling..." he joked.

Sophie was beside herself, everyone was watching...
She sheepishly started to un-wrap her package... in slight trepidation... in awe.

There was a box... deep purple, leather clad 15 x 10 inches and 6 inches deep in dimension.
She opened it hesitantly, it was lined in white silk... surrounding a plaque with a commemorative inscription.....

Sitting inside the box was a double-barrelled, silver sterling, ivory handled derringer... with the inscription...
"It had to be you.... No.1
    Love Always Tommy"

Sophie shrieked.
"Ho my God Tommy...."
"OK, if you insist, I'll be you're... God....!"

Louise laughed, she knew what Tommy had in mind, it had been arranged.....

Tommy grabbed Sophie around the waist pulling her to him and kissed her.
Sophie blushed but never resisted.
Everyone was laughing and cheering....

"Do you think, she as fathomed out the situation now...?" Chloe asked Fred.
"You mean cottoned on..?" "Well she doesn't need to be a rocket scientist does she..."

Martha and Tommy joined Chloe and Fred....
"I think our son as grown up....?"
"Where sure our daughter as.... at long last...."
"Geoffrey, Joan, come here and join us....!"

They all knew except Sophie that Tommy was in love with her.

"Sophie I'm in love with you...." Tommy had his hands on Sophie's waist.
"Ho Tommy, I've loved you since we where seven...! Even when you pulled my pig tails." she wrapped her arms around his neck.
"That was a show of endearment" he smiled.
"I prefer this show of endearment... affection...?"
"Then this affection will continue...."
"Forever...?"
"Forever...!"

They danced the night away with their family and friends, disappearing to the garden now and again, chatting, kissing and cuddling, then returning to continue revelling.....

"They look so compatible together..." expressed Martha.

"So Delightful, so endearing..." concurred Joan.

"They certainly do...!" endorsed Fred.

So happy, joyful and glowing, it comes from the bottom of your heart...." Sniffled Joan....

"Very convivial together...." Enthused Geoffrey....

"I second that emotion" said Tommy shrugging his shoulders and smiling.

Chapter 70

"Come to think of it your Louise seems quite taken with the young man Tommy brought along..."

"She certainly does, doesn't she...? Very taken...!"

"That's lovely we could have Four Musketeers...?"

Who is he...?

"He's Tommy's team mate"

"He's Tommy's Captain actually"

"Nice boy...?

"Very nice young man...."

Freddie was taking a lot of notice of Louise, giving her a lot of attention, getting her drinks, dancing with her, and even holding her drink whilst she went to the loo.... so she was obliged to come back...

"Don't be long..."

And Louise was lapping it up; she had set her sights on Freddie and was oblivious of any other goings on... blinkered.

"Don't move... aster le vista baby, I'll be back..." she pointed at him.

"I hear you're an athlete... you look athletic....?"

"Of sorts, I'm a footballer... a very athletic footballer...!"

"So what positions do you like playing...?" Louise said flirtingly.

"I can play it straight down the centre, I love scoring, I also like laying it on, teasing, setting it up, or coming in from behind...." countered Freddie.

"Any favourite position...?"

"No... Just as long as I enjoy the game...!"

"I like a player who's adaptable... so you can play a few positions....?"

"I love being in control when I play... but I'm always up for inspiration, we never stop learning... I hear you could be a teacher...?" said Freddie

"I can teach, if the student is willing to learn...?

"I love to learn new tactics... but sometimes the student can teach the teacher..."

"I'm also Management material, how do you feel about working under someone...Freddie...?"

"I do believe I'd enjoy working under you... Lou...!"

"Work Hard... and play Hard...!"

"They call me the rock...!"

"Rock solid...?"

"Hard as nails..."

"Hmmm.... do you like to massage with oils, before you play.... Freddie the Rock...?"

"I Love a vigorous massage... be foreplay.... Helps me perform longer, they say I'm a good performer, I cover every inch of the playing surface and my shooting is very precise, hard and direct...."

"You have a hard shot...?"

"Unstoppable, it penetrates the net..."

"I'll have to come with you... and look forward to exercising together...?

"Extra time seems likely then... Louise the Player....!"

They were chatting laughing and teasing all evening....

"They're going to the garden... to get some air they said" Sophie and Tommy joked.

"Get some air...?"

"Be handy if they come up for air...!"

Sophie loved Louise like a sister, she loved Tommy as the man she wanted to spend the rest of her life with.
Now she could never imagine being without him.
Sophie had never been so happy in all her life.

The following day they all went out for lunch before seeing Louise off at the railway station.
Freddie had made a big impression on Louise...
Louise had made a big impression on Freddie...
Over the next four weeks... Sophie and Tommy where joint at the hip, always together.
Sophie going to watch Tommy play, Tommy going to see Sophie in a tournament and she won it.
They would phone Louise together, telling her all about what they were doing.

"Sophie Tommy, I am so happy for you both... I am chuffed to bits for you"
"And what about you...? ... What's happening with Freddie...?" nosed Sophie
"Freddie is lovely.... so fit...!"
"Ho yer...!"
"As he said anything about me to you Tommy....? She inquired.
"He doesn't stop bloody going on about you, I think you've bewitched him..."
"Hmmm..."
"He's under your spell Lou..." teased Sophie.
"Ditto... I've been under his..."

"Louise...!" Sophie was slightly shocked.... "One moment Lou, Tommy can...?"

"I know girlie talk, I'm off out anyway tell Louise I'll see her at my bash"

"So tell all...? What's all this the worlds your oyster...? If you've got it, flaunt it
Business...?"

"Exactly....! University of Life as opened my eyes.... I'm enjoying myself being away, free with no boundaries, and I'm getting a lot of attention...!"

"I hope it's only your eyes that are open...?"

"Ho Sophie don't be so prissy, you have Tommy and that's all you ever wanted, me on the other hand, variety is the spice of life"

"I hope your taking precautions and they are...?"

"Yes of course... I tell them to tie their feet to the end of the bed..."

"Louise stop being frivolous... and what do you mean by... Them...?"

"I'm on my apprenticeship.... learning new techniques..."

"Them...?"

"I met a boy at the University when I first arrived, he was studying economics, we had so much in common so I slept with him, which was my first time now I'm catching up on what I've missed out on...!"

"I thought you liked Freddie....?

"I do... actually I do but because you're on a diet it doesn't mean you can't look at the menu...?"

"Only look...?"

"Well... Economics, English, Maths, Philosophy, Physics and Languages... they are all interesting subjects that I've experienced and enjoyed tuition in, and booked up for more lessons....!"

"Louise you will get yourself a reputation...."

"Ho dear, it's too late for that; horse and barn door come to mind... Sophie stop with the butter won't melt in your mouth routine, are you telling me you haven't slept with Tommy...?"

"No, I haven't and I've told him I won't until my wedding night... I want to be a virgin...which he understands and respects me for...!" Sophie stated avidly.

"Excuse me why I throw up...!"

"Louise you have changed, so what about Freddie.... Have you slept with Freddie...?

"Very fit... of course and what he doesn't know won't hurt him...!"

"You're deceiving him...? Lied to him...? I thought you liked him...?"

"Ho Sophie, please grow up.... Stop being so pious and righteous..."

"What about being respectful and having some dignity, some pride in you....Louise"

"Sophie I've snared Freddie he's mine, but what I do here, well why the cats away the mice can play..."

"Snared...?"

"Yes... snared, I knew the moment I set eyes on him; I'll marry Freddie, pro footballer, the good life, just like you and Tommy...!"

"Louise how shallow... I love Tommy for being Tommy...."

Chapter 71

Louise arrived in the morning so that they could go and watch Tommy and Freddie play.

They were both making their first team debuts and the papers were making a big thing it.... "Freddie and Tommy the Deadly Duo"

Tommy scored the only goal in a 1-0 win, from a sublime pass from.... Freddie...!

Louise and Sophie and all the family were there in attendance, watching and cheering.

"I hope you have behaved yourself...." enquired Sophie.

"Sophie what I do in my time is my business...." she smiled and winked.

"And what about Freddie...?"

"Freddie will do as he's told and when he asks me to marry him... I'll be a good dutiful little wife...."

"Do you love him...?"

"Love him...!" Louise shrugged her shoulders.

"Louise you are devaluing the fundamental core emotions of a relationship and marriage.... truth, honesty, trust, monogamy, transparency, care, consideration, kindness, consistently and persistently... True LOVE...!"

"Please Sophie join the real world... true love... don't make me laugh, I'll let Freddie think exactly what Freddie wants' to believe and encourage him... with my talents"

"With your talents...Your sexuality... flirtatious and frivolous.... actions, lying, deceitfulness, manipulating, mind games... are those the talents you mean Louise." Sophie let fly.

"Thank you for the compliment....

"So please educate me, as in how you will persuade Freddie to ask you, to marry you...?" Sophie said contemptuously.

"Easy.... Freddie is an honourable boy..."

"Louise you cannot make Freddie... want to marry you..."

" If I'm Pregnant...!"

"Pregnant... are you pregnant...?"

"Sh's...!" Louise placed her finger to her lips raised her eyebrows and shrugged her shoulders.

"You would trap him, for what, to have the life style...?"

"I could be...!"

"Louise I'm ashamed of you...! That is depravity to the depths of a whole new level...! That is a disgusting, degrading act of emotional blackmail, entrapment, created and your stimulation of gluttony and jealousy... by a calculating and manipulating mind...."

"Don't judge me Sophie..."

"You have no morals" scolded Sophie.

"Please don't play the moral high ground with me"

"I'm not...! I love Tommy for who Tommy is, not what Tommy has or will have"

"Ho yer and I suppose there won't be no big wedding...?"

"Wedding...! Tommy hasn't asked me to get married..."

"....And no big mansion....?"

"No.... what are you talking about...? Even if he did, what would we want a mansion for...?"

"To suit the trappings, life style and persona of stardom"

"Stardom...! Where do you get this from, we love each other.... deeply...!"

"And if he asked you, what would you say...?"

The final whistle blew.... The game was over, everyone was cheering and hugging.

The house had been prepared for the party before they left for the game.

"The bars up and the booze is ready to flow..." enthused Tommy snr.

"The food is all prepared, we only have to lay it out... when we return" engaged Martha with Chloe and Joan beside her.

"How's the music Fred...?"

"Ready to rock and roll... Geoffrey!"

"Come on in..."

"Make yourself at home..."

"The bars that way...

And the food is over there..."

The music was rocking and the booze was flowing

"*No matter what they say, no matter what they do, Believe in what you know, what is right for you,   Don't let them put you down, ignore that silly frown, Smile back, and keep on track,   Just smile back, wink, and keep on track....*".

"*I'm looking pretty hot; I'm not kidding myself, Let's hit the floor adding up the score, If you're pretty hot and you hit my spot, We can close the door, I'm not saying no more, Think what you want, Think what you like, Where gonna party... right through the night....!*"

*"**We** are both pigheaded, we wouldn't give in, the last word to have, had to win, what a waste it would be, ho what a sin, how absurd we acted this way, the truth was all we had to say...*

*"**There** are so many nights, that I lay awake, All on my own, my heart does ache, Thinking of you, dreaming of you, Just wanting you, just me and you, And what might have been..."*

*"**We** spent so long together, travelling down the rocky road of life, Experiences and emotions we did share, some were good and some were bad, And some I'm sure you would agree, Left us totally in despair..."*

*"**Hate** is such a spiteful word, When you put it next to love, And love is what you used to say, In that kind and caring way, I love you...!"*

*"**We** try so many ways to lead the life we want, We knock on many doors, to be turned down, By narrow minded bores, How disillusioned, we become, Trying our hardest.., to be, other than a bum"*

*"**Seeing** my existence pass me by, Swimming upstream without a break,   Knock on many doors give us a chance, We won't give in, We won't go away, We'll eventually win, we'll eventually win...!"*

"Happy birthday to you, happy birthday to you, happy birthday dear Tommy....

He score when he wants, he scores when he wants....

Six foot two eyes of blue... little Tommy Jackson... he scores when he wants..."

"What a surprise the obligatory birthday cake and candles..." Tommy said to Freddie smiling.

"Come on let's dance..."
"Swing those legs Geoffrey"
"Mind my sciatica...."

The party was in full flow....

"Sophie will you come in to the garden with me please, I need to get some air" Tommy led Sophie to the garden by the hand.
"Ok...?"
"Come here..." He placed his arms around her waist and kissed her passionately....
She responded, very passionately, quivering from head to toe.

"I have a present for you...."
"For me...! It's your birthday Tommy and I have your present inside"
"You are my present Sophie, I love you...."

He slipped a single 1 carat diamond ring on to her finger.

"Sophie I could never imagine living my life without you, beside me....

....I want to look into your eyes and touch your face and tell you I love you last thing at night...

...I want your beautiful face to be my first sight when I wake up in the morning and I want to know your mine for life....." Tommy went down on one knee...
"Please make me the happiest man in the world Sophie.... and marry me...?"

Sophie screamed in ecstasy.

"Ho Tommy I love you with every breath I take... yes yes yes" and a tear rolled down her face... "YOU have made me so happy Tommy, a dream come true.....
I couldn't imagine living without you or you being with someone else..."
"I told you we would always be together..." Tommy hugged her.
"I will kill you if you ever leave me..." Sophie hugged him back.

Running back into the party she ran to everyone showing them her ring.

"Mum Dad look, look...! Tommy as asked me to marry him, Ho I'm in bits, I'm so happy, deliriously happy...."
"Sophie Darling we are so overjoyed for you" enthused Chloe.
"My beautiful daughter to be a bride..." gloated Fred...
"Ho Sophie congratulations..."
"Sophie that's so wonderful..."
"Exquisite Sophie exquisite news..." Geoffrey clasped his hands together.

Tommy and Martha where astounded.... they had no inkling this was Tommy's intention tonight, although they knew he was in love with her.

"Sweet heart that's brilliant news" said Martha.
"Yer brilliant, where's my boy..." Tommy snr looked around the room.

Tommy had been standing in the entrance of the patio doors, watching with delight at Sophie's excitement.
He walked in to a rip roaring cheer.
"Mum, Dad, you both Ok...?"
"As long as you are son, she's beautiful..."
"You couldn't have picked anyone more suited... perfect match"
"Mr and Mrs Miller I hope you approve" asked Tommy searching for their reactions.
"Certainly do Tommy son, certainly do... smiled Fred enthusiastically.
"I've wished for this day to happen and it as, I'm thrilled for both of you" sniffed Chloe, with tears running down her face.

"So he asked you and you said yes...!"
"I love him Louise"
"And I love Sophie... Louise" Tommy cut in.
"I'm so pleased for you both, I really am.... Where's my Freddie...?"
"I'm here Louise..."

Louise introduced her new man to her mum and dad
"This is Freddie mum"... "Dad this is Freddie..."
"Hello Freddie."
"Good evening Fredrick."
"Chloe, Fred, this is Freddie."
"Hi Freddie nice to meet you...."
"Well I'm Fred and your Freddie... nice to meet you son."
"Martha, Tommy, this is Freddie"
"Hello Fred how you doing, great pass for his goal, yes
Louise we do know him"
"Hello love, good game today..."

"He seems a very nice chap."
"Yes he does."
"He plays in the same team as Tommy...?"
"Yes he does."
"He's captain of the reserves."
"His he stuck to Louise...?"
"I'd say it round the other way"
"Louise doesn't seem to want him out of her sight..."
"Stuck like glue."
"Joint at the hip..."
"Me and my shadow...!"

Louise never left his side after the announcement...!
"She seems quite taken with him...?"
"Adoringly...!"
"Could there be a double wedding in the wind...?"

"Freddie don't you think its romantic... Sophie and
Tommy...?"

"Yes I'm very pleased for both of them, Tommy's my best mate and Sophie's a real Lady..."

"I can be a lady..."

Freddie looked at her "I hope so; I don't want to end up with a tart, with a mattress on her back....!"

"I'm not like that... well only with you" she said defensively and smiled at him.

"Good keep it that way... I don't do tarts with knickers labelled *next... and a bus shelter for a contraceptive...!*"

"I agree... I think if two people want to be together, it's important they can trust each other... don't you...?" said Louise innocently.

"Yes...!"

"Do you trust me Freddie, my rock...?" she asked naively.

"Do I have any reason not to...?" Freddie quizzed.

There was a change in Freddie... more astute and assertive....

"As Sophie told him...? As Sophie told Tommy..? As Tommy told Freddie...?

No he hasn't been out of my sight all night..."

"No no reason at all, I'm all yours, why do you ask that...?" she was nervous

"I may be laid back and easy going Louise but don't ever take me for... *mug on my forehead and welcome walk over me on my chest"*

"Best you don't force him into a corner Louise.... because you won't like what comes firing out, that's why he's our captain....." interjected Tommy smiling and taking his arm... "Let's have a beer Fred" and led him away.

Sophie confided in Louise "I want to get married as soon as possible, because we want to start a family...!.
"Me too...!"
"Louise"
"Only joking, only joking" she raised her hands in surrender.

Louise cuddled Sophie and whispered "I always knew you would end up together, I am really pleased Sophie."
"Thank you Louise..."
"We are the Three Musketeers, One for all ... All for one" stated Louise.

The party continued into the early hours....
Sophie and Tommy where sitting in the garden watching the sun rise....

"Do you think Louise is serious about Freddie...? She never left his side, except when I grabbed him for a beer..."

Tommy you know I want to be a virgin on my wedding night...?
"Yes I know" He confirmed, slightly shocked and concerned.
"Louise won't be...!" Sophie declared.
"Come again...?"

"Louise is sleeping around at University; she is also sleeping with Freddie. He doesn't know what she is up to, she as a bad name at Uni and doesn't care"

"Louise is sleeping around...?" Tommy was astounded.
"Yes... she has turned out to be a right little slut...!"
"What about Freddie...?"
"She as designs on Freddie... long term...!"
"Long term...! But in the mean time, she is on a mission an apprenticeship... and as a mattress stuck on her back, what do they call her.... easy lay...?"

"That's how she put it... and taking pleasure in every module she applies herself too."
"And what am I suppose to do now, tell my best mate the girl he's infatuated with is a right old slapper and grass up my other best friend , who turns out to be a right little slut...the slapper in question..."
"Wait and see I've spoken to her, just wait and see..."
"How lucky I am to be with you Sophie, I love you and we will always be together...!"
"I suppose you are" she said innocently, teasingly, trying to defuse the tension.

"You know what, if Louise had taken up sport; she would have been a second hand dart board, which had experienced plenty of pricks in it.... plenty of use...."

Chapter 72

The following morning there were the compulsory hangovers, breakfast and coffees....where served...

"Louise if you're going to make the train, we had better leave"

"Yes I know Freddie... are you coming all the way, with me....?" she smiled.

"Don't you stop...!" enraged Tommy....

"What...?" replied Louise Shocked and shaken by his response...

"Forget it" mellowed Tommy.

"What was that about...?" enquired Freddie to Louise.

"Ho nothing, he probably as a hangover...." she threw him a smile.

"Are you two coming with us to the station...?" she looked at Sophie and Tommy.

"Tommy...!" quizzed Freddie...

"Yes of course we are, you are my best mate Freddie and we are seeing my other best mate off to University. The infamous University of Life, a Louise: so much to learn with so many Masters to please. Must be hard working under all of them... giving them all your attention. Jack of all... Master of none...."

Louise looked at Tommy... sternly.

"Tommy you ok mate...?" asked Freddie concerned with Tommy's tone and words.

"Ha the Master Freddie, our Captain, Captain Freddie, who we play under because we respect him.... really respect him" Tommy looked at Louise with disgust in his eyes.

"I don't suppose I'll see you for a while, I really do have to knuckle down this term if I want to pass out with respect and honours...!" she said glaring at Tommy and then passing her attention to Sophie, as she boarded the train with Freddie.

"Respect and Honours...!" smirked Tommy.

"Guess not, but we can speak on the phone" interrupted Sophie light heartedly, trying to calm the atmosphere and the tension.

"I suppose you will both be busy, organising the wedding" Asked Louise trying to change the subject.

"Yes we will...!" snapped Tommy

"Hope I'm invited...?" and the train pulled out...

Chapter 73

"Hi Sophie..."

"Blimey Louise you've not been gone 3 hours, what's wrong...?"

"I had to phone you, have you said anything to Tommy about me...?

"Why...?" Sophie countered.

"Why...? Because he was very off with me and Freddie kept asking me what was wrong between us on the way back, did you...?.... Have you...?"

"Yes I did."

"Why...?"

"He deserved to know Louise, to be honest you are acting like a slut, your acting like a tramp, what has happened to you...?"

"As he told Freddie...?"

"I asked him not to...!"

"Please beg him not to... Please Sophie... please...!"

"That depends on you Louise."

"What do you mean...?"

"Well that's simple, if you're going to carry on acting like the local bike, anyone for a ride; WE won't want you at the wedding, and Tommy won't allow you to ruin Freddie's life and career."

"Sophie how could you say that...?"

"Tommy's mine...! I'm going to marry him and no one will spoil that, certainly not you."

"I know Tommy's yours."

"Well the way your acting, you might just try it on with my Tommy"

"I would never do that, why would you say that...?"

"If the Cap fits, then ware it...!"

"I would never ruin your relationship together; I would never try to split you and Tommy up...."

"Good because I would kill you if you did...."

"Sophie don't say that, you're scaring me, I love you and Tommy like family, I promise you."

"Then clean your act up, for your own sake..."

Chapter 74

Over the next few months' things happened very quickly....

All of the invitations were sent out, the caterers were informed of the menu, flowers ordered, cars booked....

"Ho Tommy look at this... see what I've found a big manor house, set in acres of grounds and a lake, it has a licence to marry on site... Civil Ceremony...."

"That's amazing, so spectacular; I bet it's busy...?"

"It's got available dates...!"

"Like when...?"

"Like end of the season."

"I bet it's expensive..." he quizzed.

"Expensive... Ain't I worth it...?"Sophie glanced at Tommy.

"Yes of course, book it if that's what you want" he surrendered.

"They do everything Tommy; they take care of everything, "*Your-day Our-day Services.*"

"Golden Service no doubt."

"Don't you want to marry me Tommy...?"

"Yes of course I do..."

"Good... because if you jolted me now, I'd kill you Tommy Jackson... mmm *Sophie Jackson*... I like that"

"Book it Sophie, just book it, I don't want you killing me, skinting me maybe..."

"Stop joking Tommy, we can afford it easily."

"So the dates been set then...?"

"In stone..."

"Sophie's got her way then...?"

"As if there was any doubt about that..."

"The weddings been booked then...?"

"A bit soon, isn't it...?"

"Ten months to the day...?"

"At least not nine months...!"

"No, it's not for that reason..."

"Sophie wanted it..."

"And what Sophie wants....!"

"So quickly...?"

"In the closed season..."

"She wants to start a family."

"Ho Tommy, please... please take a look at this... darling."

"What's that then...?"

"Look at this Hotel."

"Hotel... I thought you had picked the venue...?"

"Our Honeymoon sweetie, look at that beach."

"Beach...? Where...?"

Bali... Nusa Dua beach... what a place what a Hotel...5 stars...!"

"Bali... 5 stars...?"

"Look at that sunset... Ho Tommy we must book it...please can we...? Ho we must"

"5 stars.... We must...?"

"You do want us to have an unforgettable honeymoon.... don't you....?"

"Yes of course"

"I'm worth it baby..."

"Tell me...Why was the Wedding booked so soon... and in the close season...?"

"So that they could go away on honeymoon..."

"Where's that to...then...?"

"Bali"

"Bali...!"

"Nusa Dua beach"

"Nusa Dua Beach... 5 star no doubt...!"

"But of course, it would have to be...."

"Who picked that...?"

"Who do you think...?"

"Does Tommy have any say...?"

"By all accounts... NO...!"

"Tommy, we had better go out house hunting...?"

"House hunting...?"

"Yes darling house hunting, we can't be living with parents, can we...?"

"No your right, that makes sense... why didn't I think of that...?"

"All under control sweetie"

"Sophie I don't want to live to far away, I have to travel into training and get to the club"

"Of course not"

"Nice house, three beds... detached maybe....?"

"Ho Tommy... look at this one..."

"Ho no...!"

"Tommy it's beautiful."

"No surprise there then..."

"I've found a five bed-roomed en-suits detached house, lounge, dining room and study, bespoke fitted kitchen, conservatory, gym and a pool, 2 acres of mature gardens, gated with its own sweeping drive"

"And why didn't I see that one coming round the corner at me, straight on the nose..."

"We can afford it..."

"We can...? Can we...? But we don't need it now Sophie... Do we...?"

"I thought we were going to start a family."

"Ho right book me in, put the dates in my diary, make sure the temperatures right, on tap, knock out a football team...!"

"Ho Tommy you do love me...? You do want a family and you do still want to marry me.... don't you...? We are getting married...?"

"Of course I do who else could I love...? Who else would I want to marry...?"

"We are getting married aren't we...?"

"Sophie we will always be together"

"So they have bought a house...? Stated Tommy astonished...

"Yes" replied Martha

"Already... they have bought a house...?"

"Yes.... Five bed roomed en-suit, lounge, diner, study, bespoke fitted kitchen, gym, pool, and conservatory...!"

"That all...?"

"2 acres and gated sweeping drive..." continued Martha

"Bollocks, whose idea was that...?

"Guess who...?

"Well I don't have to be Sherlock Holmes do I, Sophie! What's wrong with that girl?

Chapter 75

"Tommy and Freddie The deadly duo..."
"The golden boys from the East End..."
"Poetry and Motion..."
"Future of England..."
"Me and My Shadow..."
"King and Prince Regent..."
"Telepathic Talent..."

The newspapers loved them.

The boys where becoming a firm fixture in the first team...

"England Under 21's call up for Tommy and Freddie..."
"Jackson invited to train with the full England squad."

"It would only be a matter of time before he gets his first full England cap, a future England captain"

Sophie was doing extremely well at work and also winning trophies and England recognition.
"Sophie Miller will surly go to the Olympics...."
"No Nerves Sophie..."
"Golden Girl Sophie..."
"Dead Shot Sophie..."

The press where having a field day and once there connection was made

"The Golden Couple of Sport...."

"Hot Shots...."

"Ho yes, we are getting married, in the close season" Sophie had quoted.

Interviews, advertising offers and photographers wherever they went...

"Ho Tommy I'm so happy."

"I could do without all this media cover; I just want to play football"

"Ho... Well now sweetie, we are now celebrities, so get use to it...."

"Sophie... what's happened...?

"Get use to it, Tom."

"Sophie its killing me, I don't want this limelight."

"Ha where's frigid Louise...? The bike as run out of oil, she's no longer doing rides..."

"Na... she's gone all bashful"

"She's been round the world ...twice... United Nations..."

"That's what I heard..."

"She's become a hermit."

"She is working very hard."

"Studying and passing exams."

"She is setting new standards."

She was also making the press for her academia and of course the connection was found.

"The Three Musketeers"

"The Three Amigo's"

"All for One~One for All"

Her relationship with Freddie was going from strength to strength and she told her two friends they were very much in love...

She confided in Sophie...

"I've stopped playing the field; I really have cleaned up my act Sophie...."

"Is Freddie aware of your past indiscretions Louise...?"

"Sophie you make me sound like a slut..."

"If the cap fits..."

"I lost my way...

"You lost your way... mmm... doesn't sound like it... but you certainly lost your knickers..."

"Sophie I made a mistake or two..."

"Or Two...!"

Louise threw Sophie a look...

"Are you going to tell Freddie...?" Sophie interrogated.

"No I haven't... Have you told Tommy...?" queried Louise.

"Yes... You know I told Tommy...?"

"Why...? Why do you want to spoil my future with Freddie...?"

"Freddie is Tommy's best mate; don't you think he deserves to know...?"

"But Freddie loves me; Sophie he told me so... so he doesn't know... he can't know...?"

"NO... he can't know... can he..."

"Tommy didn't tell him...?"

"I asked him not to...! That's Tommy doing as he is told..." Sophie smirked... "But perhaps he should..." Sophie continued tormenting Louise.

"Please don't... I made a mistake.... I do love Freddie...." Squirmed Louise...

"You Love Freddie... and what about all the trappings... and the glamour...?"

"What trappings Sophie..."...."I love Freddie for being Freddie" Louise smiled.

"You owe me big time Louise, so what's your agenda now...?"

"No Agenda Sophie, now just love, dreams and desires.... in being together... I hoped one day there would be Four Musketeers...!"

Chapter 76

"Tommy can I have a word please...?"
"What do you want Louise....?"
"I know you are ashamed of me...?"

Tommy looked down...

"I'm also ashamed of me, to yourself be true, isn't that what they say" Louise said sincerely.
"To the point Louise..."
"Please forgive me, forgive my indiscretions, I know not what I do, I am but human... fallible"
"Philosophy, poetry...? Queried Tommy...
"No, I'm begging for redemption from you, one of my two best friends that I love as a friend. In allowing me the chance to have love with another friend... who is also your best friend"
"Redemption Louise....! you give yourself redemption, if you can forgive yourself and learn to love yourself, without arrogance, you are able to forgive others and love others, allowing others to love you...."
"So can you forgive me...?"
"Who am I to forgive you...?"
"Tommy, please...!" she held her hands out.

Tommy took Louise's hands into his; he pulled her close and cuddled her....

"We have been the best friends since we where kids and I've loved you all that time. I can't say I understand your actions, perhaps I'm not meant to. What I do know is I love you for who you are. I love You Louise, I love Sophie, and I suppose I Love Freddie my mate"

"I love You Tommy...I always have, I love Sophie and I love Freddie your mate, my mate....."... *"The Four Musketeers...?"*

Sophie had watched the interaction between Louise and Tommy from a discreet distance.

"So what's your game Louise, you playing up to my Tommy....? I told you not to....!"

Chapter 77

"Come on Louise if we hurry up Tommy's mum will have a fry-up on the go...."

"Freddie for God's sake, at least let me get off the train before you start rushing me down the road, worrying about filling your stomach"

"I want to get a good lining inside me..." *"For tonight's the night, its Tommy's stag night"*

"It's 8.35 Thursday morning and your singing about going out and getting wrecked tonight, let's enjoy the day love...?

"The seasons over my sweet, I, we, can let our hair down, where are you going on Sophie's hen party...?"

"No idea... where are you lot going...?

"Hitting the town I think..."

"Taxi...."

"Where are we staying...?"

"I'm at my mums, you're at Tommy's."

"No snuggling up together in bed then...?"

"No...! My Mum and Dad are not that liberal, so Not until Monday...." Louise winked at Freddie, and then pecked him on the cheek... "You are going to come in and say hello..."

"Not necessary, I know for a fact there is communal breakkie going on at Tommy's... 9am sharp, a Martha special...."

"You sneaky snake, you're the sneakiest, that's why we left so early...?"

"I'd like to call it adapting and improvising, tactical advantage."

"I'd like to say it's you looking after your stomach first, hank marvin are we, el Captain...?"

"Sophie Tommy... Louise and Freddie are here, roll call, breakfast, chow, grubs up, nosh is on the table" bellowed Martha.

"Hello Hello, grubs up, good timing..."

"Hello"

"Come on in..."

"I'm so hungry my belly feels like my throat's been cut...!"

"Takes me back to being in the mess... ha Chloe...?"

"Martha's cooking is far superior"

"Tip Top nosh; eat your heart out Savoy Brassiere..."

"You dig in Geoffrey love, you dig in..."

Chapter 78

"So Sophie where are we going tonight....?"

"We are having a meal in town, a little Italian then there's a live band on, in the Three Kings... conveniently for us they have a disco afterward going on until 3am... late enough...?"

"Magic...?"

"Magic... I'm going to need some Magic Potion to keep me going until that hour..!"
Groaned Chloe...

"Rubbish, you're a right little goer once you get going..." Laughed Joan...

"That's the trouble, it's getting her going..." taunted Martha...

"I'll give you a jump start if you want...?" teased Fred frivolously, raising his eye brows and smirking at his wife.

"More like some three in one oil... To loosen her up" Ribbed Tommy snr...

"That also sounds up my street...!" continued Fred grinning from ear to ear.

"Ho I say... Now now, you'll embarrass the dear lady" defended Geoffrey

They all looked at Geoffrey smiling....

"Ok Ok ... you're embarrassing me, I know I'm a prude..." And he laughed...

"And we wouldn't change you for the world" they chorused...

"Thank you Geoffrey, a true gentleman protecting my honour against these ruffians..."

"He's my knight in shining armour..." *Joanie whispered.*

Chapter 79

"So Tommy where we off to....?" Quizzed Freddie...

"Well it won't be the Three Kings..."

"Na that's been confiscated...."

"Sequestered...."

"Seized by terrorists"

"Three Kings is our domain" demonstrated Geoffrey indignantly.

"Now now Geoffrey old son, slow down tiger..."

"That's it... they've ruffled his feathers..."

"He will launch a counter offensive to re-establish territorial rights and tenure..."

"The United Nations will intervene and come to a common conclusion, in settling rights to the Three Kings..." declared Joan.

"How say you...?" countered Geoffrey.

"Permitted Trespass, treaty of short lease, in ownership..."

"Invasion of Human Rights...! Our Human Rights have been infringed."

"There are two bars, each to their own, we will concede and sit or stand with free will in the bar that you don't use, accepted...?"

"With due diligence, of territory..."

"Concurred....There is a No man's land, a separating wall with an archway, which can be, but must not be infiltrated...!"

"Accepted a pact is drawn, Peace in our time" declared Geoffrey grinning.

"Peace in our time...! You tyrant..." summoned up Joan smiling.

"You haven't lost it *Joanie* darling, you gave me a close run."

"We would have relinquished our rights of trespass and surrendered into going elsewhere... *Dearest*"... *"And our side will be renamed the Three Queens...."*

They hugged each other... lovingly, respectfully, adoringly..... Mutual admiration...

The audience where in awe, cheering, clapping and laughing....

"That's our regular bar, that's your quarters, for the evening" pointed Fred.

"Ok general..." retorted Martha

"This is a great night."

"What a brilliant band."

"Great music, real classic tunes...!"

"Come on let's dance some more girls" said Chloe.

"The Three in One oil is working..."

"It's not oil; it's a large Gin and Tonic...!"

"That's her tenth large Gin and Tonic...!" laughed Martha.

"Ho mum I'm so happy" said Sophie.

"Darling I'm so happy for you...."

"We are all so happy for you and Tommy, Sophie."

"And what about you Louise, with Freddie...?"

"Yes spill the beans Louise"

"Yes darling tell mummy, what's going on with you and Freddie...?"

"I love him so much...!"

"And Freddie...? How does Freddie feel about you...?"

"He told me, more than once, he loves me also..."

"And and...!"

"And nothing..."

"Do we...? Are we...? Going to have the *"Four Musketeers*...?"

"Ok gentlemen resumption to normal activities."

"Yes now where playing on home ground."

"Our home ground as been infiltrated..."

"It's not right being in the same pub on a stag night and a hen party..."

"What do you think you're going to get up to...?"

"It's not the point, its tradition."

"Hum bug..."

"They don't sell hum bugs... have a brandy"

"Golly good idea."

"His will power, as got the breaking strain of a tooth pick...!"

"Well son... Saturday afternoon you will be a married man, I'm so proud of you."

"Thanks dad."

"And don't jilt Sophie or upset her, we'll have the forces gunning us down...!" Tommy nodded at Fred and they all laughed.

"No Dad... I love Sophie I adore her, we will always be together."

"So Freddie what about you and Louise...?"

"Yes my name sake what's going on with you two love birds...?"

Geoffrey stood upright and his attention was taken up, into Freddie's answer...

"You're embarrassing him and the old wigs ready with pistols at dawn" roared Tommy snr.
"No... Not at all... I'm not embarrassed and certainly have no intention of deriding Louise or insinuation of any incivility to infuriate and insight Geoffrey, so to demand satisfaction in defending his daughter's honour, with pistols or words drawn at dawn.
I'd lose... It's quite simple Gentlemen.... and I say it loud and clear... I respect Louise; more so, I love Louise very much...!"

Silence prevailed and they all looked at Geoffrey in apprehension of his reaction....

Geoffrey cleared his throat twice...

"Young Fellow well said...! Tell me now Fredrick would you partake in a brandy with me...?" Geoffrey glanced at the others, smiling proudly... "You lot should take a leaf out of this honourable chap's candour and majesty ... would you all like a top up... on me."
"My pleasure sir...yes please" smiled Freddie.
 "Yes yes yes..." they all roared "*here we go, here we go, here we go, get them in... Geoffereeeey.... Geofereeeey Geoffereeeey Geoffereeeey, get them in... Geoffereeeey.*"

Both parties spent the evening in their allocated areas getting pleasantly drunk, dancing, laughing, a few tears, drinking, laughing, and dancing, a very satisfactory night for all.

Louise and Sophie cuddled up in bed chatting about their hopes and dreams for the future....

"I am so happy Louise, in two days time; I'll be Mrs Sophie Jackson."

"Sophie I am so happy for you and Tommy."

"And Freddie...?"

"I love Freddie so much, I hope he asks me to marry him, I'd say yes in an instance."

"Good then you can leave Tommy alone" Sophie smiled at Louise... "Night night"

"Tommy I'm going to ask Louise to marry me on the Sunday, after your wedding...?" Confessed Freddie....

Chapter 80

"My head is splitting..." moaned Freddie.

"Me too..."

"This room is spinning"

"Me too..."

"I'm not made to drink alcohol..."

"You could have fooled me; it looked like you thought it was going to run out"

"It's that Geoffrey... a bad influence"

"Your future father-in-law you mean..."... "Do you remember what you said...?"

"Yes...! I'm going to ask Louise to marry me...!"

"Go for it Fred, I think you will make a great couple."

"Do you think your mum will have one of her famous breakkie on the go...?"

"Blimey you recovered quickly..."

"I'm Hank Marvin...."

"You're always Hank Marvin."

"Then I might pop over and see Louise"

"You're not seeing Louise today, if I can't see Sophie you can't see Louise, any way its bad luck for me and you, as my Best Man and you must protect me...!" Tommy smiled at Freddie.

"That's your bad luck, not my bad... Why is it my bad luck...?" Freddie looked at Tommy puzzled and inquisitively.

"Because it's an old East End superstition....! that if the best man gets to see is other half, knowing its bad luck for the groom to see the bride to be the day before the wedding... it evokes and empowers evil actions... to follow..." Tommy spoke mysteriously

"What evil actions....? Empowers...! Evokes...! What evil actions...?" Freddie asked curiously and with some trepidation in his voice.

"I'll inform me mum and the consequences of such a selfish action by you, would be......... No famous breakkie from my mum...."

"Tart... you're like a big kid... in-corrigible...!."

"Thank you I accept that compliment... Mum any chance of a fry-up please... we are hank marvin...?"

Chapter 81

"Louise why is the room spinning...?" asked Sophie sorrowfully.

"It may have something to do with the copious amounts of Champagne you shovelled down your throat... Sophie"

"Well a girl only gets married once, may as well get used to it... the good life from now on... the golden couple."

"Is it Tommy you love and want or what he can provide for you...? Asked Louise...

"I've got it all Louise, I've got him...." said Sophie arrogantly.

"Sophie you accused me of stretching the parameters with Freddie, wanting him for all the materialistic trappings and what have you done Sophie.

The trappings of an ego warrior, Lavish Wedding, Spectacular Honeymoon, Palatial Home, what an hypocritical, charlatan you are, so disingenuous, a ridiculous extravagance of over baring pretence, a pompous, pretentious expenditure for the on lookers...."

"Ho and what are you insinuating...?" Sophie said sarcastically... "You're only jealous Louise, I've got Tommy, Tommy's mine and not yours, and I'm worth it all..."

"Insinuating... I'm not insinuating, I'm telling you... you're infuriating... You have such an elevated, highly inflated ego. It is condescending, a profuse, obnoxious, patronising pretence... all bravado...!"

"Be careful of what you're inciting Louise.... your spitting close to the wind" flared Sophie.

"You're a megalomaniac Sophie... Me, me, me, pomp and grandeur...!" squared up Louise.

"You don't know how much of a maniac I could be Louise, if you try to take what's mine...!"

"Do we really know you... Sophie...? Does Tommy really know you Sophie...? Perhaps he should know...!" Retaliated Louise...

"People who poke their noses in where they don't belong... Mmm.... Don't lose your nose to spite your face Louise and don't lose your head Louise and do something you regret..."

".....You don't want to get caught in the crossfire...!" she raised her eyebrows and grinned.

Chapter 82

The two girls were up early....
Not having too much sleep...
You could cut the tension with a knife.......

"Remember Louise this is my Wedding Day and Tommy and I will always be together, He said we would always be together....!"

 "Come on now a good breakfast will sort everyone out, settle us down..."
"We have a long day ahead of us, so we will need some substance...." Chloe affirmed.
"Bacon sausage egg toms and beans..."
"... Bread and butter ... tea or coffee..."

Mr Miller was practising his speech time and time again, driving everyone crazy....

"Fred now please put a stop to it, you will be eloquent, articulate and fluent my love...!" Encouraged and confirmed Chloe.
"Yes Chloe ... I've practiced enough... it will be brilliant..." mellowed and surrendered Fred, smiling.

"Come on darling let's get dressed....
"I'm going up..."

"The hairdresser as arrived, come on girls it's time to get your flowing locks done..." "The beautician's here"

"Let's get those nails done"
"Pedicure dear..."

"Ok all done...."
"Now it's time to put your dress on..."

"Fred you look so handsome" said Chloe.
"Thank you my love, you look quite ravishing you're self."
"Here comes Sophie...!"
"Tread carefully darling as you come down those stairs"

"Sophie your bride's gown looks stunning, you look like a princes."
"A super star....!"
"Wow Sophie you look magical..."
"Enchanting..."
"Sophie darling you look like an actress... so beautiful"
"Lace Satin and Diamonds.... fit for a queen"
"How long is that train? You'll need the royal engineers to carry that up the aisle..."

"Chloe it time you left for the church with Louise.."

"You look lovely Louise by the way...."

Fred Miller and Sophie waited until they witnessed Tommy and Freddie leave, then they left for the church....

"Tommy you ready to leave" asked Freddie.
"Yes I am mate"

"Well you two have scrubbed up nicely" said Martha proudly.

"And you don't look to bad, neither Tom...." she winked at her husband.

"And you my lovely are still as beautiful as the day I met you..."

"It's time for us to go Martha..."

"Don't hang around too long, you two"

The manor house was splendid and all the guests had arrived, as well as the press.

All the chairs were set up in equal pews, where the guests could congregate, with a centre aisle for Sophie and Fred to walk down, to the Altar.

It had been beautifully arranged inside, a Magnificent White Marque, with open sides.

Decorated with chandeliers, dangling from the rafters, candelabras, and flowers: Roses; Red, White, and Blue.... pink, purple, violet, white bougainvilleas....

Lotus petals and Orchids...

An eight piece band was playing...

Chorus singers.... were singing in harmony...

Two dozen white doves flying above...

The gardens were sublime...

Tommy and Freddie stood at the erected altar in the Marque.

"It's a beautiful sunny day for it Tommy..."

"You're always so cool and calm Freddie..."

.

The whisper had gone out, Sophie had arrived.

The wedding march began....
Da Da DaDa, Da Da DaDa......

"Here we go Tommy" smiled Freddie "Come on straighten up."

The vicar was standing in front of them, ready to start the ceremony.

Sophie walked down the aisle on her father's arm, step in step, Louise just behind holding the train.

"Ho she looks like a film star..."
"What a beautiful dress..."
"Fit for a queen..."
"She is gorgeous..."
"She and Tommy are so suited..."
"He adores her..."
"He absolutely loves her..."
"She is enchanting..."

Sophie arrived at Tommy's side and glanced towards him from behind her veil.
They smiled at each other.
"I love you Sophie..."
"I love you Tommy..."

The Vicar coughed politely and started the ceremony...
Nodding to both parties, with a big broad smile on his rosé cheeked, jolly face......

"Dearly beloved, we are gathered here today, to witness...............

Serenity personified.

"Does anybody present find just cause, that this couple should not be joined in holy matrimony....?"
"I pronounce them Man and w..."

Sophie broke from her trance state of psyche, bemused disorientated.....

Chapter 83

Tommy and Louise were standing right in front of her.... at the Altar....

"Tommy and Louise are getting married..."...
"They are getting married..."...
"What about me...?"

Her eyes moistened up... and tears began to flow down her face...uncontrollably...

With her left hand Sophie held her bouquet and her small satin bag.
Discreetly with the other hand being free, she undid the bag and slipped her right hand inside, searching.... getting hold...

Simultaneously the vicar said "I pronounce you man and ...."
Sophie screamed....
"Why isn't it me....?"
"...it could have been me..."
"...IT SHOULD BE ME...!"
"It should be me..."

Those words echoed around the church...
"Why isn't it me...?"
"...It could have been me..."
"It should be me..."... *"It should be..."*
"It should be ...."
"It should..........."

"It…"

The vicar stopped instantly in his tracks, startled at what he had heard and indeed the shock of the outburst...

The thoughts that came into his mind, *the abruptness, the vicious assault, the indignation, and the infiltration of the words he had witnessed...*

At a tranquil loving ceremony, a Wedding Ceremony....

"Ho my God in Heaven... Sophie... My Child Please...! Please Sophie...!" his words turned to silence as the fear, the trepidation, the horror.... The eventuality....

"No..."

The Vicar Smythsom knew in his heart the conclusion of what was set before him.

The feeling inside him was overwhelming... carnage.... there was no going back...

He heard it in the brutality of her words, he could see it in the blank expression in Sophie's eyes... her eyes where Cold.... Black.... Soulless....!

"In this house of God, how could this be....?"

Mr and Mrs Jackson, Tommy's parents, Mr and Mrs Childs, Louise's parents and Mr and Mrs Miller, Sophie's parents where all standing in the front pews, in loving anticipation of this momentous event.

As instead of that, each and every single one of them stood staring... at each other, speechless... motionless... paralysed.... *"What is happening here...?"*

They became witnesses, point blank bird's eye view witnesses, as this horrendous catastrophic turn of events unfolded before they're very eyes...

Engraved into their memories... etched into their very minds... forever.

The silence in the church was deafening all and sundry where looking at each other... quick glances at each other.... then at Sophie... shaking their heads, shrugging their shoulders, pulling faces, grimacing at each other... mouthing the words *"what's happening...!"* in deathly silence.

Then returning their attention back on to Louise, Tommy and Sophie, in disbelief at this intrusion.....

Fixated to the spot they stood on, rooted to the ground.

Louise and Tommy both turned and looked at Sophie.

From the small satin bag, that she was clutching securely with her left hand....

Sophie took a firmer grip and pulled out the double barrelled, silver sterling, ivory handled derringer, with the inscription, "It had to be you, No.1 love Tommy" Sophie had had it engraved.....

Sophie raised her right arm into the firing position and aimed her gun straight at Louise, in a matter of seconds... no nerves, without any compunction compassion or thought..... She pulled a trigger... One Shot ... One Bullet... Carnage...!

A Deathly shot, lethal, straight between the eyes.

Louise slumped to the ground like a lead weight; Tommy looked down at his wife to be, going down onto one knee to cradle his Louise, holding her in his arms, blood spurting from the crater missing from the back of what was her head, showering him.

In the full realisation of what had taken place *"my Louise is dead; Sophie has just shot her, Sophie has murdered my Louise, on our wedding day."*

Tommy's eyes where moist and tears where rolling down his face.

He looked up and back toward Sophie "WHY SOPHIE...?"... "WHY...?" Shock, disbelief, Anger, started to erupt from within Tommy.

His face was becoming distorted.... "Whyyyy.................."

Sophie was emotionless, not a flicker of remorse, she stared at the two of them slumped down on the floor of the church. She had kept her arm aloft in a straight rigid position, the firing position.

At the same time with a slight adjustment of her arm, Sophie's awareness had taken her pose and aim, now directly at Tommy.

Sophie yelled... "It should be me... it should be... it should be meeee....."

"...And YOU Tommy.... You said... WE would always be together..."

One Dead Shot... One Fatal Bullet... straight into the middle of Tommy's forehead...

The back of Tommy's head.... Exploding....!

Blood and fragments of his skull and brain tissue cascaded, discharging over the Reverend Smythsom.
His cassock was sopping, dripping wet, sodden.
His face and hair where drenched, stained and entwined with particles of Louise's and Tommy life......

The Reverend had buckled and collapsed to the floor, resting onto his knees.
His head bowed and his arms drooping beside him, his hands placed on his lap, palms facing outward, rocking slightly back and forth... ebb and flow.

He was facing the congregation, yet blinded...
He could recognise nothing, just a blur before him.
The Reverend was in such a traumatized state of mind.
His brain was unable to comprehend what he had witnessed.
Consciously and sub-consciously he was in total rebuff, denial.

Sophie started to walk... she was edging slowly forward, towards her *two best friends;* they lay there, before her in pools of blood, unrecognisable......
Crouching down as so close to touch, Sophie's hand rested on Tommy's....

"Come on Tommy, stop messing about, get up..." Sophie smiled.

"Tommy come on, we are getting married today..." she whispered.

"Come on..."

"Tommy...Tommy...!"

"Get up....."

"Are we getting married...?"

"Tommy... Tommy..."

The congregation where frozen to beyond the conception of what they had witnessed, shell shocked. Speechless, Noiseless... in their cries for help, their screams of anguish, and their pleas for peace...

Chapter 84

There had been arranged a small Police attendance at the wedding, this was purely as precaution as Tommy was a professional footballer and had his own fan base.
Some of his team mates, his Manager and staff were also present.

The wedding had been arranged by Louise with Tommy's blessings, to be a low key affair, so as not to seek publicity...
They could never have foreseen the catalogue of events to come....

The Police officers on duty where standing outside the church guarding the front doors, protecting those inside.
A few more Officers where situated in and roaming around the grounds, a mere formality, as no imminent threat was considered.
When the first shot went off their attention was alerted, looking at each other.

"Ha Charlie was that a car back firing" stretching his neck and purveying the area he could see.
"There aren't any cars close enough or moving" Charlie claimed...

The second shot so quickly after the first, sent echoes resounding around the interior of the church.
This time the sound grabbed their concentration levels and attention...

"That is not a car backfiring... That's coming from inside the church"... "Radio it in to Control, get some back up and support down here, that's gun fire..."

The Police Officers on duty converged on to the main entrance of the church; the others surveyed the immediate vicinity to see if there was any unusual activity, also covering any of the other exit doors...

The Two Officers tentatively entered the Church... unaware if there was any live ammunition coming their way......
Once they had observed, diligently, assessed and calculated the situation, they dashed up the aisle. Ready to dive for cover in the event of more fire....
The Officers advanced up the aisle until they reached the Alter, and detained her, standing side by side of Sophie as she was kneeling on the floor.

One had retrieved the gun that Sophie had dropped, the other Officer taking the bag off of her, searching inside to make sure there were no more weapons concealed.

They had acted in full professional mode up to this point.
Then, when the situation was controlled, it became apparent to them, what they were seeing.
They witnessed at close quarters, the full contents and depravity of the chaos and slaughter, butchery in front of them. Macabre

The site was quickly secured; Detectives from the Local Police station arrived very promptly, arresting Sophie, radioing in for more superior support and specialised back up.

Also requesting some ambulances..... The pathologist and forensic officers arrived...

As would be expected some press where in situ to report on the wedding day, a low key group, but once the incident leaked, it became a swarming with press Bees on honey....

Chapter 85

The video recorder stuttered....

The three children were sitting on a blanket in the garden, sharing a bowl of crisps and coke, laughing, giggling, so playful.

Sophie was then seen on the screen, so many years ago..... Firing a water pistol at Tommy and Louise, both feigning to full down, and die....

Mrs Miller screamed uncontrollably.......

Chapter 86

In the Police investigation of the brutal murders of Louise Childs and Tommy Jackson, there was no contradictory evidence and no sane defence, of this anal felony.

When interviewed, Sophie Miller never spoke.
She was formally arrested and charged with murder on two accounts.
There were enough collaborating, independent witnesses to substantiate this.

"Sophie Miller you are being charge with the indictment of the murder, on the two accounts of, Louise Childs and Tommy Miller" the clerk of the court proclaimed.

At the trial of Sophie Miller, the evidence was overwhelming; eye witnesses gave evidence of their accounts of what happened.

Their individual evidence of which was given under oath, in the witness box, confirmed the events of that fateful day.

It was as cruel as the events of the day it's self for them all to relive...

Chapter 87

Martha broke down in tears ... on a numerous number of occasions, as she reiterated the events leading up to the "Wedding Day".
The devastation of the Day it's self. The love she had for her beloved son, and his wife to be.

She spoke of.... "They had their own dreams, of having their own children."
"Indeed we shared with them, our dreams, of having grandchildren."

Martha never raised her eyes in the direction of her *friends*, Fred and Chloe.
Only the once she spoke of the vindictive selfish brutality of Sophie's actions...

"My baby boy, my son, she shot him in meditated cold blood, as she did the love of his life, his wife to be, on their wedding day, because she couldn't have him, because he didn't want her..."
"Murderer...!"

"Why...?" she screamed at the end of her evidence.

Tommy snrs voice croaked and broke when he spoke of the love he had for his son, and Louise the plans they had made and the life they wanted to live together.

"Tommy was my pride and joy, my boy, my son, who loved life..."

"He and Louise had talked of their future together, of their wedding day, having children..." Tommy snr sobbed...

"How proud they wanted to make us... us...!"

"They teased; we are going to make you Grandparents.... loads of times..."

He even spoke of the fondness they all had for Sophie and the love the Three of them shared... one for all... all for one...

"The Three Musketeers.... They loved her..." he snivelled pointing at Sophie.... "We all loved her...!"

"We will never come to terms with what happened on that day...."

"She murdered my son..."

"Why...?

"Because he didn't want you... he loved Louise...you selfish, vile... scum..."

He did look in the direction of Fred and Chloe and asked them one question.......

"Why...?"

Chapter 88

Geoffrey was use to being in court only on this occasion he was the one in the witness box, under oath, he gave his evidence of the events of the day.....

His love for his Louise and the expectations of Louise's and Tommy's future and that of the friendship and love they all had for Sophie.

"My beautiful daughter, I love her... You, so much and always will, you will always be in my heart..."
"She loved her Tommy... it's all she ever wanted... and they planned their wedding day, and to be together forever..."
"The future..."
"To have children, to give, my *Joanie* and me.... Grandchildren..."
"They talked... of their love and friendship... we saw them grow together... toward Sophie Miller..."
"We all cared for Sophie... deeply"
"Obviously that wasn't enough for her though, she wanted what she could not have, and if she could not have it, no one could..."

Geoffrey never wiped the moisture from his eyes and the tears dropped down his cheeks...

"My daughter Louise and my future son-in-law Tommy, were brutally slain.... both shot dead, through the head, on their wedding day... by her.... Sophie Miller"

"How could this happen" he was heard to whisper.

At the end of his evidence Geoffrey broke down... in uncontrollable floods of tears.

Joan Childs entered the witness box; she took the oath and swore on the bible to tell the truth, the whole truth and nothing but the truth.
She did this with clarity and strength....

"My darling daughter Louise, who I love so much, met at an early age with Tommy, and Sophie, she loved them both, and they became known as the Three Musketeers"
"Her love for Tommy grew to being, in love, as did Tommy's love for Louise..."
"They were both so very much in love"
"They planned the rest of their life together"
To live, to love, to bare children, to give Martha, Tommy, My Geoffrey and me Grandchildren.... to be old Grandparents... she would say..."
"They included her..." pointing at Sophie... in everything they did... she was a part of their future..."
"Sophie Miller... shot and killed Louise Childs and Tommy Jackson, at the Alter on their wedding day, with a gun they bought for her as a gift..."

"Why Sophie...? Did you ever love Louise...? Could you not bare her to be happy and in love with Tommy... He was in love with Louise.... Couldn't you be happy for them...?

Only once glancing at Fred and Chloe shaking her head she asked.....

 "Why...?"

She then collapsed on to the floor, sobbing her heart out...

Chapter 89

Fred Miller entered the witness box, he spoke when giving evidence of the events of the day in a very subdued and quiet manner, remorseful, tearful, for the loss his daughter had brought into the lives of those he thought she loved.....

"There are no excuses for these actions..."
"There are no words to defend them..."

"We have also asked the question..."
"Why Sophie...?"
"Why this carnage...?"

"She is our daughter...
"We love our daughter..."

"We love Louise and Tommy..."
"We are so sorry..."

Fred never once took his eyes from his beloved Sophie

From his own time in service Fred had never wished to witness such actions again.

As he finished his evidence he also bowed his head... and cried so many tears...

Chloe was the last to enter the witness box, she spoke of the day with sincerity and humility.... repentant and apologetic of the actions of her beloved daughter, toward who she considered, was an extension of her own family, Louise and Tommy.

For the grief-stricken regretful and penitent actions that took place that day... at the hand of her Sophie...

"I know no words will ever help to heal the distress, memories and pain... that you all, we all live with."
"We offer our compassion and regret to you"

Chloe firstly watched her daughter, and then took her attention to the Jacksons and Childs as she finished, she bowed her head.

"We are so sorry... we loved Louise and Tommy"

Tears rolled down her face...

"Why Sophie... why darling...."

The evidence that was given under oath, swore on the bible, by the parents of the three children never varied, it was exactly the same.

Chapter 90

Sophie was put in the witness box to give her the chance to give her side of what happened that day, although she had never spoken since the "Wedding Day."

The Prosecuting QC commenced....
"Sophie Miller do you have anything to say in defence of your actions.....?"

Silence, she stared straight in front of her....

"I put it to you... "The Three Musketeers".... as you were affectionately known as...
 "One for All"..."All for One" was the inscription, inscribed on the Gun Case, that which they, Louise and Tommy, had bought for you, on your 18th birthday with Love.

"Inside the case was a Gun... to which you are no stranger, "No Nerves Sophie...!"... "Dead Shot Sophie...!"
"These are titles... names bestowed on you by the public and media... By which you where affectionately and publicly known..."
"Is this true...?

Silence, she stared straight in front of her.... blank eyes...

".. A Double Barrelled Sterling Silver, Ivory Handled, Derringer...
There were three of you, only one remains: "Le Cadeau de l'amour"..... "The Gift of Love"

He paused...

"With which you slay them, assassinated them, and massacred them, wilfully." "Premeditated murder of Two helpless, defenceless, young lives, who where so much in Love on their Wedding Day, the happiest day of their lives..."

He paused

"You are a cold blooded, calculating, emotionless vessel, which should never be free, in your lifetime ... To have the opportunity of inflicting upon decent human beings, and committing such an anus crime again!"

Sophie never blinked an eye lid... an Emotionless Vessel.... Silence...

Her defence claimed "Diminished responsibility, on the grounds of insanity".

Chapter 91

The Reverend Smythson never gave evidence at the trial....

The Reverend had suffered a nervous breakdown, as a direct result of what he had witnessed and encountered.

A complete mental, emotional, and physical close down.

Not a twinkle of light in his eyes...

The Reverend was sent to a sanatorium belonging to the church.

Where he was nursed and lived out the rest of his life until he died, 5 years later.

The Reverend Smythson had never spoken again, in the remainder of his lifetime.

Chapter 92

Sophie Miller was found guilty, by a unanimously decision.

Given her psychiatric reports she was diagnosed, "Clinically Insane," Sophie was sent to a Mental Institution.

The Judges summoning up was.... short and precise, this was purposeful ... to save any further pain in the direction of those present;

"That Sophie Miller would be taken from this place to a place of incarceration for the rest of her natural life, under strict supervision."
"By my recommendation there will be no parole, or even reviews for parole or early release."
"In this unprecedented case Life means Life".

Sophie left the dock attended by two officers, she was led down the steps to the holding cells, where she was quickly transferred to a Security Police van, destination, privileged information.
As the van with Police escorts left the court a hostile, vengeful crowed had gathered at the gates of the court.
This had been a very high profile case with much media coverage
The crowed of angry people banged on the side of the van with their fits and boots, some spiting at the blackened out windows.

"Murderer ...! Murdering Scum...! Assassin...! Hang her...! Lynch her.....!

Chapter 93

Tommy and Martha Jackson carried on living in their home; they could not bring themselves to leave.

There were too many good, loving memories, of young Tommy.... and there aspirations for his and Louise's future... individually and Together.

They could still feel him around in the house.... present...
His presence, his laughter, his smell... his energy.....

"He's here Tom, I can sense him... smell him, and I heard his voice earlier... he said... *Dad...*"
Tommy would choke up and tears would swell in his eyes.
"I know love; so can I, I thought I heard him earlier as well, moving around upstairs in his room. I swear I heard him call out mum..."

They would snuggle up on the settee... consoling each other...
"Love you boy..."
"Love you son..."

"Love you Mum..."
"Love you Dad..."

"We Love you...."

"Please forgive her..."
"Please forgive them..."

"Forgive them..."

"Forgive them...."

"Please........

They would look at each other, mystified... and tears would roll down their cheeks...
"How...Tommy... How....?

Tommy's room was left exactly the same, as he had left it ... on his "Wedding Day"

Chapter 94

Geoffrey and Joan Childs had also decided to remain in their home, why would they want to leave.

The lovely memories there, the good times, and the bedroom belonging to Louise with her possessions intact.....

On occasion they thought they could smell Louise's favourite perfume, the one she wore on her Wedding Day.......

"She's here Geoffrey.... I can smell her..."
"Louise's bouquet *Joanie, it's radiant my dear...*"

They would here the stairs creaking, foot steps...

"You look so beautiful darling... I love you..." Geoffrey's eyes would well up...
"Louise darling your here... you're so beautiful... I Love you..." sobbed Joan...

"Listen closely Geoffrey... listen to our beautiful daughters words..."
"Dad you'll have my mascara running... ruined..."
"Mum how do I look...?"
"Mum Dad....I love you..."

"WE love you..." They would say in unison

"Please forgive her...."
"Please forgive them....."

"Forgive them..."

"Forgive them..."

"Please..."

"How... Louise.... How...?"

The Childs and Jacksons consoled each other in their bereavement and grieving.

They never spoke to the Miller family again...

Chapter 95

On the rare occasion, the subject would be broached...
When the Jacksons and Childs where comforting...
consoling, grieving, their loss together...

What can we say to them..."
"It wasn't your fault...!"
"We forgive your Sophie...!"
"Let's grieve our losses together...!"

"I don't think so..."
"I could never find that compassion..!"

"What could they say to us...?"

"Sorry..."

"I'd wring her scrawny neck if I ever got my hands on her...!"

"And that makes you as bad as Sophie..."

"Judge, don't judge me....! Not on this one..."

"I'm not, I would walk in your footsteps gladly.... in fact I do daily..."
"Geoffrey....!" Exclaimed Joan
"I'm sorry my love, they are emotions, anger, revenge....hurt pain sorrow.. Loss..."

"I know I feel the same... but that is not what Louise wants...Is it?"

"No... It is not, and that is what differentiates us from Neanderthals...and wild beasts... compassion, magnanimous...the will to listen... and hear...

....But my heart is still broken Joanie..." and he broke down in tears... sobbing

"We all feel the same, and you wouldn't have to twist my arm up my back....snarled Martha... then breathed deeply "but that isn't what my Tommy wants.... is it Tom...!" she said calmly looking at her husband...

"No love, not from what we have heard..." and his eyes moistened and tears trickled down his face...

"How can we forgive her....?"

"How can we forgive them...?"

"How....?"

"How indeed...."

They looked at each other... knowing....

"What have you heard...?"

"Have you heard.... Please forgive her...?"

"Please forgive her.... Please forgive them...?"

"Yes we hear Tommy saying that..."

"We hear Louise...asking us..."

Gradually they felt more comfortable... opening up, sharing their experiences... confiding...

And this deliberation continued.....

"How....?"

They stayed and mourned the spirit of the lives of their beloved children and the love they had for each other...................

Chapter 96

Fred and Chloe Miller left their beautiful home by the dead of night without a word, never once venturing out of the house, in fear of bumping into their estranged neighbours.

No inclination had been given to those around of their pending intention.

One week after the court case ended, "there will be no appeal" the trial was over.

They vanished with a "For Sale" sign appearing over night.

Trying to sell their property as quickly as they could, willing to take a loss on the value.

There was no value for them, in living there anymore.

Never speaking to their neighbours again.... never being able to look them in the eye....

They moved as far away as possible.

"What can we say to them Chloe... we are sorry our daughter murdered your children" lamented Fred.

"It wasn't our fault Fred, we never expected her to react this way and we never pulled the trigger...!" exclaimed Chloe looking, searching for any excuse to gain an understanding and a get out clause for what had transpired.

Fred looked at his beloved wife.... sorrowfully regretfully...

"And who do you think they will blame... Sophie or US...? Most likely all of us, notwithstanding the fact..." Fred paused... "It was us who encouraged and taught her how to use a missile of destruction, to fire a lethal weapon...!"

They never returned.....

The Millers bereavement and grieving was never achieved, and continued on their own... in their own solitude...Until....

Chapter 97

Sophie Miller was sent to a high security Hospital, where she lived out the remainder of her life.

Sophie would spend her days sitting in an armchair, gazing out of a window looking intently, searching as if she was waiting for someone to turn up.

She sat in total silence; she would bath, dress, eat, drink, and nothing more, just sitting in her chair... rocking to and fro........waiting. Never indulging or encouraging conversation with others. Supreme isolation, in a crowded world...

Sophie existed for the rest of her life in the institution, in near total silence.

As it was reported and witnessed by the staff at the hospital, that for that one week leading up to the date of the anniversary of... "The Wedding..."
Sophie would be heard to be talking to herself...
Talking to herself.... of her, "Tommy"...

"He's MY Tommy...!"
"How in Love WE are...!"
"How WE would always be together...!"
"Tommy said, WE will always be together...!"
"WE are getting married...!"
"Tommy Loves ME...!"

And it was reported that on the morning of "The Wedding" Sophie would be heard to say.... just the once...

"We are getting married today...?"
"Are we getting married today...?"
"Tommy..."
"Tommy.....!

Then she returned to her unspoken blanket of silence........... Rocking to and fro...

Except for the exception of that one week, until she died....

Sophie fell to sleep that night and went to spirit, peacefully, to the next life, on the First Anniversary of her "Wedding Day"

The staff on duty that night, said they thought they heard Sophie speaking in the night, she was heard to say...
"Hello I've been waiting for you; you have come for me...!"

Chapter 98

Their love lived on in Spirit, in the next life as;

"The Three Musketeers..."
"One for All ~ All for One"

Chapter 99

Fred and Chloe where the only ones to attend Sophie's funeral, they chose it that way...

"Fred love can you smell Sophie's perfume wafting around..."
"Yes love I thought at first it was my imagination... then I thought maybe you had sprayed yourself..."
"No I haven't .... I thought maybe you had sprayed it on your hand... for comfort..."
"No..."

"I've felt her presence Fred.... I thought I felt her touch me..."
"Me to love, she appears to be around us... I can feel her..."

"I have heard her speak Fred... I've heard her voice....words..."
"I thought I was going crazy or it was my imagination... so have I Chloe, so have I..."

"What have you heard...?"
"I heard the words... please help them..."
"Please help us..."
"What have you heard...?"
"The same as you, quite often..."
"Yes often..."
"Nothing more Fred...?"

Fred looked at Chloe....

"Yes love more..."
"Tell me, what have you heard Sophie saying..."

Fred looked at his wife... puzzled
"It doesn't make sense... I'm confused... I don't understand what she wants us to do, I don't even know if it's her or my grief or my imagination" and tears rolled down Fred's cheeks

Chloe looked at her beloved Fred... and her eyes filled up, and tears flowed.
"Does she say, learn to love again... move on, forgive and share with others... "

Fred nodded crying uncontrollably...
Chloe took Fred into her arms, cradling him tightly...

"Does she say love, unconditional love..."
"Yes... Yes... you have heard her...?"
"Yes Fred I have..."

"How Chloe...? How...?"
"I don't know Fred... but that's what she wants..."
"Then we will find a way...."

That night they lay in bed.... and heard:
"Show them, help them, and love unconditional love"
"Love..."
"Unconditional Love..."

"Share unconditional Love......."

Chapter 100

6 Months after Sophie's funeral;

"Fred love, answer the phone my hands are wet..."
"Hello Miller residence, can I help you...?"

"You can if that's Fred Miller..."

Fred froze then looked at Chloe; she caught his stair and expression....

"Tommy, Tommy Jackson... is that you...?"

Chloe scuttled up to be beside her husband, looking intently into each other's eyes as she approached him... they cradled the phone between them... listening... hearing every word....

"Yes it is..."
"How? ... How have you obtained our number..."
"The Wig as his uses, he as contacts..."
"Geoffrey...Geoffrey is with you?"
"Yes... as well as Joan and Martha..."

"Why, what can we do for you" Fred regained is statue, military training inbuilt.

"We have been talking and we all decided it's your round... "

Tears welled into Chloe and Fred's eyes....

"Fred is Chloe with you... its Geoffrey..."
"Yes she is..."

"Jolly good, that's the way it should be, now old chap, no beating around the bush, we are aware of your circumstances... and we are all in the same boat... and we are still grieving as we know you are..."

"Yes..."

"Something quite profound as happened to all of us, and we wish to carry out our children's wishes.... and share with you and Chloe...

"And that is....?"

"None of us will ever understand, the events in life, that change our lives forever, but to try to forgive, for forgiving is a virtue, and this is what our children have asked us to do...."

"Wow Geoffrey that's deep"... questioned Fred...."Asked you to do....? "

"And so are your pockets..." Tommy injected...

Fred and Chloe grinned...

"Yes dear chap... it is and it takes some getting your head around it..." emphasised Geoffrey..
"And we have..." stated Tommy

"Fred is Chloe listening in? its Martha and Joan..."

"Yes she is... Hello Martha... Joan... its Chloe, what's this all about...? we are mystified...?

"Mystified..... Yes as where we... our children are trying to help us... to teach us"

"Help us..! Teach us?"

"Yes...!"

"What exactly...?"

"Forgiveness and Unconditional Love...."

"Ok... I can accept that... We want to accept that.... please explain"

"We feel that we need to grieve, to grieve together, to help each other... as the true friends we were... we are"

"If we can that would be brilliant...."

"We can, we can help each other... and then learn to help others..."

"The ripples affect my Dears..." Geoffrey said profoundly

"The pebble in the pond..." Tommy stated earnestly

"Chloe Fred... its Joan... it's very simple; if we the adults of today do not learn, then the children of today will become the adults of tomorrow... we must learn.."

"Yes... when can we meet and start..."

"Now... right now....if you open the door, we are sitting in the car outside..." said Martha

"And could do with a wassa...." Tommy shouted

Chapter 101

"You never did sell your house..."
"No you did not, strange that..."
"No offers..."
"No takers..."

"No..."
"No interest at all...."
"Some viewers..."
"Lots of viewers..."
"No bids...,
"No takers..."

"Perhaps that's the way it was meant to be...."
"Perhaps you where never meant to sell it..."

"Strange that... we never thought about it in that way......"
"Perhaps we weren't..."

"Perhaps it's time to move back home..."
"Yes... Move back home..."
"Yes... We think you should move back home..."
"Yes... Where you belong..."

Fred and Chloe smiled... their eyes welled up and tears rolled down their checks...

Martha, Joanie, Geoffrey and Tommy smiled back... mirroring their friend actions..

And nodded knowingly...........

"Yes it's time we did..."

Tommy Jackson	}	
	}	Young Tommy Jackson
Martha Jackson	}	
Geoffrey Childs	}	
	}	Louise Childs
Joan Childs	}	
Fred Miller	}	
	}	Sophie Miller
Chloe Miller	}	

Printed in Great Britain
by Amazon

63138618R00234